The Good Sister

Maggie Christensen

Dedication

To a special aunt who was the inspiration for this story

Also by Maggie Christensen

Oregon Coast Series
The Sand Dollar
The Dreamcatcher
Madeline House

Champagne for Breakfast

Sydney books
Band of Gold
Broken Threads

Check out the last page of this book to see how to get
a free download of one of my books.

Prologue

Isobel – 2015

I was always the good sister.

I lean back in my favourite armchair and sigh looking at the words I've written. It may not matter anymore, but I want to get everything down, just as it happened. Maybe knowing what I do now, I'd have behaved differently – maybe not.

If Doctor Ramage is right, I don't have much time left, but maybe long enough to make things right. Not for me, but for my namesake Isobel – Bel as she calls herself these days – my sister Nan's daughter; the daughter I might have had if…

My name was never shortened. Father wouldn't permit it. He regarded it as common. But this Isobel is of a different generation and she likes the shortened version.

I twist the garnet ring on my finger, the tears trickling down my cheeks. It's all I have left, all except the memories.

It began seventy-five years ago when I was only twenty. It would take another forty for me to discover the truth.

'Are you Isobel MacDonald?'

In the hours when sleep won't come, I can still hear that shrill voice echoing through my head. It was so long ago I should have forgotten it, relegated it to the past where it belongs. But now that I know my days on this earth are numbered, I need to tell someone my story. My only remaining relative is young Isobel who had the sense to leave this godforsaken land for fresher pastures. Maybe she'll understand why I behaved as I did and allow me to die in peace, to believe what I did was right – that I *was* the good sister.

One

Bel climbed out of the black taxi and stood looking up at her childhood home while the driver unloaded her case. The house hadn't changed much. It was still an imposing structure guarded by black railings, its oriel windows gazing down on the River Kelvin with what had always seemed to her a jaundiced expression. The grey stone facade she remembered had gone, replaced by a patina of soft pink sandstone. Bel supposed it had always been there, underneath, hidden by years of smoke and dirt.

She'd read about the transformation of Glasgow, but now it was right in front of her eyes and she was astounded at the metamorphosis. Bel hadn't been home since her mother's death more than thirty years earlier. She had to expect to see changes.

'Your case?'

Bel turned in surprise. She'd been so absorbed by the old house that she'd forgotten the taxi driver.

'Thanks.' She fumbled in her bag for the fare, paid the driver, then picked up the case and mounted the steps. They didn't seem nearly as steep as she remembered.

The faded lettering on the enamel centrepiece of the bellpush brought back memories, its surrounding brass plate showing signs of wear but still as bright as ever. Bel remembered polishing it till she could – to use her granny's words – see her face in it. She followed the

3

now faint instruction to *press*. A bell chimed in the distance.

A gust of wind rustled some leaves in the gutter. Bel shivered. She'd all but forgotten how cold it could be in Scotland, even in summer. From the other side of the door came the sound of footsteps and the tap-tap of a cane. The door opened to reveal the tall figure of Bel's aunt. A loud Scottish voice greeted her.

'Hello, hello. Aren't you a sight for sore eyes? Come away in. You'll be needing a cup of tea.'

Bel dropped her case and stepped into an enveloping hug. She inhaled the remembered violet fragrance of the Evening in Paris cologne that had always been her aunt's favourite. 'It's good to be here at last,' she said, returning the hug. Then she held the older woman at arm's length and studied her. 'You haven't changed a bit.'

But, as she'd expected, there was a frailty about the old woman that hadn't been there on Bel's last visit all those years ago.

'Och, away.'

The familiar Scottish expression took Bel back to her childhood. Almost as tall as Bel, Isobel still held herself erect, albeit with the aid of a walking stick. Her now completely white hair was fashioned exactly as Bel remembered, the long plait coiled into a tight bun at the back of her head. Her eyes had lost the piercing blue, which, when Bel was a child, seemed to see everything. Now they were rheumy and partially hidden behind a pair of half-moon glasses, and the skin on the cheek which had touched Bel's was papery thin.

'In here.' The older woman led the way through a door on the left of the wide hallway. As she followed her aunt, Bel glanced up at the imposing staircase she'd slid down as a young child, and descended more elegantly in her teens and early twenties, before she'd made the decision to emigrate.

'Oh, it's just as I remember it!' Bel looked around the large room. The wide oriel window was flanked by two floral-covered armchairs between which sat a low table piled with books and papers. So, her aunt was still an avid reader. Opposite the door, partially hidden by a sofa covered with a multitude of cushions, the old fireplace had been boarded up to house a gas fire with artificial coals, while on the other side of the room sat the old sideboard. The place still smelt the same too – an odd mixture of furniture polish and an elusive aroma Bel couldn't quite identify, one unique to her childhood home.

'You still have it!' Bel walked over to run her hand across the well-worn surface of the sideboard. 'I remember this so well.'

'That old chiffonier is part of the family,' Isobel said fondly. 'But I don't know what'll happen to it when I've gone. No-one wants good furniture these days. It's all that Ikea stuff. And there's no family but you, and you're on the other side of the world.' She laughed hoarsely, the laugh turning into a cough and she leant heavily on her cane as she tried to regain her breath.

'Are you all right? You'd better sit down.' Bel led her aunt to one of the armchairs and settled her into it, covering the old lady's knees with a tartan travelling rug which had been hanging over its back. 'I should've thought.'

In her excitement at seeing her aunt and the changes to the old house, Bel had almost forgotten the reason for her visit. Aunt Isobel had written detailing her illness and asking Bel to visit "before it was too late". She wanted Bel to help her "sort things out" before the inevitable.

'I'll be fine in a wee minute,' her aunt said, breathing heavily. 'It just gets me that way sometimes. I'm sorry you had to see me like that so soon after you got here. Some days are better than others, and I've been having a good day.' She wheezed a little, then raised her head. 'Maybe if you could fetch me a glass of water? Through there.' She pointed to the door leading to the hallway. 'The kitchen's where it always was. I spend all my time down here. I can't get up the stairs these days. But you'll find your room up there. I had Betty make it up.'

'Won't be a tick.'

But Bel's progress was interrupted by a wheezy instruction, 'And if you could just put the kettle on while you're there.'

Bel smiled. Aunt Isobel had always been a little formidable, even though she'd tried so hard to be friends with Bel and her mates. She hadn't changed.

Opening the door, Bel found herself in a familiar corridor leading to the old kitchen. She filled both a glass and the kettle wondering what had happened to the rest of the house and where her aunt slept. It was a big house for one person.

*

By the time Bel returned, her Aunt Isobel had regained some colour and was sitting upright in the chair clutching the rug. She allowed her niece to help her guide the glass to her lips, then pushed it away. 'It's my lungs,' she gasped. 'They're going to be the death of me,' she chortled, reminding Bel of an old friend and client back in Australia.

Heather suffered from emphysema and sounded exactly like Aunt Isobel, including the same sense of humour. 'Too many cigarettes,' the older woman continued. 'No one told us they could cause this. But I've had a good innings, not like some. They're all gone now.'

Bel followed her aunt's eyes to the sideboard, the top of which was covered with family photos: her mother, aunt and grandparents – all now dead.

'Don't know how I managed to outlive them all, especially our Nan,' she said, referring to Bel's mother. 'They say the good die young, so what does that say about me?' she chuckled and coughed violently into a handkerchief.

Bel couldn't be sure, but thought she saw a trace of blood on the white cotton. Before she could comment her aunt spoke again.

'Is that tea ready? I could fair be doing with a cup. One sugar and plenty of milk. And you'll find some ginger snaps in the tin by the stove. I remember you used to like them.' Her voice was coming clearer now, so Bel felt more confident to leave her while she made the tea.

She smiled as she poured the tea and set out the biscuits on a flower-rimmed plate. The last time she'd eaten a ginger snap had been right here in this house. As a child, she'd cracked them with her elbow to see if they'd break into three pieces so she could make a wish. Bel hadn't thought of them for years. She was touched her aunt remembered.

'Now, how are you really?' Bel asked, when their cups were empty and she'd eaten several of the biscuits to please Isobel. Her aunt had refused to have any herself saying they were too hard for her false teeth to manage.

'So-so. I've defied all the doctors and specialists so far, but I know I can't do it for much longer. I don't expect to make a hundred. The Queen can save her stamp,' she laughed, then her voice took on a more serious tone. 'I don't think I'll see the year out. That's why I wanted you to come. There are some things I want to set straight before I go, and there's someone I want you to meet. I need to make sure everything's done the way I want it. I…' She began to cough again, but waved away an offer of more water.

Bel half-rose, unsure how she could help. How on earth had her aunt been managing to live on her own – to take care of herself?

'There's a bottle of whisky over there in the sideboard,' the hoarse voice instructed. 'I'll have a wee tot and you may care for one yourself.'

Bel hurried across the room and opened the door of the sideboard to discover the bottle of a good malt whisky hidden behind some boxes. It had always been tucked away like this – kept for medicinal purposes only. Some things never changed, except she guessed the "medicinal requirements" were called on more often these days. There were some glasses there too, crystal. Most likely Edinburgh Crystal, Bel thought, recalling how, as a young woman growing up in Glasgow, she'd had it instilled in her that crystal was one of the few good things to come out of Edinburgh. As a child, she'd mentally added Edinburgh Rock to the list too, loving its soft crumbly texture and the way the pink and yellow sticks melted on her tongue.

She poured her aunt a generous measure, hesitated before pouring another smaller one for herself, then joined Isobel by the window. It was close to six o'clock and still bright outside. Bel had always loved the long light summer evenings in Scotland; something she missed in Sydney where the sun set much earlier all year round, even during daylight saving.

'There's a steak pie in the fridge. It only needs heating up. And some potatoes and peas… I'd planned…' Isobel's voice died away and she took a sip of her drink. 'Ah, that's better. Nothing like a wee dram to perk me up.'

'I can manage dinner,' Bel said.

Steak pie – always the standby for special occasions in the family. She guessed her arrival counted as that. Since her mother had died, there was only Aunt Isobel left here in Scotland and Bel herself on the other side of the world.

At one time, this house was teeming with life – her mother, two aunts, grandparents and a couple of great aunts who'd lost their fiancés in the First World War. Now it seemed like a ghost house.

'Not just yet.' Isobel's claw-like hand grasped Bel's. 'First I want you to tell me about your life down there in Australia. Letters don't say everything. I want to picture it.' She closed her eyes while Bel sipped her own drink and began to speak.

'I live in Sydney. In a place called Cremorne. My house is quite different to this one, smaller, red brick with a veranda all around and separated from the road by a white fence. It's within walking distance of Sydney Harbour. As you know, I have a dress shop just like you and Mum had – I call it a boutique.'

She saw the old woman smile and continued, 'It's in a classy suburb called Mosman not far from where I live. I've been lucky that a friend called Jan is minding it for me while I'm here. She's had a rough time, lost her elder son, but is managing to get through it.' Bel paused remembering how Jan had arrived in her shop to apply for a temporary position. Now the two were firm friends and she had no qualms in leaving Jan in charge for however long she needed to stay in Scotland.

'It's a world away from all this,' she continued. 'The weather for a start. We get a lot of sunny days and it can be very hot in summer – and humid, which can be pretty awful, so most homes have air-conditioning and sometimes fans too. I don't think I could survive the summer without them. We also have big storms, often after a really hot day. Then there are the beaches. Not like those here, or even in Europe. We have long stretches of golden sand and big waves. Lots of surfing and we have to watch out for sharks.'

'And your little dog?'

'Toby's still there, and Jan's looking after him too. Her younger son, Andy, loves him and begged to be allowed to be in charge of him. So, everything there's being taken care of and I can stay for as long as you need me.'

At those words, Bel felt her aunt's grasp loosen.

'You'll miss him and your home.'

'I guess so, but there's so much here that's different, very different from what I remember. And I'll be too busy spending time with you, so I won't miss it too much.'

'Mmm.' Isobel's voice was fainter. The older woman had dozed off. Bel gently removed the glass which was dangling from her aunt's hand, stood up and stretched. She was tired after the long flight, but was determined to stay awake until a decent hour. That way, she'd be sure of a good night's sleep and would hopefully wake up refreshed.

Now that her aunt was asleep, Bel decided to investigate her room. Climbing the stairs, she pushed open the door to what was now clearly the spare bedroom, all set up for her with a single bed, a heavy old wardrobe and chest of drawers. It smelt musty from lack of use, though intermingling was a hint of lavender. Someone, no doubt the mysterious Betty, had placed a vase holding a sprig of lavender on the bedside table. Bel smiled.

She began to unpack, hanging the few items she'd brought with her in the old mahogany wardrobe, storing the smaller items away in the tall chest of drawers and laying her Kindle and iPad on the bedside table. Closing the wardrobe door before she left the room, Bel caught sight of herself in the fly-spotted mirror. *Not too bad after such a long flight.* She examined her tall figure so like her aunt's but topped with the smooth helmet of silver hair, instead of the coiled white plait. A closer inspection showed her the havoc the trip had wrought. Her eyes, usually a clear blue like her aunt's, were red from tiredness and the skin on her cheeks appeared dehydrated. She grimaced. Nothing a good night's sleep wouldn't fix.

When she made her way back to the kitchen Bel found the steak pie on the middle shelf of the fridge. This one was shop-bought, judging by the wrapping. It was unlike those she remembered from her childhood, served in an enamel ashet provided by her grandmother and filled by the local butcher. Bel also managed to unearth potatoes and a tin of peas. She turned on the oven and peeled the potatoes, reflecting how little had really changed in all these years.

Apart from the newish refrigerator and a few appliances, it was still the kitchen she'd grown up with. The same old gas stove sat against one wall with the metal rack above where Bel remembered the dinner plates sitting to warm; the green cupboards against the other wall hadn't changed at all. The kitchen table sat in the middle of the room where it had always sat, it's smooth surface showing the result of many scrubbings over the years. The tile-patterned linoleum was now faded, wearing thin in places and curling up slightly on one corner. It all felt so familiar yet strange. It was as if she'd travelled back in time.

Bel thought the kitchen seemed to be stuck in a time warp. Given the state of her bedroom, she was guessing the rest of the house hadn't changed much either, only the curtains changing with the seasons as they had throughout her childhood – velvet for winter and floral for summer.

She set the table and returned to the living room to sit by the window, turning her chair to enjoy the view across the river to the Botanic Gardens which used to be a favourite spot where she could escape the confines of her family and this house.

Bel hadn't found it easy growing up in this house surrounded by adults, and had taken every opportunity she could to get away. Finally, in her mid-twenties she moved all the way to the other side of the world. Her childhood hadn't had been unhappy, quite the opposite, but the house full of adults was also full of rules and expectations and she'd been glad to leave those behind.

That and the broken heart she'd been at pains to keep secret. It had been a relief to find the independence she hungered for and to start afresh in a new country.

There was a movement beside her.

'I must have dozed off. Did you…?'

'Dinner's on and should be ready soon.'

'Good girl.' Isobel picked up her glass and raised it to her lips again, beamed and leant forward. 'It's so lovely to have you here. I don't get out much, but we must try to do a few things. Maybe…'

'Don't worry about me. I can see Glasgow any-time. I'm happy just to spend time with you.'

'You're a good girl,' Isobel repeated and slumped back into her chair. 'Matthew will be here tomorrow. He's the one I want you to meet. He takes care of things for me.' She nodded. 'He's a good man, clever too.'

'Matthew?' Who was Matthew? Surely Aunt Isobel wasn't going to try to introduce her to someone she deemed *eligible* for someone in her sixties? Bel had tried marriage once and wasn't about to get involved with a man again at her age.

'Matthew Reid. He's my lawyer. A lovely young man.'

Bel breathed a sigh of relief. *Her lawyer. Of course.*

Two

Bel – 2015

For a moment Bel lay still. She missed the shrill birdcalls and the early morning snuffing of Toby, her little westie, back home. All she could hear was the gush of water in the distance. She opened her eyes and blinked at the unfamiliar room, the large wardrobe looming over her like a giant ready to pounce. Of course, she was in Scotland, in the old family home, and the water she heard was rain pouring down outside. Yesterday's sunshine had disappeared. Glasgow had decided to put on its special summer weather for her.

She rose, pulled her wrap around her and, drawing back the curtains, peered out of the window. A sorry sight met her eyes. It must have been raining all night. Water was flowing in the gutters, the pavement was covered with puddles and passing cars were creating waves as they sped through the sheet of water lying on the roadway.

Bel turned back into the room, shivering. She was reminded again how cool Scotland could be, even in June. Picking up her toiletries, she went to the bathroom for a quick wash, then dressed quickly in a pair of blue tailored pants topped with a pink striped shirt.

Once she'd fixed her make-up and brushed her hair into its usual neat style, Bel felt ready to face the day. Making her way into the kitchen she was surprised to see her aunt already seated at the table with a steaming bowl of porridge and a pot of tea.

'So, you're up at last! Did you sleep well?'

'Yes thanks.' Bel crossed to give the old woman a kiss on the cheek. 'And you?'

'I don't sleep much at night. I suppose it's because I nap during the day. One of the nuisances of getting old. But I've always liked the early morning, even as a young girl.' She paused, gazing off into space, then seemed to return to the present. 'Make yourself something to eat. There's porridge, if you like it, or bacon and eggs in the fridge. And help yourself to a cup of tea. I suppose you like that fancy coffee? I've never taken to it.'

'Tea'll be fine, thanks. And maybe some toast if there's bread.'

'You won't get fat on that. You're like me. One of Pharaoh's lean cattle.'

Bel smiled at this saying which she remembered from her childhood when she had indeed been thin… tall and thin – what her grandmother had called a skinny Lizzie. Taking a seat opposite Isobel, Bel realised again how like her aunt she was. Both had the same tall build with wide shoulders and a long face with a square jaw. Bel remembered her aunt's black hair in years gone by, just like her own had been before it turned to its present silver. But Isobel had kept the long hair of her youth, whereas Bel had chosen to keep hers short and neat.

'You'll meet Matthew today,' Isobel reminded her, pushing aside her empty bowl. 'He'll be bringing over some papers.'

'Right.'

'You're looking very smart. A good advert for your shop. What do you call it again?'

'Isabella.'

Isobel smiled. 'Our name, though you've fancied it up a bit. I suppose they do that over there. Your mother, Kate, and I had no such notions.'

'I liked the name of the shop you three had. Plain and Fancy.'

'It suited the times.' Isobel's eyes closed as if remembering bygone days, then snapped open again. 'Now, we need to get breakfast cleared away. My cleaning lady comes this morning and she doesn't like to find the breakfast dishes still on the table.'

'Keeps you in order, does she?' Bel chuckled at the thought of anyone trying to keep her aunt in order. 'I can do some cleaning up while I'm here.'

'No, no. That would annoy Betty even more. She has her ways, her set times for everything and does everything I need in her two days. It doesn't do to get in her way or upset her routine. She'll be doing the living room first. We'll be talking with Matthew in there and there are some nice chocolate digestives in the pantry. He likes them with his tea.'

Obviously a much-liked and spoiled young man. Bel cleared the table without a word. She'd barely finished and was emptying the teapot when there was a loud ringing in the hallway and the sound of a door opening.

'That'll be Betty. She's been with me for years and has her own key, but she always likes to give me warning that she's arrived.'

Sure enough when the door closed there was a loud, 'Hello there. It's only me,' followed by the arrival of a short wiry woman in her fifties, dressed in a yellow raincoat and wielding a dripping umbrella. 'It's fierce out,' she said in the soft lilting accent of the Highlands. 'I'm drookit and thought I was going to be blown away coming up the road. This'll be your niece, then?'

Bel was conscious of the woman's eyes examining her. 'I'm Bel.' She held out a hand.

'I'll no shake it till I've dried off. No sense in both of us being sodden. I'll just take this off and get started, shall I?' She looked at Isobel as if for confirmation, but didn't wait for a reply and proceeded to remove her wet garments and carry them back into the hall.

'She's a canny woman,' Isobel said in her absence. 'Came to me after your mum passed away and she's been with me ever since. Every Tuesday and Friday without fail, except for when her man had his accident and was in hospital for three weeks. Even then, she popped in when she could between visiting him. I don't know what I'd do without her these days.'

'Now then.' Betty was back wearing a wrap-around overall and carrying a bucket with several cleaning implements and bottles sticking out of it. 'You're not going to sit in here, I hope. I can't get on with folks under my feet. And you said you had yon solicitor man coming today too. So, I'll need to be getting the room ready for him.'

'That's right,' Isobel answered. 'We'll get out of your road. There are some things I want to show you,' she said to Bel. 'In my room. We can go in there while Betty's doing this part of the house.'

Isobel rose and, picking up her cane, slowly led Bel into her bedroom. Bel gazed round the room which had once been the dining room. Clearly reading Bel's thoughts, Isobel answered her unasked question, 'Yes, this was the old dining room. I tend to eat in the kitchen these days and it made sense to turn this into my bedroom. It saves me the stairs. It's all shut up there now, except for your room. Maybe you'll be wanting to look around, but no one's been up there for years, other than Betty.'

Bel stifled a smile, imagining the dust and cobwebs she'd find if she ventured beyond her bedroom.

Isobel settled herself in a chair by the bed and indicated to Bel that she should pull up a small stool. Once Bel was perched awkwardly at her aunt's side, Isobel drew a well-worn photo album from a drawer in the bedside table. The cover was faded leather in a shade that had most likely been red, and was cracked from use and the passage of years. Isobel patted it like an old friend.

She opened the book at the first page and rubbed her forefinger lovingly over the photo. 'I want to show you this so you can understand what life was like back then,' she said, 'Here we are, the three of us. I was twenty in this photo, your mum was nineteen and your Aunt Kate was twenty-four. My, we thought we were the bee's knees in those outfits.' The picture showed three young women similarly dressed in spotted dresses topped by three-quarter length jackets with wide shoulders. The waists of the dresses seemed to be pulled in as they were very narrow. Their hair was coiled up behind their ears and all three were wearing hats sporting little feathers.

'You all look very elegant,' Bel said, peering at the three figures. 'That's Mum in the middle, isn't it? And you're on her right? Were you going somewhere special?'

'We were. We were all dressed up to attend the Empire Exhibition.'

'The Empire Exhibition – in Glasgow?'

'It was held in Bellahouston Park and was the most exciting thing we could imagine. I remember that summer – it rained and rained – but it didn't stop us. We travelled all the way across town to see the exhibit. There were pavilions from all over the empire and an amazingly high tower. I seem to recall it was over four hundred feet high.'

'Wow, what happened to it?'

'It was demolished the following year. Such a pity.' Isobel shook her head. 'It was 1938. What a year that was. It was a year before the war began, a year where we all thought we were invincible, that the world was our oyster. Your mum was walking out with your dad, Kate had just completed her business course and was all set to be a career woman and…' Her voice trailed off.

'And you, Aunt Isobel? What were you doing?'

'I was being good.' Isobel suddenly closed the book with a snap. 'I'm sorry, dear. I thought I could do this, but I'm not ready to… It may be best you read it. I've written it down. It's all in here.' Isobel reached back into the drawer to take out a sheaf of papers covered in spidery writing. 'Take these back to your room. Young Matthew will be here soon. I'll just see how Betty's doing and make sure she has the kettle on.' Leaning on the arm of the chair, she eased herself up, grasped her cane and slowly made her way out of the room, leaving Bel staring after her in astonishment.

By the time Bel had taken the papers to her bedroom and returned to the kitchen, the kettle was boiling away. Betty had laid a tray set with an embroidered cloth with three gold-rimmed china cups and saucers, and a matching plate containing a stack of chocolate digestive biscuits.

'We'd better be away through. Betty's done in there, and he'll be here in a minute.'

Smiling inwardly, Bel followed her aunt, curious to meet the young man who occasioned such minute preparation and appeared to be such a favourite of both her aunt and Betty.

'Here he is!' Isobel had taken her usual chair by the window and angled it so she could watch the road.

Bel glanced out to see a low-slung sports car draw up. Clearly young Matthew wasn't short of cash and was a bit of a lad. She wondered how Isobel had discovered "young Matthew" and why she'd chosen him when there must be many more conservative and experienced lawyers in Glasgow.

The sound of the bell was followed by Betty's hurried footsteps and a loud, 'I'll let him in,' before the door was flung open and Betty announced with a flourish, 'Mr Matthew.'

The man who entered the room was nothing like Bel's imaginings.

For a start, he wasn't young. He was closer to her own sixty years and towered over Bel who'd stood up to greet him. Wearing the typically Scottish tweed jacket with a checked open-necked shirt and a pair of jeans, he looked as if he'd be more at home in a paddock than in a drawing room or office. His dark thatch of grey hair was shot through with silver and glistened with raindrops, and his square-cut jaw lent him a determined appearance. She supposed he did have an office, no doubt somewhere in Glasgow, but obviously made house calls too. He immediately went over to Isobel and planted a kiss on her cheek.

'How's my best girl this morning?' he asked.

'All the better for seeing you. Are you not wearing a coat in this rain?'

'Too tough. I left my umbrella in the hall. Didn't want to leave puddles on your good carpet.'

Isobel chuckled. 'I want you to meet my niece. She's all the way from Sydney, Australia.' Her outstretched hand gestured in Bel's direction.

Matthew turned his glance towards Bel who had been listening to this exchange with amusement. 'So, this is Bel.' He held out his hand to shake hers and she felt his eyes rake her up and down. 'Another braw MacDonald lassie,' he said at last.

Bel couldn't help but feel he'd overdone the Scots accent for her benefit and reddened. 'I grew up in this house,' she said defensively, though not sure why she felt the need to explain herself.

'Of course you did. Matthew knows that. I filled him in on his last visit. So you can stop pretending to be a yokel.' Isobel directed her last remark to Matthew.

'Your aunt's told me all about you – how proud she is of you, Very successful, aren't you?.' Matthew's eyes, which Bel now saw were the hue of dark chocolate, twinkled as he spoke as if daring her to contradict. Why did she feel as if he was throwing down a challenge?

'Now sit down, both of you. Betty'll be bringing in the tea,'

'I can fetch it,' Bel offered, eager to leave the room and regain her equilibrium.

On her way to the kitchen, Bel stopped for a few seconds in the hallway, hands to her flaming cheeks. What was the matter with her? Why did she have the impression her aunt's solicitor was mocking her? Was it the way he'd spoken or some tacit message she'd seen in his eyes? She met Betty at the kitchen door, the loaded tray in her hands.

'I'll take it, Betty,' Bel said, her cheeks cooling as she relieved the woman of her burden.

Back in the front room, her aunt and Matthew were chatting about some local identity who'd been featured in that day's paper. Bel placed the tray carefully on a low table and poured the tea.

'Matthew takes his black with two sugars,' Isobel instructed, 'and I'll have mine with one and milk.'

While they were drinking tea, and Matthew was making a hole in the plate of biscuits, Isobel inquired about Robbie and Fiona, who Bel gathered were Matthew's children or grandchildren. This appeared to be a regular routine in which both engaged. So it wasn't until the cups were empty and Betty had been summoned to clear them away, that the real purpose of his visit became apparent.

Isobel straightened her back and began to speak. 'Matthew here knows my wishes. He has it all written down. I want you to know them too, so there won't be any mistakes.' She nodded. 'He's helped me write a living will. The law's a bit of an ass about this in Scotland, so I want you to make sure it'll be upheld if – when – I'm no longer able.'

'You mean you want to refuse medical treatment?'

'In a nutshell. I've had a good life. When my time comes, I don't want the doctors trying to keep me alive with all their medications and interventions. I want to go peacefully. I feel it's going to be soon and…'

Tears began to well in Bel's eyes. Why hadn't she visited before now? Why had she been so caught up in her own life that she'd kept postponing a trip to Scotland? But in her heart of hearts she knew. She'd been afraid – a sixty-year-old woman afraid of the memories this house held for her.

Matthew must have recognised Bel's anguish. He held out a large handkerchief which she clutched gratefully, throwing a teary smile in his direction. 'Thanks.' She made an attempt to return it, but he shook his head.

'Dinnae fash yourself,' Isobel said in a brisk voice. Bel smiled inwardly at the Scottish term for worry she hadn't heard for years. 'It comes to us all and I'm ready to go. And, if possible, I'd like you to be here when my time comes. Matthew here is a good man, but he's not family. You're all the family I have left. That's why I wrote to you and why you're here.'

Bel studied her aunt. She looked so well, so alive, sitting upright in her chair, the watery light from the window illuminating her hair like a halo. It was difficult to accept that she was calmly discussing her demise. She swallowed and took a deep breath. 'I'll stay as long as you need me, Aunt Isobel. You know that.'

'I know nothing of the sort,' the older woman replied. 'That's why I had Matthew come along this morning. I needed you to understand a few matters. There's this house for example.'

'The house?' Bel glanced around the room. The rain appeared to have stopped and the sun had moved and was now throwing a fine shaft of light across the faded carpet. Bel remembered it had once been bright with a floral pattern.

Matthew cleared his throat. 'What your aunt means is that she has willed it to you, along with certain responsibilities.'

'Responsibilities?' Bel repeated, thinking she sounded like a parrot. 'Maybe you could explain?'

Matthew looked at Isobel as if asking her permission to continue. She nodded.

'Over the years your aunt has donated to several charities. One of those...' he hesitated.

'Oh, for goodness sake, man! What he's trying to say, Bel, is that I'm leaving the house to you with certain conditions attached. I know you won't want to live here. Your life's in Australia now. But I would ask that you – and Matthew – set up the house as a home for disabled children and their carers. It would need some modification, but...'

'Your aunt has already had plans drawn up.'

Bel's eyes moved to Matthew at his interruption. She felt an ache in her throat. How did Isobel know about Bel's own commitment to helping disabled children back home – or did she? Was this simply a coincidence? 'I'd be happy to fulfil your wishes,' she said, 'but surely it won't be soon? I mean, you're looking so well and...'

'I do put a good face on it, don't I?' Isobel said with a smile, brandishing her cane to emphasise her words. Then her face became more serious. 'But, according to Doctor William Ramage, I don't have long. My lungs are filling up with fluid and it seems I'll drown or something equally terminal. So...' she took a long breath, 'I want you two to get to know each other.'

Bel cast a furtive glance at the man who was now regarding her with what appeared to be amusement. Just what was Isobel suggesting? Surely there was no further need for Bel and Matthew to talk until the worst happened. If her aunt was to be believed, then she – Bel – would still be here when Isobel passed away. That would be when she and Matthew needed to liaise, not before, not now. But she'd counted without the man himself.

'Sounds like a good plan,' he said, rising and planting a kiss on Isobel's cheek. 'Maybe you'd care to come for a drive tomorrow – weather permitting?'

Bel felt her mouth fall open. 'I…' she began, intending to refuse, to explain she'd come to spend time with her aunt, not to go gallivanting around the countryside with a solicitor who looked more like a farmer.

But before she could utter another word, her aunt intervened. 'Capital idea. You can show her that bothy of yours,' she said, turning to Bel and adding, 'Matthew has a place out towards Loch Lomond. That's why he looks so disreputable.' She chuckled. 'Pretends to be a man of the land, instead of a respectable lawman. Sometimes I think he's missed his calling.'

'But…'

'There's no Mrs Reid. If that's what you're thinking.' Isobel chuckled, then burst into a coughing fit.

Bel hurried to provide her aunt with a glass of water and, without quite knowing how it happened, by the time Mathew left, she'd agreed to go for a drive with him next day.

Matthew's visit appeared to have tired Isobel out so, while she was having a nap after lunch, Bel retired to her room and, picking up the sheaf of papers, began to read.

Three

Isobel – 1938

'Let's go and have our fortunes read tonight.' My sister Nan, brimming with excitement, was clearly going to brook no refusal. 'I've heard this woman is really good. She lives only five minutes away. I've already set up an appointment, but we need four girls to go. You *will* come, won't you?'

It was the last thing I wanted to do. I was on my feet all day at the hair salon and when I got home I liked to put my feet up and have a cup of tea. I didn't believe in fortune tellers anyway. I thought it was all a load of old rubbish, a way of cheating young women like my sister out of their hard-earned cash with stupid notions of meeting tall, dark and handsome heroes who'd sweep them off their feet, just like they saw in the cinema or read in *True Romances* or *True Story*.

'Say you will. It'll be fun. Jeannie's coming and you could ask Eileen, couldn't you?'

I sighed. I knew I was going to have no peace until I agreed to go along with this. My best friend, Eileen, would agree. She was always up for anything.

'Okay. I'll telephone her,' I said reluctantly. Our telephone was relatively new and we were still thrilled with the novelty of being able to contact our friends from the privacy of our own home, even though Father cautioned us from using it too frequently.

*

The four of us were giggling and pushing each other with a combination of nerves and excitement as Nan rang the bell. It was a dank November night and the rain was belting down. We were anxious to get out of the weather while being unsure what we were letting ourselves in for. Eileen was just asking, 'Do you think this is the right place?' when the door opened and we were shown into a small lounge room.

After waiting impatiently, sitting on an overstuffed sofa which had seen better days, we took turns to go into an adjoining room while those of us left behind chatted nervously and drank cups of tea.

When my turn came, I picked up my empty teacup as I'd been instructed, and entered warily. The room looked as if it had once been a bedroom. The floral curtains were drawn across the solitary window, and the woman we had come to see was sitting in front of a low table opposite an empty chair. I perched on the edge of a low chair and handed over my cup, wondering what on earth I was doing here.

The woman bent her head over my tea cup pretending to see goodness knows what in the collection of soggy tealeaves stuck to the edge of the cup.

Okay, I thought, *bring on the dark handsome stranger and let's get this over*.

'…Who's Bob Smith?'

I stared at her without speaking. I'd been letting the woman's voice flow over me, when the name grabbed my attention. Okay, it was a very common name, but I didn't expect to be given an actual name. It would be all too easy to disprove.

I shook my head. This wasn't supposed to happen. She was supposed to talk in generalities; the tall dark man from across the sea, weddings and babies. That's what I'd expected when I stood at the dark green door with my three friends just an hour earlier.

Her voice reverberated around my head as I gazed down at my hands. I tried to ignore the ringing in my ears and looked up at the face opposite me. She was a small woman whose faded blonde hair lay in wisps around a prematurely wrinkled face, the brightly coloured earrings and the red lipstick making an incongruous statement. Her eyes, behind gold-rimmed spectacles, seemed puzzled and the red mouth opened and repeated the words, 'Who's Bob Smith?'

She peered at me, clearly taking in my shocked expression. 'You haven't met him yet, then? You will, and you'll think you're set for life.' She stared into the teacup again. 'He'll leave you. It won't last.' She put the cup down. Short and sweet, I thought, shaken despite my cynicism.

I didn't wait to hear any more. 'Thanks,' I muttered and left. Back in the lounge room, I prepared to fend off questions and thought of what I'd been told. There couldn't possibly be anything in it, could there? I put it out of my mind. The woman had said it wouldn't last anyway.

'What did she tell you?' It was Eileen, always the loudest. Sometimes I wondered why she was my best friend; we had so little in common. My mother always said it was because she dared to do the things I'd like to do, but I knew that there was more to our friendship than that.

We'd met on our first day at primary school. I'd been hiding nervously among the coats in the cloakroom when she'd caught sight of me and pulled me out to join in the class line. It seemed she'd been doing that ever since – pulling me out of hiding, that is.

'Well?' Eileen's voice had become impatient. I shook myself and tried to think of what to reply. I certainly wasn't going to repeat the name I'd been given. That would just be asking for trouble. I knew I'd never hear the end of it.

'Just the usual,' I replied, shaking back my hair. I'd been trying a new style, at Eileen's urging, and it wasn't working for me. My naturally straight black hair defied every attempt to fashion it into anything stylish.

'There is no usual. Don't be so coy.' Eileen's eyes flashed, and I knew I'd have to come up with something fast or she'd never give up.

'She said I'd meet someone, a man, tall, dark hair and that it wouldn't last,' I improvised.

'Mine's going to be blonde,' Nan interjected, 'and older.' I turned around. I'd missed hearing about my sister's fortune while I was listening to my own.

'Maybe that one with the blond curls in the choir,' I joked, only to see Nan blush. It was true that there was a tall blond fellow in the church choir who'd been giving her the eye, but I hadn't thought she was interested. Well, well!

At that point Maisie, the spey-wife, emerged from the bedroom. 'Is that all of you now?' she asked. She looked different in the brightly-lit living room, surrounded by the shabby three-piece lounge and side tables filled with family photographs; less fey somehow and more ordinary. It was odd to think she'd spent the last few hours pretending to foretell our futures.

We bundled ourselves up in the hats, scarves and gloves we'd taken off only a few hours earlier and went out again into the dreary night. The rain had stopped, but the remaining clouds hid the moon and stars leaving us to find our way home by street-light.

'It's going to freeze tonight,' predicted Jeannie. She'd been quiet all evening, but chose now to become chatty. 'I think she was good, don't you?' She turned to Nan, her best friend. 'I'm glad you let me come along,' she added to me, as if I'd had anything to do with it.

*

'You were very quiet on the way home. Did she say something you didn't tell us?' Nan wanted to know. We were back in the living room drinking cocoa by the fire. Mother and Father were in bed, so we were whispering. The room was still warm, though the fire was dying down and the embers cast long shadows around the room. They flickered across the solid furniture which had been in the family for generations.

We huddled close to the fireplace, like we had as small children when we imagined shapes in the flames and the thought of being tall enough to reach the top of the mantelpiece was unimaginable. The difference was that now we huddled there so that the smoke from our cigarettes went straight up the chimney. Mother and Father would kill us if they caught us smoking.

'Just thinking,' I replied, hoping that would satisfy her. I had no intention of giving away any more details. Bob Smith! She might as well have said John Brown or some such. 'Well I'm for bed. I have an early start tomorrow.'

I lay very still in bed pretending to be asleep. I shared a room with Nan and our other sister Kate. We were all old enough to have our own rooms, and the house was certainly big enough, but we liked being together and often used the darkness to share confidences. The barnlike dimensions of the upper level of the old house echoed in the night. When we were younger, Kate had scared us with stories of ghosts, though none of us had ever seen or heard one.

Kate hadn't gone with us to the spey-wife. She had more sense, I thought. She was determined to *make something of herself* as our mother put it. What she meant was that Kate was the clever one. She was the oldest and had always been given more responsibility. Afternoons spent playing in the garden were not for her; she had work to do. She was actually only four years older than me in age, but light-years older in her attitude. She worked at the local cooperative like Nan, but had almost completed a business course. Then, as Mother said, the world would be her oyster, and she wouldn't have to put up with these stuck-up customers anymore.

I could hear the gentle snores of my two sisters, but was too excited to fall asleep immediately myself. The name Bob Smith kept going around and around in my head. It was all very well to rubbish fortune tellers and tell my sister that it was all a lot of codswallop but what if…?

I lay there imagining meeting this Bob Smith. What would he be like? Tall, dark and handsome, of course. And where would I meet him? It would have to be some romantic setting, like the couples in *True Romance* magazine. Maybe he'd save me from drowning, or from a runaway horse, or … It didn't occur to me that there was little chance of drowning or meeting a runaway horse in our part of Glasgow.

I closed my eyes tight and hugged myself.

I was twenty and had never had a real boyfriend. I'd kissed a few boys in kissing games at church socials, but had always wiped my lips afterwards and pretended it hadn't happened. They hadn't meant anything to me.

Nan was the pretty one with her blonde curls, blue eyes and pointed chin. I was… I thought about that. I suppose I wasn't exactly plain but there wasn't much you could do with a long face and straight black hair. Now that I was grown up I tended to wear my hair in a roll behind my ears, not very glamorous, but it was too long to leave down in the salon and the clients expected us to look neat, *soignée* Lillian called it, but then it *was* her salon.

*

It was a few months later and I'd completely forgotten about the evening and the spey-wife's prediction. I'd attended a couple of church dances and had been walked home by boys I hoped never to see again. Eileen telephoned me at the salon, her voice shrill with excitement.

'I've just met this gorgeous guy, and he's got a friend.'

'Not again.' I'd been down this route before and discovered that gorgeous guys usually had friends who were not so gorgeous. Eileen's idea of gorgeous wasn't mine anyway. 'I told you I wouldn't be in it again.'

'You've got to come. You'll like him. He's a teacher.' A teacher. Was that supposed to be an incentive? Sounded staid and boring to me.

'Well, what do you say? Saturday night? We're going to the cinema.' Eileen clearly couldn't understand my silence.

'Okay,' I replied slowly, trying to work out if this was a good idea or not, but unable to come up with any excuses. Eileen knew I had nothing else planned because we usually spent our Saturday nights together.

*

Although I wasn't expecting to like this blind date, sure he'd be like all the others Eileen had produced, I took more care than usual with my appearance. I borrowed a skirt and bolero top of Kate's and managed to coil my hair into some resemblance of the latest fashion. Father had refused to allow us girls to bob our hair, so I was stuck with these long locks. I donned my hat and gloves, checked myself in the mirror and rubbed a touch more rouge into my lips before slipping out the door.

Eileen was waiting for me at the corner and we walked quickly to catch the tram that would take us into Sauchiehall Street.

'We're meeting them outside the Odeon,' she said, beaming. 'Oh, I know you'll like him.'

'Have you met your fellow's pal?'

'No, but Alan says he's quite a catch. You're too fussy by half,' she added, referring to my rejection of the "good sorts" her own short-lived romances had produced in the past. 'And they're showing the latest Clark Gable. You said you wanted to see it.'

I sighed. It was true. Clark Gable was my pin-up, and I'd been dying to see his new film.

When we reached the cinema, there was a long queue stretching along the side of the building and no sign of the two men. 'Do you think…?' I began, wondering if we should take our place in the line, when Eileen grabbed my arm and pointed to two figures crossing the road.

'Here they are,' she said, her voice rising with excitement.

As the men came closer. I gasped. One of them could have been Clark Gable himself with his dark hair brushed back from a wide forehead and a neat dark moustache. He had to be Eileen's date. As they approached, I turned my gaze to the other. He appeared pleasant enough, a pretty ordinary sort of guy with sandy-coloured hair, freckles and a wide grin. He looked as if he might be good company for an evening at least.

But when they joined us, it was the sandy-haired fellow whose arm Eileen took. 'This is Alan,' she said with a grin, 'and this is…'

'Bob,' the Clark Gable lookalike said, taking my outstretched hand. 'Bob Smith.'

Four

My mouth dropped open. Bob Smith! The Clark Gable lookalike was called Bob Smith and he was the *friend* who was to be my partner for the evening? My head was whirling. The spey-wife's words going around and around. *Bob Smith. It won't last.*

'Are you all right?'

Eileen's elbow nudged me back into the present. Somehow, I managed to unglue my tongue from the roof of my mouth. 'Hello, I'm Isobel MacDonald. Pleased to meet you.' I gulped. How inane. *What must he think of me? Of course, it wouldn't last. It wouldn't last past this one evening. What guy wanted to be stuck with a tongue-tied fool like me?*

But he took my hand, held it firmly and smiled. 'Pleased to meet you too. Alan didn't tell me his doll's friend was such a looker.' I saw him glance across at his pal with an expression I couldn't identify and was about to say his friend hadn't met me when Alan gave a loud guffaw.

'Didn't want to disappoint you if she turned out to be a plain Jane.' He reddened. 'We'd best get in the queue.'

Bob tucked my hand in his arm, and the four of us joined the others waiting in line. 'Warm enough,' he asked. I nodded, still unable to speak. *He thought I was a looker?* I felt a fluttering in my stomach. My hand was pressed tightly between his arm and his chest. I could feel the warmth from his body through my glove. I couldn't believe

I was standing here, on an ordinary Saturday night, in the middle of Glasgow, arm-in-arm with this handsome chap.

Eileen and her fellow were absorbed in each other, so it was left to Bob to try to make conversation with me. He began by asking where I worked. My stilted responses soon became less self-conscious as he expressed interest in my hairdressing experience and the training I'd undergone.

I discovered he lived further along Great Western Road in what I'd always thought of as the classy suburb of Milngavie. But he didn't sound posh. Bob was easy to talk to. He told me he was a Physical Education teacher which explained his good physique. For a moment, I pictured him in shorts and singlet with his broad shoulders and long legs, then brushed away the bold image.

All the time we'd been chatting I hadn't noticed the line moving slowly forward, so it was with surprise I saw we'd reached the front of the queue. While Bob and Alan bought our tickets, Eileen whispered, 'What do you think? He's a real he-man.' I barely had time to reply before the men turned back to us, tickets in their hands, and ushered us through the door into the darkness of the cinema.

I was relieved to find we were sitting in the middle of the theatre. I'd been afraid that Eileen and Alan intended to sit in the back row so they could canoodle. We slid past a row of knees to our seats, and I dropped into mine with a sigh of relief.

The lights dimmed completely, and the film began. I was enthralled and quite forgot the man beside me as I thrilled to the love duel between Clark Gable and Spencer Tracey imagining myself in the story being enacted on the screen. If I was my namesake, the beautiful Jeanette MacDonald, I knew which one *I'd* choose. When they sang the final rendition of *San Francisco*, I felt my eyes water and was surprised when my companion offered me his handkerchief.

'Thanks,' I muttered. 'Sorry.' I patted my eyes and handed it back.

'Keep it,' he said. 'You may need it again if the next film's a sad one.'

I trembled with excitement. Did this mean he intended to see me again? I glanced at him out of the corner of my eye. He really *did* look like Clark Gable. Except Bob had a slight cleft in his chin and a small scar above his right eyebrow. It made him seem more approachable, more ordinary, more human. Clark Gable would always be my pin-up, but he was a matinee idol, not a flesh and blood man, not a man who'd lend you his hankie, who might even kiss you.

Heat flooded my cheeks at this daring thought, and I attempted to hide it by bringing the handkerchief up to my face and pretending to blow my nose. 'I'll wash it before I give it back,' I assured him and saw him smile.

Once outside the cinema, I turned towards the tram stop, but Eileen had other ideas.

'Why don't we have an ice cream?' she suggested. I was happy to do anything to make the evening last longer, and the men both agreed. So, despite the cool evening, we were soon walking along the road eating the ice cream cones we called pokey hats. We were still eating our cones as all four of us clambered to the top of the tram which would take us back home.

When the tram reached our stop, I expected Bob to continue with the ride back to Milngavie and was preparing to say my goodbyes. To my astonishment, he rose with the rest of us. 'Better make sure you get home safely,' he said, as he helped me down from the vehicle and tucked my hand into his arm again in that gesture I found so intimate.

By the time we reached the turn off to Kelvin Drive where I lived, the other two had lagged far behind us. I turned, intending to speak to Eileen, but they were too wrapped up in each other to notice.

'They'll be fine,' Bob laughed, as we swung left into the wide road from which the river was partially hidden by bushes. I didn't talk much on the way along, wondering if he intended to see me again, if he'd want to kiss me, and what I'd do if he did. Bob, however, appeared to have no such qualms and kept up a running commentary on the film we'd seen and others he'd enjoyed recently. From his chatter, it seemed he was an inveterate picture-goer, making me wonder if he took a different girl to each one.

'This is me,' I said, slowing down and stopping at the foot of our steps. I checked the windows to see if anyone was looking out, but all I could see was a dim light behind the curtains on the ground floor. Upstairs was in darkness, which could mean my sisters had already gone to bed.

I shivered a little as a sharp breeze blew up and I removed my hand from my companion's arm. We stood awkwardly facing each other.

'Thanks for walking me home,' I said, ready to escape up the steps to the familiarity of the house. I wasn't used to being walked home by a good-looking fellow like this one and wasn't exactly clear on the protocol. The boys from the church socials seemed like children by comparison.

'Can I see you again? There's a good film on next week too.' I could see Bob's breath form a cloud in the cold air. Trying to disguise my enthusiasm, I thrust my hands into my pockets, my handbag hanging over one arm.

'I'd like that,' I murmured, inwardly exulting. He wanted to see me again! I didn't care what the film was. I was thrilled to be offered another date. He put a hand on my shoulder and leant forward.

As our lips met, I felt as if this was what I'd been waiting for all my life. His moustache brushed my top lip and his mouth was soft on mine. The kiss was over almost before it had begun, but the sensation lingered – a tingling impression that something momentous had happened.

'So, next Saturday. Seven-thirty. I'll meet you at the Odeon again?'

I nodded.

He tipped the hat he wasn't wearing and walked off whistling, leaving me gazing after him in a trance. I touched my lips with one finger, reliving his touch, the kiss that had been so different from any I'd had before. I had no desire to wipe this one off; I wanted to enjoy the tingling senaation forever.

I almost skipped up the steps, pausing before I went in to get rid of the wide smile which I knew must be on my face.

'How was it?' Nan turned from where she was sitting by the fire, reading the latest copy of *The People's Friend*. She tossed the magazine aside as soon as I walked in.

'Okay.' I tried to subdue my excitement, but couldn't stop my lips from curving up.

'Was the film good? What was he like? How did...' Her questions followed in quick succession, not giving me time to reply.

I laughed and removed my coat and gloves, dropping them on a chair before joining her by the fire. 'I need to thaw out. It's pretty cold out there.'

'Don't stall. It was that Clark Gable film, wasn't it? Was he gorgeous? Did you swoon?'

Relieved it was the film she was interested in, I launched into a detailed account of the plot with descriptions of Jeanette MacDonald's lavish dresses which seemed to satisfy her. I kept the information about my own Clark Gable to myself.

'Where's everyone?' I asked, when I'd run out of superlatives to describe the film.

'In bed. I was about to go too, but I waited up for you.' Nan yawned. Then something seemed to occur to her.

'The *friend* Eileen's chap brought along. Another drag?'

I felt my face redden. 'He was okay.'

'Oh? And…?'

'He's invited me to the pictures next week.' There, I'd said it. Now I knew I'd be in for a heap of teasing from both of my sisters.

'But you'll miss the dance,' Nan wailed.

In my excitement at being asked for another date, I'd completely forgotten the church dance which, till tonight, had been the highlight of our social calendar.

'You don't need me. Jeannie will be there, and Eileen.'

'But…' Nan pouted. 'We always go together. What'll I do if Jeannie clicks?'

'Maybe you'll click too. What about that tall guy in the choir? He's sure to be there.' I watched my little sister blush.

'He wouldn't be interested in me. He goes about with an older crowd.'

'That shouldn't matter if he likes you. I've seen the way he stares at you when you're not looking.'

'But do you know what he said?'

'What?' I was beginning to find this conversation tedious. I wanted to go to bed and think about my own new fellow, if that's what he was.

'He said he'd ask me out but I was too young. And he called me Young MacDonald! As if I was a child.'

I couldn't help smiling at Nan's outraged expression.

'See, you're laughing at me too. It's not fair, I hate being the youngest.'

'Well, that's not something that can be changed in a hurry. Come on. It's time we went to bed. It'll be morning and the church bells'll be ringing before we know it. And you'll be in the choir along with what's-his-name,' I added mischievously.

'It's Colin,' she said, dreamily. 'Colin Davison.'

I grinned as we put the guard around the fire and turned out the lights before heading upstairs to bed.

That night, it was no faceless he-man who filled my dreams. I hugged the knowledge of Bob Smith to myself as I relived every minute of the evening, culminating in that kiss. Had I been too forward? Would he think me loose?

I didn't care, but vowed to be more circumspect in the future. I'd behave like any other properly brought up Presbyterian girl would and offer my cheek for his kiss next time.

Five

The day promised to be fine. Weak sunlight peeked through the clouds of the previous day, shining on the still wet pavements and making the puddles sparkle like diamonds. Mindful of the cool summer days and aware she was to be driving in a sports car, Bel dressed in a pair of pants topped with a long-sleeved cotton tee-shirt in her favourite shades of pink and purple.

She had sat up reading her aunt's story till late last night, travelling back to the years before she'd been born, smiling at the description of her mother as a young girl in the throes of her first crush. That guy in the choir had become her father. It was difficult to recognise the man she barely remembered as the cheerful fellow who'd stolen her mother's heart, but people did change.

And Bel discovered she had more in common with her aunt than she thought. She, too, always believed telling fortunes and such like were a load of rubbish, but what a coincidence for her to actually meet Bob Smith.

Her eyes had started to close just as the tale was becoming interesting, and she was looking forward to reading more that night.

When Bel entered the kitchen, it was to find her aunt sitting exactly as she had been the day before. Isobel looked up, a wide smile on her face. 'You're ready, then?'

'I thought it might be a bit cool in the car.' She poured a cup of tea and helped herself to a piece of toast before joining her aunt at the table. 'No point in asking how you slept, I suppose?'

'None at all. I'm thinking you'll be wanting to get away – you and Matthew. It's a lovely day for a trip up to Loch Lomond.' Her lips turned up in what Bel thought was a sly grin. 'When's he picking you up?'

Bel swallowed quickly, thinking her aunt was all too interested in her trip with Matthew. What was that all about? She was beginning to wish she'd refused his invitation, even though it would have been rude.

'Half-nine. Will you be all right on your own?' It was a stupid question. Aunt Isobel had been living on her own for years.

'Bless you,' the older woman replied. 'I have my routine. Grace will be round at eleven for a cuppa. She does the flowers at the church and always drops round on her way home.'

Suddenly Isobel's earlier comment struck Bel. 'Loch Lomond? That's…'

'Where Matthew has his place. I wanted you to see it. You'll understand when you get there.'

Bel regarded her aunt in dismay. 'But he didn't say… You – he – mentioned a drive. I didn't…' She pressed her lips together. There was something going on here, something she didn't understand. It felt as if her aunt and this Matthew were in cahoots in a private joke, one which involved Bel. As someone who liked to be in charge, she hated this feeling.

She'd travelled to Scotland at her aunt's request, expecting to be holding the hand of a bedridden, dying woman. Instead, here she was, being subtly managed by the woman who, although purporting to be at death's door, seemed pretty hale and hearty, *and* in league with an enigmatic Scottish solicitor.

She finished her breakfast and rose. The enigmatic one would be arriving soon, so she'd better fetch her bag and a jacket in case of a change in the weather.

As if reading her mind, Isobel placed her cup in its saucer, rattling the china. 'Remember how changeable the weather can be here. You'll need a rain jacket or some such and you don't want to keep the man waiting.' She nodded towards the clock hands clearly pointing to twenty past nine.

By the time they heard Mathew's car draw up, Bel had followed her aunt's suggestions and was anxious to leave. It was strange how, even at her own advanced age, her elderly aunt could make her feel exactly as she had as a teenager. Although she'd only arrived the day before, Bel was suddenly anxious to get out of this house which, despite being empty except for one elderly woman, still gave her the claustrophobic feeling it had in her youth.

'You're ready?' Matthew greeted her as she opened the door. 'I'll just say hello to your aunt before we go.' And he made his way through the house, as if he did this every day, Bel thought, as she followed on his heels.

This morning he was dressed much as he had been the day before, the only difference being the absence of a jacket. His hair was tousled, leading Bel to believe she'd been right to imagine they'd be driving with the top down. Today, he had his sleeves rolled up to the elbow revealing tanned sinewy arms, from which she quickly averted her eyes, before again thinking it odd for a supposedly conservative Scots solicitor to look more like someone who spent his life outdoors.

Bel swung her long legs into the tiny car and waved to her aunt as Matthew shut the car door before moving around to the driver's side and sliding behind the wheel.

'It's a bit tight,' he apologised with a grin. 'But wait till we get out of the city traffic and you'll see why I choose to drive this jalopy when I can. I keep the company car for business and your aunt's become more of a friend than a client over the years. I think she likes to imagine that if she were younger, or I were older…' He chuckled. 'And who knows. She's clearly been a bit of a knockout in her time.'

Bel couldn't think of any reply, so remained silent, glad of her short hair as the breeze rippled through it. It had been years – another lifetime – since she'd driven in anything like this, and she couldn't stem the feeling of exhilaration as they sped through the morning traffic. It seemed no time before they'd left the city streets behind and were driving along the A82 through Dumbarton and heading towards Balloch and Loch Lomond.

'My wee place is part-way up the loch, at Inveruglas,' Matthew explained.

The name brought back memories – memories of hiking holidays, of staying in youth hostels, of carrying a heavy rucksack along the side of the Scottish lochs. The low white building at Crianlarich which was always their first port of call, the hostel at Rowardennan, a popular stopping place, situated as it was on the eastern bank of the loch and having fantastic water views, its turrets making it appear like an ancient castle. And the remote building at Glen Affric, eight miles from the nearest road.

'And you live there alone?'

'Aye,' Matthew said shortly. 'When I'm not being overrun by the grandkids.' Then his mouth turned up in what Bel took to be a smile. 'If we're going to be spending any time together you'd best start calling me Matt. Matthew is a terrible mouthful. Your aunt likes it, but...' he hesitated. 'I'm Matt to my friends.' He was peering through the windscreen so Bel couldn't see the expression in his eyes, but wondered when they'd advanced to the status of friends.

*

'Here we are.'

To Bel's surprise, when the car stopped, it wasn't outside the small farmhouse built from the local grey stone she expected, given Isobel's references to a bothy and a croft. The home was a modern edifice of wood and glass rising up from the heather and gorse-covered terrain and appearing to be part of the landscape with the mountain looming high behind it. It was set back from the road and surrounded by a dry-stone dyke, much like those they'd driven past on the way up the lochside. But that was the only traditional thing about it. Behind the wall, Bel could see a neat garden in which roses and some smaller plants she couldn't identify appeared to be struggling for existence.

'Aye, it's a bit windy for them,' Matt said, clearly seeing the direction of her gaze. 'But they do their best. Hamish doesn't help either.'

At his words, a small white dog appeared as if from nowhere and, positioning itself on the inside of a small wooden gate, began barking furiously.

'I hope you don't mind dogs,' Matt said, getting out of the car and stretching. 'He's a...'

'West Highland Terrier,' Bel finished for him. 'I have one just like him at home. Toby.' All of a sudden, a rush of homesickness flooded her. What was she doing here? Travelling to a country she'd vowed never to set eyes on again, visiting an aunt she hadn't seen for years, driving up Loch Lomond with a stranger. She shook her head in bewilderment. It was as if some nameless force had taken hold of her, brought her here for its own purpose and was now taunting her with a dog like little Toby who must even now be wondering why he'd been abandoned back in Sydney.

She realised her companion was looking at her strangely. 'Sorry, did you say something?'

'I was asking how old your dog is. Hamish is just a puppy. He's still to learn how to behave properly. I got him for company, and the grandkids love him. If you come inside, I'll explain a few things and you'll see...'

By this time, Bel had managed to extricate herself from the confines of the car. It was a relief to stretch her legs after being so cramped, and she was glad she'd dressed warmly as a stiff breeze blasted across the ground almost propelling her into the gate.

'So, you're a dog person.' Matt led her through the gate to be greeted ecstatically by Hamish, who alternated between running circles around the pair and trying to climb up their legs, his tongue hanging out to show his approval. 'I always say you can trust a body who likes the wee craiters. I cannae abide cats. Always remind me of their big cousin, the tiger.'

Bel smiled inwardly at the sweeping statement which dismissed all cats and cat-lovers, and also at Matt's occasional lapses into broad scots. It was such a long time since she'd been exposed to the vernacular of her native tongue. It was odd, but somehow it made her feel comfortable, as if she'd come home.

Walking up a wooden ramp, Matt unlocked the door and Bel followed him in through the wide entrance to a large hall which was full of light. Looking up, she could see the blue of the sky through tall windows which reached up to the high roof.

'Come on through,' Matt said, directing her through the hallway to a spacious kitchen-living area – what she'd call a family room. The floor was of smooth grey slate – no rugs to soften the hard surface – and the room was casually furnished with soft armchairs and sofas, their covers reflecting the gold and purple tints of the gorse and heather outside. At the far end, sliding doors opened out onto a wide deck overlooking the loch.

'This is lovely,' she exclaimed, her eyes roaming around the room, in which nothing seemed to be out of place. 'It looks…'

'Unlived in.'

It was true. Apart from a few books and papers lying on surfaces, there was little evidence of habitation, so clear and wide were the floor and spaces between the pieces of furniture. But, despite this, there was an ambiance about the place, a warmth that had nothing to do with the temperature, though the sun shining through the glass did provide a degree of heat. Bel reflected that with so much glass in this climate you'd need good double glazing. She couldn't imagine what it'd be like in winter.

'Sit yourself down. I'll make us a cuppa and explain. Then you'll understand why your aunt was so keen for me to bring you here.'

Bewildered, Bel did as he instructed, dropping into a comfortable armchair with a view of both the loch and the mountain. She watched Matt busy himself behind the kitchen bench, while Hamish settled at her feet, having decided she provided no threat. Noting the collection of high-tech gadgets and the way he appeared quite at home there, Bel decided Matt was clearly a man who'd been fending for himself for some time. She wondered how long he'd been on his own and what had happened to his wife before reminding herself it was none of her business. She was here at her aunt's directive, not as a friend or guest of the owner.

'Here we are. Thought you might like a proper coffee.' Matt handed her a mug of black coffee and offered a plate of shortbread fingers. Gratefully taking the mug, she accepted a piece of shortbread, shook her head at the offer of sugar and milk, took a welcome sip of the beverage and sighed with pleasure. She'd been missing her daily shot of caffeine.

'So,' Matt said, evidently in no hurry to provide the promised explanation. 'Australia, huh? How do you find it?'

'A better climate than this place,' Bel replied, cupping her hands around the mug.

'How long have you lived there?'

'Close to forty years. I was pretty young when I left home. Eager to get away.'

'And you've never been back? Never hankered for home?'

'Not till now – apart from a flying trip for Mum's funeral. Sydney's been my home for a long time. Longer than Scotland was.'

'Hmm.'

Matt seemed to consider this, then surprised her. 'I went there once. Australia. Saw the Great Barrier Reef, Sydney Opera House, Bondi Beach. I was a regular tourist. Can't say I had the urge to stay.'

Bel was becoming impatient. She could feel her level of irritation rising. 'You wanted to explain something?'

'I did. Look around you. What do you see?'

Bel let her eyes roam all around the room, out to the deck and back to the hallway and entrance. What was she supposed to be looking for? She hesitated, then finally spoke. 'You have a lovely home, but it's very empty.'

'Ha! Got it. It's designed that way. When Fiona – my granddaughter – was seven she was in an accident. We thought we were going to lose her.' His voice broke. He paused, and brushed a hand over his eyes, but not before Bel had seen them fill with a profound grief. 'She survived. However, she's been in a wheelchair ever since. That's why…' He waved his hand to encompass the room in which they were sitting. 'I keep the place tidy to give what she calls her *chariot* room to move. That's the reason for the ramp too, and the wide passageways. I had this place built to accommodate her needs.'

'Ah!' Bel was gradually coming to understand why Isobel had been so eager for her to visit. 'You're familiar with the modifications required to…'

'The modifications needed to make the old house in Kelvin Drive suitable for the purpose Isobel has in mind. It won't come cheap.' He rubbed his chin. 'I knocked the old place here down and started from scratch. You won't be able to do that, nor would you want to.'

Bel wasn't too sure about that, but remained silent, aware that, given the potential historical value of the old house and its proximity to the neighbouring buildings, he was right.

'However, it can be done with a good architect. Isobel has been doing her research and you'll find she has it all worked out. She wants you to know her wishes and to see what I've done here for wee Fiona. Not so wee, these days.' He gave a lopsided grin and dragged his hand through his hair. 'She'll be twelve at the turn of the year and off to the high school. She's bright as a button. Keeps us all on our toes. Determined to beat her brother in the academic field. Robbie's more sports inclined. Made the school first eleven in rugby last year,' Matt said with some pride. 'Takes after my dad. The talents seem to have skipped a generation.'

So, there was method in her aunt's apparent madness. She wasn't trying to throw Bel together with her unusual solicitor. She merely wanted her niece to see what needed to be done, if and when... Though no doubt more a matter of when. If Isobel was to be believed, her health was on a downward spiral.

'How long have you been Aunt Isobel's solicitor?' she asked.

Matt rubbed his chin and seemed to be considering. 'Must be around thirty years now. It was just after dad died. She contacted my uncle first — it was originally his firm — then seemed to prefer me to the old man.' He grinned. 'I was better looking in those days.'

Bel smiled politely, though she couldn't help thinking he was still a handsome man. Many of his age had let themselves go, given in to what was often called middle-age spread. Matt didn't seem to have a spare ounce of flesh on him. With his broad shoulders, long legs, tanned face and arms, his still thick hair showing just a hint of silver streaks among the grey and his penetrating brown eyes, he could well be described as the man every sixty-year-old woman dreamed of. But not this one, she reminded herself. She was long past dreaming of a man, let alone an eccentric Scot.

Six

Bel – 2015

When Bel returned, Isobel was eager for an account of her trip and nodded appreciatively when she described the house and its adaptations in detail. 'But it's a modern home. I don't see how it can be done here,' she said finally, despite being reluctant to talk of the things that could only happen when Isobel had passed away.

Her aunt, however, had no such qualms. She reached into a bureau drawer and pulled out what looked like a set of plans. 'It's all here. I've had it drawn up and costed. Though likely you'll find things a bit dearer when the time comes. I had these done a few years back, when Matthew and I first talked about it. Take a look.' Isobel passed the large sheets to Bel, who unfolded them on the table and examined them carefully. They were very thorough. Every detail seemed to have been considered and allowed for.

When she said as much, her aunt smiled. 'I didn'ae ken what you'd really be like, or if you'd even come back. Young Matthew helped me find the right man. He did a good job, didn't he? It's all ready for when…'

Bel folded up the plans again. 'Well, we won't be needing them just yet.' She couldn't get used to her aunt talking about her own death as if she were going off on a trip and needed to make sure everything was in order before she left.

'So,' Isobel began. The pair had eaten and were sitting by the window with a cup of tea. 'You and Matthew. How did you get on?'

'Fine. He seems a nice man. He told me about his granddaughter, and he has a little dog, just like my Toby.'

'Aye. He's that fond of the wee thing. It's company for him when the bairns aren't there, and of course they dote on it. It's the same breed as yours, you say? Isn't that something?'

Isobel had an innocent look on her face, but for some reason, Bel felt her aunt had known this all along. *What was going on here?*

'And what do you hear from Australia? I'm thinking you must have been on the email. You'll be wanting to keep tabs on that friend of yours. What was her name?'

'Jan,' said Bel, realising she hadn't opened her iPad since she arrived. Of course, there would be emails from Jan who'd promised to be scrupulous about keeping in touch. Sydney seemed so far away, not just geographically. Here in Scotland, Bel felt she'd entered a different world, a world where anything could happen. She gave herself a shake. What nonsense! 'I'll go and check now,' she said, rising and putting her cup down on the low table.

'No need to rush off.'

'No, but you're right. Anything could be happening back there. I should check.'

Once in her room, Bel turned on the iPad, waiting impatiently while it booted, then again while the flurry of emails appeared. She smiled. As promised, Jan had sent one every day. She opened and read them quickly: reports on sales, anecdotes about favourite customers – Mrs B's oldest granddaughter was being married and she'd purchased her wedding outfit, Edna from the bank was preparing a wardrobe for her first cruise, and Rita from the bakery sent her regards and was dying to show off her holiday photos.

Then there was a more worrying one. Bel's old friend and good customer, Heather, hadn't been well. She was also a good friend of Jan's sister, Anna, whose boss and mentor she'd been at Northern Beaches Grammar for many years. Heather had taken early retirement due to ill-health, but some time convalescing plus an extended overseas trip had given her a new lease of life and she'd been filling in at the school again. Now, it seemed, she'd taken a turn for the worse and was in hospital. Bel bit her lip, regretting she was so far away and unable to visit. It reminded her how fragile life could be. Heather and Isobel both suffered from the same complaint – and were equally stubborn.

On a happier note was a short email from young Andy, especially touching as he included a shot of Toby, tongue hanging out with the caption *Missing You* typed in bright letters in a balloon coming from the little dog's mouth. Bel smiled again. It was as if she was there and could feel her pet's wet tongue licking her toes.

She fired off a quick reply, then turned off the device with a sigh. For a few moments, her surroundings had faded, and she'd been back home in Sydney, but now she returned to the present, the darkening skies outside the window reminding her she was in Scotland.

'We're in for another deluge,' Isobel greeted her when she came back downstairs. 'And you'd better top up that cup. Your tea will be cold.'

Bel did as she was bid and settled back in her chair.

'Will you be seeing Matthew again?' Isobel enquired with a smile.

'I don't expect so, unless you have business with him.'

'Well, we'll see about that.' Isobel's reply was enigmatic, leaving Bel wondering if she'd been right to imagine her aunt had another agenda for her, one which included Matt and which had little or nothing to do with the house and her inheritance.

'Now there's someone else I think you'd like to see while you're here.' She pointed a finger at Bel. 'Remember Mary Anderson?'

'Mary?' Bel's eyes widened at the name. Mary Anderson had been her best friend all through primary and high school. The pair had spent every available moment together – sat together in class, been in the same Girl Guide troupe, gone dancing every Saturday, shared tales of the boys they met, backpacked around the highlands in school holidays and taken their first trip to France together. Bel remembered a few double dates which had them almost at each other's throats, and the time they'd both fancied the same boy who, it turned out, didn't know either of them existed. But through it all they'd remained friends, sworn to be lifelong buddies. What had happened? Bel racked her brains. She'd gone to uni while Mary…

'She's still there – in the old house.' Isobel's voice interrupted Bel's memories. 'Never married and looked after her folks till her mother passed away. Not long after your own mum. She drops in to see me regularly. You should look her up.'

Mary Anderson. So, she was still here, hadn't married.

'She never moved out?'

'Not like yourself. Being the youngest, she ended up caring for her parents in their old age. Now they're both gone and she's rattling around in that big house on her own.'

Bel stifled a grin. Her aunt's house was exactly the same size as the Anderson's, and she lived alone, too.

'I haven't see her since we left school – when I went to uni and she…'

'Went to the Dough School,' her aunt finished, using the local term for the Glasgow and West of Scotland College of Domestic Science. 'It's a university now too – the Caledonian University.'

'Hmm.' Bel wasn't sure she wanted to look up old friends, try to resurrect friendships that had been dead for over forty years. She was a different person from the young girl who'd lived here, in this house. She'd moved on a long time ago. What would she and Mary have in common these days?

But Isobel wouldn't give up. 'It'd do you good to catch up. See someone your own age. You don't want to be sitting here with me every day waiting…' She didn't finish the sentence, but Bel silently finished it for her – waiting for her aunt to die was what Isobel meant.

She sighed. There was no escaping. 'I suppose I can give her a call,' she said. 'Do you…'

'Her number's in the book. Right there by the phone. But she'll be calling in. Wednesday's her day at the library. She keeps me supplied with reading matter.'

Bel exhaled slowly. So, she wasn't going to have any choice in the matter. She decided to change the subject. 'I've started to read your…' She wasn't sure what to call it – a diary, a memoir, a piece of fiction, a fantasy?

'You have?' Isobel shifted uncomfortably in her chair. 'I don't know, I didn't…'

'If you didn't want me to read it, why did you give it to me?' Bel asked testily.

'Things were different then,' was all her aunt said. 'You'll have discovered…'

'Bob Smith. The name sounds vaguely familiar.'

'It's a common enough name. I thought so at the time. That's why...'

'And he really did look like Clark Gable?'

'His very image.' Isobel's eyes glazed over as if she could see him there in the room. 'He was so handsome, his slicked-back hair as black as night, his moustache – I suppose what you'd call sexy – tall, broad-shouldered. And his eyes – as deep brown as chocolate – and like dark pools. A girl could lose herself in those eyes.'

Bel experienced a flicker of recognition. She'd seen just such a pair of eyes recently, eyes whose memory she'd tried unsuccessfully to forget.

'And was he the love of your life? What happened? You didn't marry. Did he die in the war?'

'You don't really want to talk about that.' Isobel rose and began moving around the room aimlessly with the help of her stick as if to stop her niece from pursuing her questions.

But Bel was curious and determined to bring it up again. Aunt Isobel had always been affectionate but distant to her as a child; not as loving as her mother but more demonstrative than her Aunt Kate who'd died when Bel was in her teens – another victim of smoking. No doubt the answer lay somewhere in what Bel privately now called the *Isobel Saga*. She'd read more tonight.

Having grown up in the fifties and sixties, she'd always accepted the fact that the war had happened, and changed lives – her own father had survived, but had returned a changed man, so her mother had said. His death, when she was only five, had resulted in her having been brought up in a house run by women after her grandfather had died.

She'd never felt curious about the war years, how people felt, how her parents' generation coped and survived. Now she had a burning desire to know more. Maybe this was her opportunity.

Seven

Isobel – 1938

I don't know how I made it through the week. The image of Bob Smith flickered behind my eyes as I washed and set hair. I could hear his voice in my ears as I made polite conversation with clients, and I longed for each day to be over so I could curl up in bed and dream about him. I could hardly wait for Saturday.

Fortunately, my sister Nan was absorbed in her own daydreams of the blond-haired choir member who'd stolen her heart and her hopes for the church social, while Kate was more interested in the columns of figures she was memorising for her forthcoming examination.

The only one aware of my crush was Eileen, who'd been quick to contact me after the cinema to find out how I'd fared with her beau's friend. Of course, I'd played down my infatuation, saying he seemed all right, but she'd wormed out of me the fact that I was seeing him again.

'It's tomorrow, isn't it?' she said as we walked home together on Friday evening, sharing her umbrella.

'What is?' I asked, pretending indifference.

Her elbow bumping mine almost sent me flying. 'Clark Gable.'

'His name's Bob.' I giggled.

'But you have to admit he has the look of your idol.'

'Maybe a bit.' I tried to hide my eagerness. 'What are you and Alan doing tomorrow?'

'The church social,' she sighed. 'I wish you were going to be there too. It's such a staid affair. Why don't you drag Bob along? If there are four of us we can liven things up.'

'I don't know him well enough,' I objected, knowing that to turn up at the social with a stranger would set all the tongues wagging – my sister's most of all. 'Nan'll be there – with Jeannie,' I said, to deflect her attention from me.

'And I suppose she'll be sighing over that lad again?'

'I think he likes her, too. Just wait. One of these days he'll be walking her home.'

We parted at my corner, and I ran the rest of the way home, trying to avoid the puddles and holding my bag over my head to protect my hat. *Why did it always seem to be raining?*

*

By Saturday night, I was up to high doh, as my mother would have put it. I hadn't been able to concentrate all morning. Luckily the salon closed at lunchtime or I'd have been a nervous wreck.

I took my time getting ready, choosing my outfit carefully and spending so much time in front of the mirror that Nan had to push me aside to check her dress for the dance. Kate barely looked up from her books as Nan and I tripped downstairs and popped our heads through the kitchen door to say we were off.

We walked along together, but at the end of Byres Road, Nan peeled off in one direction while I went the other way to catch the tram into town.

Sitting on the upper deck of the vehicle, I fidgeted with my gloves. *What if he isn't there? What if he hadn't meant it? What if he forgot?* I almost got off early to catch another tram home, but managed to stop myself. It was only a date, after all. So what if he didn't turn up? No one would ever know if I didn't tell them.

By the time I reached my stop, I'd almost convinced myself he wouldn't show, so it was a shock to see him standing outside the cinema, a cigarette between his lips and his hands in his pockets. I stood watching him from across the road, enjoying the almost illicit sight of him before he raised his eyes and noticed me. I waved and ran across the road skirting the cars parked by the kerb.

'I thought you weren't coming,' he said, throwing the cigarette to the pavement and grinding it with his foot. Then he smiled, a smile that lit up his face. 'It's good to see you, Isobel. I've been looking forward to tonight.'

'Me too.' Feeling bold, I linked arms with him as we joined the queue which stretched all along the wall, just as it had the previous week. Despite the large number of cinemas in Glasgow – I'd read there were over one hundred – this one was always busy.

It felt different this week – just the two of us. Standing together in the line, it was as if we were in a cocoon. The buzz of conversation around us seemed to disappear as Bob asked me how I'd spent my week. His tales of the schoolboys he taught seemed exciting by comparison with my suburban ladies, but he didn't appear to mind and made me feel I was the most interesting thing that had happened to him all week.

I don't remember what the film was about. What I do remember from that evening was the thrill of Bob's hand holding mine, the rough texture of his jacket against my arm and the shock and disappointment when the lights went up and I realised the evening was almost over.

*

That was only the first of many such evenings, some spent with Eileen and her beau, some just Bob and me. As the winter progressed into the spring and summer of 1939, our outings varied from trips to the pictures to walking in Kelvingrove Park, listening to music at the bandstand or sitting watching the passing parade. The papers and the radio talked of the possibility of another war, of the dangers of Germany rearming, but we ignored the negative news, absorbed as we were in the wonder of our own romantic idyll.

It was on one of those evenings, one of the long, light, summer evenings when we'd walked around and around the park talking about nothing in particular, that Bob suggested sitting on the grass. At first, I objected, remembering the courting couples we'd passed – couples who seemed to think nothing of canoodling in broad daylight with what seemed to me to be gay abandon. That wasn't the way I'd been brought up. A chaste kiss at the end of an evening, or one stolen in the back row at the pictures was one thing, but that type of loose behaviour in a public place was something else entirely.

So, it was with some trepidation and a lot of wheedling on Bob's part, that he finally persuaded me to settle somewhat uncomfortably in the shade of a tree. At first, I sat up primly, my legs curled under me and my hands clasped in my lap. We continued to talk quietly and watch the passers-by. Then, I remember, he took my hands in his and I was conscious of a distinct flutter in the base of my stomach. I'd felt this way before when his kisses became more passionate, but then it had been at our front door through which I could escape any further embrace. Here in the park, there was no such way out.

Holding my hands firmly, Bob leaned over to kiss me. As our lips met, the flutter in my stomach became stronger. For the first time, he pressed his tongue between my lips and I experienced the strangest sensation. It was as if I'd turned to jelly. It made me want more of whatever he was offering me. It made me…

I pulled away, suddenly understanding what my mother had warned me about, what men wanted of women, what we must save for marriage, the difference between good women and bad women. I suddenly knew that there was no difference in the way we felt, in what we wanted. The difference was in how we responded when tempted.

'No, Bob,' I said, regretfully. 'We mustn't.' I drew my hands away. I pulled down my skirt which had become rucked up to my knees and looked around hoping no one had seen. I was shaking and wasn't sure why.

'Let's get you home then.' His voice was brusque, unlike his usual joking tone.

What had I done wrong? Surely I'd behaved the way he'd expect any good girl to behave? I puzzled over this as we walked home in silence, unwilling to be the first to speak. When we reached home we stopped, and I waited for my usual goodnight kiss, surprised only to receive a peck on the cheek.

'Be in touch,' Bob said as he strolled off, my confused eyes following him. What did he mean? Why hadn't he suggested another date? We'd been courting for months. Surely it wasn't going to end like this?

I opened the door slowly, and had started up the stairs when Nan called out to me. I stopped mid-step intending to ignore her, but she called again, her voice so filled with excitement I was forced to head back down and into the lounge where she and Kate were drinking cocoa.

'You'll never guess,' she trilled, pirouetting in the middle of the floor as if she was the doll in one of those new-fangled music boxes. 'We were walking in the park. Then we sat down on a bench. Colin got down on one knee and...,' she burbled.

I stopped listening. Nan was in the park? She and her fellow and goodness knows how many other people I knew. What if they'd seen me – seen us? What would they think? Would I be branded as one of those loose women they talked about in hushed tones? Would...?

'You're not listening!' Nan almost stamped her foot in annoyance.

'Yes I am.'

'What did I say, then?'

'You were with your fair-haired fellow in the park.'

'And?' She hopped from one foot to the other in excitement.

'And?' I realised I must have missed something – something important – while I was worrying about being seen.

'He proposed! We're to be married! We're going to look at rings next week!' Nan spoke in exclamation marks as if the world had swung on its axis which, for her, I suppose it had. She'd been keen on him forever and had been hoping against hope he'd pop the question. Ever since he'd brought her home from the church social, that same night I went to the pictures with Bob. Of course, I knew he'd noticed her long before that. I guess he'd been waiting for her to grow up.

And she had. I'd been too engrossed in my own romance to notice that my wee sister had suddenly bloomed and now... *she* was the one who was engaged – and it should have been *me*!

I sat down with a thump. Nan's life was about to begin, just as mine seemed to have come to an end. I tried to sound pleased for her and listened with half an ear as she and Kate debated as to when the wedding would be – not for ages yet, they predicted. Our parents would insist on a long engagement. She was still pretty young. Meantime I was wondering how soon I could escape upstairs. Though, of course there would be no privacy there, unless I could manage to get undressed and into bed before she and Kate came upstairs. Maybe

I could feign sleep and evade their questions about my own evening and predictions about Nan's future.

Fortunately, Nan's excitement had blunted her usual curiosity about my evening. I was lucky. Despite my disappointment in Bob, I managed to fall asleep as soon as my head hit the pillow, so was saved the expected inquisition when my sisters finally made it upstairs.

*

The week passed with no word from Bob. My spirits were low, and I found it hard to hide my own disappointment in the face of my sister's growing excitement. The parents were pleased about Nan's fellow – a good churchgoer, in the choir and from a family they knew and liked.

Bob had never received such acclamation, coming as he did from the posher end of town and being a much more unknown quantity. Maybe they'd known something I hadn't. I thought of the old phrase "Handsome is as handsome does". I'd never understood it till now. I should have known he was too good to be true, too good for me – or not good enough? That's what Mother would have said if she knew. But she didn't. I hadn't told anyone.

Friday came too soon that week. Funny how the weeks dragged when I had a date with Bob on the weekend, but this one had passed in a flash.

Eileen and I were sitting in the park eating lunch when she nudged me. 'Has he asked you yet?' Her eyes held a gleam of something I couldn't identify.

'What?' I took another bite from my sandwich and pretended to be indifferent.

'You know,' she said.

'If you're talking about Bob, he hasn't asked me anything.' How could he ask me anything if he didn't call or see me? Eileen knew about Nan's engagement. Did she think I was going to be next? Follow my wee sister down the aisle. Fat chance! I was forgetting that only a week ago I'd imagined it would be me sporting a bright diamond on the third finger of my left hand. I could barely look at Nan's without feeling a trace of envy, which I was at pains to hide.

'Well,' she said, lowering her voice, even though there was no one to hear us. 'My Auntie Betsy and Uncle John were planning to take their two boys away for a week to Largs. They go to the same boarding house every year. It's right on the seafront. The boys have developed chicken pox so they can't go, and Auntie Betsy has offered me the rooms. What do you think?'

What did I think? What did it have to do with me?

My face must have shown my bafflement, because she immediately added, 'You and me, Alan and Bob, the four of us, a week away together.'

'Oh!' A week earlier I'd have been over the moon, but now? 'I don't...'

'Alan's going to sound out Bob, and I said I'd talk to you. Bob hasn't said anything?'

'I...' I cleared my throat. 'I haven't spoken to Bob.' I looked down at my hands, still holding the half-eaten sandwich. I hadn't told Eileen about last Saturday. She'd have laughed. Although she wasn't one of what they called *loose women*, she'd probably have gone along with Bob, and hoped no one saw her or found out. That's where we were different. But it didn't stop us being best friends.

'Oh, well.' She dismissed my week of despair with a grin. 'It's the end of the school year. He's likely been busy. Maybe Alan hasn't had a chance to ask him either. You *will* come, won't you?' Her appealing eyes met mine. 'Father'd never let me and Alan go by ourselves. He'd imagine us getting up to all sorts.' She giggled as if the thought of what she and Alan might get up to was the funniest thing. 'You will, won't you?'

I nodded, my throat too tight for words. I couldn't let my friend down, though I was sure Bob would refuse. I'd be the odd one out again, relegated to being Eileen's cover for a week away with her boyfriend.

But miracles do happen.

That night, just as we were closing up, a tall familiar figure walked into the salon, twirling his hat with one hand and a cigarette in the other, looking impossibly suave and handsome as ever. I blushed and tried unsuccessfully to control the butterflies in my stomach.

'Hey there, how's tricks?' He grinned, and I was lost again. All the sensible advice I'd been giving myself about forgetting him flew out the window. This was Bob. He was here. He hadn't dumped me. I was in heaven!

'Walk you home?' he asked.

I couldn't grab my bag quickly enough. Shouting goodnight to the others and grinning from ear to ear, I walked out proudly on his arm. What had I been thinking? Of course, he respected what some might have called my prudishness, but what I knew was just how any well-brought up girl should behave. I blessed my parents for their good sense in teaching me the right way to conduct myself. Maybe soon Nan wouldn't be the only sister with a ring on her finger.

It was a warm evening, and we were in no hurry, so we dawdled along arm-in-arm like any other courting couple. When we reached the end of our road, Bob stopped suddenly, lit a cigarette and turned to face me. 'Did Eileen mention Largs to you?' he asked, awkwardly shifting from one foot to the other and taking a long drag on his cigarette.

I could have done with one myself to calm my nerves. I was in the habit of smoking in private – when my parents weren't around – but there was no way I'd light up in the street.

'She might have.' I wasn't going to make it easy for him, even though I was dying for him to suggest we should go too.

'Alan said they'd only be able to go if we went with them.' He took another draw on his cigarette and flicked the ash into the gutter in a gesture I admired.

My mood immediately collapsed. I felt crushed. So, he was only doing this to please his pal? He really hadn't meant to see me again.

I could feel my eyes begin to water, and my face must have fallen, because he immediately gave that cheeky grin of his and said, 'It'd be a lark, wouldn't it? The four of us off on holiday together. What d'you say? Will your parents agree?'

My relief was palpable. A bubble of excitement welled up and I gave him a big smile. 'I'll have to ask them.'

Bob threw his cigarette to the ground and stepped on it, then squeezed my arm, before tucking it into his and pressing my fingers affectionately. He pulled me close as we walked on and whispered what I suppose could be called sweet nothings into my ear. I was walking on air. Not only was my chap back, he wanted to spend a whole week with me by the seaside. The only drawback was I had to get my parents' permission. But Eileen would be there too, and maybe my folks didn't need to know about the boys.

Eight

Bel – 2015

A week passed, then another. One day was very much like the next. Bel did the shopping for her aunt and reacquainted herself with Byres Road. It had become much more cosmopolitan, and now boasted a number of book and charity outlets as well as coffee shops and restaurants.

She was intrigued to see a familiar pub, The Curlers Rest, still existed. As a student, Bel had spent many an afternoon there, having escaped from classes, drinking half-pints of beer and putting the world to rights. The place had been old then, so how old must it be now? It appeared to have had a facelift. It now catered for meals and was open all hours. Other old favourites, the Aragon and the Doublet, which she'd visited less frequently, were still there too. Glasgow hadn't changed much. From the preponderance of student scarves on the street, it seemed students hadn't changed much either.

On other days, Bel renewed her love affair with the Botanic Gardens, though Isobel had only been able to accompany her on one of these trips, pleading tiredness or lack of interest, telling her niece, 'You'll enjoy it more on your own,' and refusing to be swayed into accompanying her.

Bel enjoyed strolling along the pathways of her youth, recapturing memories of the times she escaped the confines of her restrictive home to enjoy the relative freedom in the garden's open spaces. Now, it was just pleasant to feel the breeze in her hair and to be reminded of Australia among the tree ferns and palm trees in the large glass house known as the Kibble Palace.

Bel's aunt had been urging her to contact her old school friend since, by accident or design, she'd managed to be out each time Mary had visited. But today there was going to be no avoiding her. At exactly two o'clock, the doorbell gave its familiar ring.

'That'll be her now,' Isobel said, rising and grabbing hold of her stick.

Bel made an attempt to forestall her, but her aunt waved her away. 'I'll be infirm soon enough. I can still answer my own front door.' She tottered off, her uneven gait almost belying her words. Bel watched in silence, knowing how much it meant to her aunt to maintain at least a semblance of independence and wondering how changed her old school friend would be.

Forty years was a long time, a time that had changed Bel herself into a different person from the shy child and rebellious teenager Mary had known. She heard the front door open and close, the indistinct sound of voices in the hallway, then they came closer and the door opened to reveal her aunt and a short, plump, grey-haired woman wearing a brightly-coloured tent-like dress and sandals.

Bel rose to greet her old friend, seeing the warm eyes and smile she recognized in the now blurred features of the older woman.

'Bel! I'd have known you anywhere.' Mary's voice hadn't changed, the same melodious tone that had made her popular in the church choir as a young girl, then later in the folk scene around Glasgow as a teenager.

'You still look the same too,' Bel replied, though if she'd met Mary in the street she would most likely have walked past without recognising her. Her once slim friend had ballooned in middle-age and now resembled the mother she'd lived with for so many years.

'My voice is probably the only thing that hasn't changed,' Mary replied ruefully, looking down at herself. 'But look at you. You haven't gained an ounce. You're just like Isobel here.' She glanced fondly at the older woman. 'I don't know how you MacDonalds do it. But you're not a MacDonald, are you? It was your mother who was the MacDonald and you were Isobel Davison. I heard you married over there, too.'

'Married and divorced a long time ago,' Bel replied.

'Now, let me get you two a cup of tea,' Isobel said, turning to leave.

'I can…,' Bel began, but her aunt had already walked out the door and was tap-tapping her way along the hallway. Bel looked at Mary and raised her eyebrows in despair.

Mary laughed. 'She's an independent old biddy. You're lucky. But…' She hesitated. 'I don't know how much she's told you about what her doctor says.'

'Enough. That's why I'm here.' She sat down again, and Mary joined her, choosing a large armchair and clearly feeling very at home.

'So,' Mary said, 'it took Isobel's being at death's door for you to come back to Glasgow? You never wanted to return, to come back to live here?' She didn't wait for an answer, but continued, 'I suppose you live a life of luxury over there in the sun and can forget all about us poor folks here in the land of your birth.'

Bel took a deep breath. She'd wondered if she and Mary would have anything in common, but hadn't expected this sort of bitterness. She counted to five before replying. 'Our lives took us in different directions, Mary. Aunt Isobel tells me you still live in the old house and your parents are gone. I was sorry to hear that. You never moved out?'

'Sorry they're gone or sorry I still live there?' A touch of Mary's old sense of humour appeared as she sighed. 'No, I never had the chance. Remember how we planned to leave home, flat together, maybe go to London. It seemed the place to be back then in the seventies. We lost touch after school, when you went off to uni. I went to the Dough School and became the general dogsbody at home. Cathie married so that left me when Mum got sick. And when I began cooking more – and eating more – I became…' She looked down disparagingly again at her body. 'Well, what you see now.'

'I never meant to lose touch.' Bel experienced a feeling of guilt. Had she contributed to her friend's unhappiness? Would Mary's life have been different if she'd…?

'Not your fault. When you went up the hill, I deliberately made other friends. I didn't think you'd still want to know me. I was very aware in those days of the difference between me and the people you'd meet at uni. Daft now. The Dough School is a uni too. Makes you think, doesn't it?'

There was a sound at the door and Bel leapt up to open it and let Isobel wheel in a tea trolley carrying not only tea, but a selection of buttered gingerbread and chocolate biscuits. If Bel stayed here for long, she'd no longer be "one of Pharaoh's lean cattle". She was amazed at how Isobel had retained her trim figure. The Scots were renowned for their love of sugar and all things sweet, and her aunt was no exception.

'Catching up, girls?' Isobel asked as she set the trolley beside her favourite chair and began to pour the tea. 'Bel, can you pass these to Mary while I catch my breath.' She indicated the tea and plates of food, while putting a hand to her chest and breathing heavily.

'Sure.' Bel complied, feeling guilty and wishing she'd insisted on making the tea herself. She was finding it difficult to gauge just how much help to give Isobel – when to insist and when to accept the other's independent spirit. It was a tough call. It must be hard to give up your independence, to allow someone else to do what you'd rather be doing for yourself. She hoped it never happened to her, realising that, in Isobel's position, she had no niece or other relative to call upon. What would that mean? A nursing home? Perish the thought!

'You shouldn't have, Isobel,' Mary said, in what seemed to be a well-worn objection as she helped herself to two large pieces of gingerbread and a couple of biscuits. 'If I take these now, you'll no' need to come back,' she said to Bel. 'Your aunt always provides so much with her afternoon tea, I can barely eat anything for the rest of the day.'

'Och, away with you,' Isobel said, clearly taking Mary's words as a compliment, and reminding Bel of her own mother's baking and typically Scottish hospitality.

When she was growing up, it was considered the height of bad manners for a hostess to be frugal in her offerings or for a guest to refuse what was on offer. And the baking always contained lots of butter, sugar, and eggs, ingredients which rarely found their way onto Bel's shopping list back in Australia.

'Your aunt's been keeping me up to date with all your news,' Mary said, when all three had consumed their fill and the teapot was finally empty. 'You have a dress shop? You didn't stay with teaching, then? Isn't that what you went there to do?'

'Yes, it's a long story.' Bel wasn't sure she wanted to go into her personal history right then. She looked down at her hands, wondering how much she could get away with saying, or not saying.

Her aunt seemed to sense her discomfort. 'The two of you'll have plenty of time to share your stories.' She turned to Mary. 'Have you my books? I'm right out of reading material, and if it wasn't for Bel being here, I'd be champing at the bit.'

Mary started fossicking in a bag at her feet and drew out three books. 'Here you are. I managed to get the latest Ian Rankin for you this week.'

'Good girl.' Isobel took the books and examined the cover of the topmost one. 'He sets them all in Edinburgh, but despite that, he writes a good story. You should get into some of our local authors while you're here.' Isobel pointed at Bel as she spoke. 'Caro Ramsay or Stuart McBride. If you enjoy blood and guts, that is.'

Bel laughed. 'From time to time I do manage to find Scottish authors in Australia, you know. And other authors do write well about Scotland like Ann Cleeves with her Shetland series.'

The three began discussing their favourite books and authors till Mary checked her watch. 'I'd better be off,' she said, rising and picking up her bags.

'I'll see you to the door,' Bel said, sensing her aunt's approval. 'I'll take these things through when I get back,' she said to Isobel, knowing full well her aunt would have preferred to do it herself, but noticing the older woman was tiring with the strain of having company.

Mary hesitated on the doorstep. 'I know you're probably busy with Isobel and everything,' she began, making Bel wonder what on earth Mary imagined she was doing here every day. 'But I'd love to have a chat about the old days, and catch up. I'd love to hear about Australia.' Bel was about to make excuses when Mary's eyes met hers and Bel was reminded of the close friendship the two had before circumstances drew their lives apart.

'Why not? You're just up the road.'

She was rewarded by a wide smile. 'How about next Tuesday? Around ten?'

'I'll see you then.'

Bel closed the door. She'd surprised herself by her acceptance of Mary's invitation. When she'd set out on this trip, it had never been her intention to recapture her earlier years, yet here she was doing just that; staying in this house, visiting her old haunts in Byres Road and the Botanic Gardens, and now agreeing to visit Mary to "talk over old times". It wasn't what she'd planned at all.

'Did you and Mary make a time?' Isobel wanted to know as soon as Bel returned.

'Tuesday,' Bel said, still surprised at her decision.

'That's good.' Isobel leaned back in her chair and coughed violently. When she regained her breath she added, 'It was Mary who helped me find young Matthew, you know.'

'Mary?' Bel asked, part of her puzzled by her aunt's choice of words. But before she could enquire, Isobel continued.

'It was when her parents were putting their estate in order, they came across Reid Solicitors in Anniesland. Donald Reid had founded the firm and young Matthew is his nephew; a family firm.' She nodded her head as if to confirm her words. 'He's served me well ever since. Yes, I have a lot to thank your old school friend for.'

*

When she had a few minutes to herself. Bel continued to read her aunt's account of her younger life. As she read, those years before the war came alive. It wasn't a time Bel knew much about – what had happened in Glasgow or Scotland as a whole. The books and films she'd been exposed to had all tended to focus on England or Europe. If she'd thought about it at all, she'd have assumed it was much the same for Scotland. But she'd never given any thought to her own family – her mother, aunts and grandparents – to all the inhabitants of this house and what their lives had been like before she'd been born.

Her aunt must have read her mind.

One morning, as the pair were enjoying breakfast together, Isobel finished swallowing a mouthful of toast, took a sip of tea and asked, 'You've been reading it?'

'I have. I read the bit where Mum and Dad got engaged. Was that a surprise?'

Isobel smiled. 'I think it was more of a surprise to Nan than to the rest of us. We could see the way the wind was blowing, but your mum was always worried she was too young for him – something he once said. But once they started to walk out together, neither of them had eyes for anyone else. They glowed with happiness. I mind well the day they bought the ring. She walked in wearing that woollen suit she'd saved up for – green it was, her favourite colour – waving her hand in the air. And there on her finger was the ring he'd chosen for her. Five diamonds! And he was right behind her. He was a handsome fellow with his fair curls and his quirky sense of humour. It's a pity you never really knew him.' She sighed. 'Theirs was a fairy-tale romance, not like...' Isobel's lips tightened, and she gazed off into space – something Bel had noticed her aunt doing more and more frequently – as if she was stepping back in time.

Bel looked at her aunt in surprise. The description of her dad was quite different from her own memories. She'd only been five when he'd died and barely remembered him. What memories she had were of a morose man who, when he wasn't at work, had sat quietly in his chair. This lively cheerful guy seemed a different person. Was that what the war had done to him? Bel had read many articles about the effects of post-traumatic stress and other war-generated disorders in soldiers returning from the present-day conflicts in Iran and Afghanistan, but had never, till now, related them to her own father.

'Did he... was he... suffering from post-traumatic stress?' she asked.

'We didn't call it that in those days, and there was some physical illness there too, but I know it was hard for your mum back then. Then you came along and you were the light of her life.' Isobel smiled. 'You were a bright sunbeam for us all after those dark days.' She looked at Bel fondly as if conjuring up those early years.

Bel shifted uncomfortably. Deep down she'd always known how much her family loved her, but as she'd grown older it was that very love which had stifled her and driven her away. For the first time in her life, she experienced a feeling of guilt. Guilt that as a teenager and young woman, she'd been too self-absorbed to realise how much she meant to them, guilt that she'd put her own feelings first, guilt that she'd left.

But on reflection, she wouldn't change the past. She'd always been grateful to her mother for respecting her desire to spread her wings and see more of the world.

'Now, what about yourself?' Isobel asked. 'You've been on your own a long time. Have you given up on men?'

Bel almost choked. This was the last thing she'd expected. She was sixty-five, not twenty-five, or even thirty, the age she'd been when she and Pete and had gone their separate ways. 'I think I'm a bit past that,' she said with a laugh. She'd put the thought of men behind her many years earlier, settling instead for a full social life, her shop and little Toby. That kept her busy and content and removed the pitfalls of trying to form a relationship which was destined to fall apart.

Bel reflected that she hadn't been lucky with men, as evidenced by her first disastrous relationship here in Scotland, her short marriage and the subsequent affairs when she'd still believed in the possibility of finding a soulmate.

A soulmate! That was a laugh, a myth perpetrated by romance books and eagerly sought after by young women, one of whom she'd once been. But no more.

'It's never too late,' Isobel continued, seemingly unaware of her niece's annoyance. 'I left it too late and I regret it. Sometimes we make decisions for the wrong reasons and when it's too late to change we realise what we lost. There's someone for everyone – we just have to recognise them and do whatever it takes to hold on to our happiness.' Isobel's voice faded away on her final words and Bel sat there wondering what the conversation was all about.

She recalled reading her aunt's memoir last night. She'd fallen asleep just as it seemed that the Bob Smith character had dropped Isobel. Served her right, Bel had thought, while aware that times had changed a lot since her aunt was a young woman. Having grown up in what had been called the swinging sixties, she'd had none of her aunt's qualms.

But *her* choices hadn't led to happiness either.

Nine

Isobel – 1939

I couldn't hide my excitement. Mother and Father had agreed to my going to Largs with Eileen after checking with Eileen's parents and aunt that it was all above board. Little did they know we were to be accompanied by two fellows. Eileen's parents didn't know either. I felt a twinge of guilt at the deception, but consoled myself with the fact that I hadn't actually lied.

When the day of our departure arrived, Eileen and I caught the tram to St Enoch station where we'd agreed to meet our companions. We were giggling nervously as we pushed through the holiday crowds, our new suitcases filled with summer dresses and the daring new swimsuits we'd bought secretly one lunchtime.

As we passed the news stand, our eyes flickered past the headlines which screamed at us; there had been a fatal mining accident, the Italian foreign minister was engaged in talks with Germany, gas masks to be provided for babies, the skies had been filled with warplanes to test Britain's defences. We shrugged off all this talk of war and disasters. It meant nothing to us. We were intent on having fun.

'There they are!' Eileen dropped her case and pointed to the ticket office where Alan and Bob were standing smoking and peering at a newspaper. For a moment, I gazed at Bob, who was looking very dashing in his flannels, open-necked shirt and fair-isle pullover. With his tanned skin and a hat tilted to the back of his head, he looked for all the world like Gable himself. I shivered. I was about to spend a whole week with him by the seaside.

It wasn't as risqué as it sounded. We weren't going to share a room. No way! Eileen and I would be tucked up in ours while the lads shared one in another part of the boarding house. But it was the first time I'd gone on a holiday without the family. It would be an adventure, and I couldn't wait for it to begin.

Bob turned around and caught sight of us, taking off his hat and pointing us out to his mate. Eileen picked up her case and we walked demurely over to join them, pretending this was an everyday occurrence, instead of the most exciting thing that had ever happened to us.

'Hello, girls.' It was Alan who spoke, his freckled face turning red with pleasure as Eileen dropped her case again and threw her arms around his neck.

I peered around surreptitiously, hoping there was no one we knew to see us and report back. But all the other travellers seemed to be too intent on their own business to give us more than a passing glance. I sighed with relief.

'You got away all right?' Bob was at my side, stroking his moustache with a nervous finger.

So, he'd been worried too? A good sign surely? I ached to touch him, for my finger to stroke his unshaven upper lip. But that would be too daring, unseemly in such a public place. Maybe later, when we were alone? The fluttering in the base of my stomach which I'd experienced before in Bob's presence was back in force. Could he tell? Were my feelings transparent?

'No trouble,' I said lightly, trying to subdue my excitement, but seeing a matching emotion in his eyes.

'Okay, you two lovebirds.' It was Alan speaking again. 'We have the tickets. We should make for the platform. Don't want to miss the train, do we?'

When the train arrived, we all piled into an empty carriage with much jostling and laughing as the boys hoisted the cases up on the racks, pretending to complain about the weight of ours. When we were finally settled, with Bob and I sitting together facing the other two, Eileen produced a packet of sandwiches.

'My mother thought we'd be hungry,' she said, 'but there's only enough for two.'

The boys laughed, and Alan drew a bar of chocolate from his pocket, 'How about we share?' he suggested. 'We can have a picnic.'

When the train drew into Largs station, we all leapt up, Bob opening the door and Alan handing the cases out onto the platform. The train had been busy, so the station platform was now jam-packed with families, fathers carrying cases, children with pails and spades, and harried mothers comforting wailing babies.

We thrust our way through the crush to the roadway where Bob hailed a taxi. I felt my eyes widen as we crowded in. Bob seemed accustomed to this mode of travel, as did Alan. In my world taxis were for weddings and funerals. Otherwise it was a bus, tram or shank's pony. The holiday was certainly starting on a high note.

We reached our destination in no time. The boarding house was right across from the beach, just as Eileen's Auntie Betsy had described. As soon as the taxi drew to a stop and the door opened, we could smell the distinctive odour of sea and seaweed. I breathed it in greedily, enjoying its pungent aroma. I wanted to lift my arms in the air and spin in circles, but contained myself, merely throwing my head back, looking up at the sky and smiling widely.

Eileen showed no such restraint, running over to the sea-wall, then twirling on her toes. 'Look, Isobel! Isn't it wonderful? Oh, we're going to have such a time!'

Our landlady for the week proved to be a buxom woman in her fifties with a tight bun who greeted us at the door beaming. 'You'll be Betsy Freeman's niece,' she said. 'And who are these two fine fellows?' She winked. I almost choked. I'd forgotten the landlady knew Eileen's Auntie Betsy. What if she told her about our companions? But I needn't have worried. The woman put a finger to the side of her nose and added, 'I'm Nellie Barton – call me Nellie – and I was young once too. I'll have no shenanigans, mind. The boys can have the room on the top floor and you girls will be just one floor up. I'm thinking Betsy doesn't know there's four of you?'

Eileen had the grace to look shamefaced.

'If we need to pay extra…' Alan offered.

'No need for that. Both rooms have already been booked and paid for.' Her eyes raked the boys up and down. Then she chuckled. 'I dare say it'll be nice to have some male company for a bit. Mr Barton passed some time back. I take it you won't be averse to a bit of female companionship?' She looked directly at Bob as she spoke, and to my surprise he actually blushed. 'Only joking,' she added. 'I'm sure you'd rather spend your time with these two young things than with an old hen like me.'

Having had her joke, Nellie showed Eileen and me to our room, before heading up another flight of stairs followed by Bob and Alan.

'Look at this!' Eileen rushed to the window that looked out onto the promenade. She opened it to the sound of the waves breaking on the sand. Then she came back and bounced on the bed. 'Can you believe it, Isobel? We're really here. Just the four of us for seven whole days.'

It sounded idyllic and it was.

*

Most days, we hurried through breakfast and dashed down to the beach where the boys had hired a bathing hut, allowing Eileen and me to undress and dress again modestly. The first day, I felt awkward appearing in front of Bob so scantily clad, and his whistle of appreciation did nothing to stem my embarrassment. But as the week progressed, I became accustomed to my new outfit, and Bob's own garment left little to the imagination, forcing me to avert my eyes when he walked out of the sea, his swimsuit forming a second skin on his tanned, well-honed body.

I'd never learned to swim, inheriting Mother's fear of the water, but as a Physical Education teacher, Bob was a strong swimmer, at home in the water. While Eileen and I played in the shallows, yelling and screaming when a big wave swept over us, the boys bravely swam out from the shore till only their bobbing heads could be seen above the waves. One day, Bob tried to teach me to float on my back and the sensation of his hands gripping my bare shoulders gave me a thrill, before I decided I didn't have the courage to continue.

In the evenings, after the slap-up meal Nellie provided, we often went our separate ways, Bob and I taking long walks, while Eileen and her beau preferred to linger in the sand dunes.

Breakfast was always a jolly affair, knowing we had another entire day to do as we pleased. But on the Friday, Alan arrived at the breakfast table carrying a newspaper and looking very serious. He drew Bob aside and shook his head as Eileen tried to grab the paper from him.

'I thought we'd decided on no news this week?' she asked, referring to a pact we'd made on the train. We'd all agreed to this when the boys started discussing the possibility of war, and the dangers posed by Adolf Hitler being appointed Chancellor of Germany.

'Nellie said she'd heard it on the wireless. I had to see if it was true.' Reluctantly, Alan revealed the headline:

Germany invades Poland. Nazi troops enter Warsaw

'So? This is Scotland. What does Poland have to do with us?'

'It's not good,' Bob said seriously, stroking his moustache. 'It could mean…'

A shiver ran up my back. I'd heard my parents discussing the threats made by the German Chancellor, the dangers of Germany rearming, but hadn't taken them seriously. Even though I knew the government was taking steps, making gasmasks available, preparing for the worst, and I'd heard about the new warships being built on Clydeside.

It all seemed like a bad dream. Surely it couldn't be true? Not now, not when everything was so perfect.

'Well, they're not going to come here, are they?' Eileen asked, gazing out the window. My eyes followed hers, and looking at the peaceful scene – only a few families on the front at this time in the morning, seagulls swooping down to retrieve last night's leftover fish and chips. It seemed impossible that all this could change just because of one man in far-off Germany.

'I think we need to take it seriously,' Bob said, his voice sombre.

Alan nodded. 'It says Britain and France are preparing to declare war. Maybe we should return home.'

'But we only have two days left,' wailed Eileen. 'Surely it isn't going to happen overnight?'

'Since Adolf Hitler was appointed chancellor nothing's certain,' Alan warned. He glanced across to meet Bob's eyes while Eileen and I looked wildly at each other. I could feel the blood draining from my face, and Eileen was as white as a sheet.

'But…' I stammered. 'Didn't Mr Chamberlain have an agreement? A… a…' I couldn't remember the word.

'A non-aggression pact,' Bob completed for me. 'He did, but that was last year. A lot of people thought he was wrong to seek appeasement, but no one wanted a war. However, it seems Hitler has reneged on the agreement. It says here…' He read from the paper, 'Hitler has derided the agreement as a scrap of paper.'

'Oh!'

'But do we need to go home early?' Eileen was still keen to stay by the seaside. 'We're going home on Sunday anyway. Why can't we stay till then? What difference will it make?'

The men looked at each other again in silence, then Bob seemed to make up his mind. 'Probably none. You're right, Eileen. We should enjoy what's left of our holiday. Put this news behind us and…'

'But it *is* serious, isn't it?' I was hoping for reassurance, but fearful there was none to be had.

'It is,' Bob replied finally sitting down to join us. 'It seems war's inevitable. We should enjoy the next two days while we can. I fear that once we return home, life will never be the same again.'

'Will you be enlisting?' Eileen asked fearfully, her eyes darting from Alan to Bob and back again. I remembered Eileen's two older brothers. They'd be in it for sure.

The men exchanged glances. It was clearly something they'd discussed. I wondered just how much they'd discussed, and how Eileen and I had been so naïve as to have ignored the warning signs.

'We may have no choice,' Alan said after a long pause. 'Bob may be in an exempt occupation as a teacher, but… we've talked about it and we both want to do our bit.'

There was silence as we digested his words. It seemed incomprehensible that we could be sitting here on a bright summer morning debating such a morbid topic.

Nellie interrupted us by appearing with a tray of plates bearing the usual bacon and egg breakfast. 'Sorry I'm late. I'm all at sixes and sevens this morning. You'll have heard the news. A terrible thing. We lived through the last one and never thought to see this day.' She shook her head and went off muttering to herself.

I looked at my plate. Although hungry when I sat down, I'd

completely lost my appetite. I only picked at my food while the others managed to wolf theirs down.

Pushing her empty plate away, Eileen looked around the table. 'Well, you won't win the war sitting here with long faces. We're still on holiday. What are we going to do today?'

'It doesn't seem right to carry on as if nothing's happened,' I said. 'Do you think...?'

'I think we should have a quiet day and head home a day early. We should all be with our families at a time like this,' Alan said.

The others nodded and I remembered Bob and Alan had brothers too. Their parents – and Eileen's – would be terrified for their boys. I grew up with tales of the last war and the devastation it had caused for families, although Father remained close-mouthed about what it had been like "over there" as he referred to it.

The four of us spent the day together, unwilling to be parted, the boys serious, Eileen and I worried, but all of us trying to put a brave face on it. After dinner, Bob suggested a film, but Eileen was all for going dancing. I didn't fancy dancing, so Bob and I headed to the cinema, leaving Eileen and Alan to head off to Barrfields Pavilion to enjoy what was touted as one of the best dance floors in Ayrshire.

The film was *Wings of the Navy*, a light-hearted spy film with George Brent and Olivia de Havilland, but with war imminent, the storyline failed to amuse us or hold our attention, and the newsreel shots of Poland being invaded were all too real. I shuddered and leaned closer to Bob, his arm tight around my shoulders. We walked back to the boarding house slowly. It was a clear night and everything would have been perfect except for the threat hanging over us, the threat I didn't want to even think about, never mind mention. Maybe if I didn't think about it, it would go away.

We stopped for a kiss and cuddle in one of the shelters on the promenade, then continued back. I couldn't help but feel a hint of disappointment. It had been a wonderful week. Bob had been very attentive, affectionate, but... he hadn't made the declaration I'd been hoping for. He still hadn't proposed. Maybe the threat of war had intervened, but surely...

I was still wondering about this as I closed the bedroom door behind me and saw I had the room to myself. Eileen and Alan must still be dancing. I yawned, stretched my hands above my head and kicked off my shoes. I was about to remove my jacket when there was a gentle knock on the door.

Surprised, I opened it a crack and was astonished to see Bob standing there.

'Can I come in?' he asked in a whisper.

I was shocked and quickly glanced up and down the corridor to make sure no one could see. Apart from Nellie's strict directives of no shenanigans, nothing in my upbringing or previous experience had prepared me for this.

'What?' was all I could say. My tongue was sticking to the roof of my mouth and I felt my stomach drop, but whether from fear or excitement, I didn't know.

'I can't get into my room.' He looked awkward and just a little hopeful. 'Alan and Eileen are...'

He didn't need to finish. I could well imagine what the other two were up to. But, while I'd always known my friend appeared to be what many called loose with her wild talk, I'd never in a million years thought this would happen. I felt myself redden as I imagined the other pair entwined, their bodies writhing. I closed my eyes to dismiss the image.

'No,' I said decisively. 'You can't come in here.'

'No? Where am I to go? Come on, Izzy. Why can't we have some fun too? Take pity on a poor guy.' Bob placed a hand flat on the door as if to push it open.

He looked so handsome, standing there smiling, smoothing his moustache, more like Clark Gable than ever. It was tempting to throw caution to the wind, to forget all of Mother's warnings, to give in to the heat spreading through my body, to..., but something, some shred of decency held me back.

'No,' I repeated. 'You can't. *We* can't.'

'But where else can I go?' His face drooped. He looked so forlorn, I almost weakened.

'You can find somewhere else,' I said and closed the door, wondering if I was making the biggest mistake of my life, but convinced it was the only thing I could do.

I stood just inside the door and listened as Bob's footsteps grew fainter, then I heard the front door slam. He'd gone.

I undressed slowly, waiting for Eileen to return. She'd be back soon and Bob could get into his own room. Everything would be back to normal, and tomorrow we'd have forgotten about it. I lay down and closed my eyes, but sleep wouldn't come. The sound of cars on the road outside seemed louder than usual. My eyes stung with tears. What if Bob didn't forgive me? What if he thought I was too prudish? I remembered the last time I'd said no to him. But he'd come back to me then, seemed to respect that decision, so…

I must have dozed off finally, because when I opened my eyes again, bright sunlight was pouring through the window. My eyes went to the bed on the other side of the room where I expected to see Eileen fast asleep. It was empty – hadn't been slept in. That meant… Damn! Where had Bob spent the night? Had he found somewhere to sleep? How dare Alan and Eileen be so uncaring, so insensitive, so selfish?

I pulled on my robe, grabbed my toilet bag and made my way down the hall to the bathroom to freshen up. By the time I returned to the room, Eileen was there, changing into her costume ready for the trip home.

'Bob gone down to breakfast already?' she asked, combing her hair.

'I don't know. He didn't spend the night here.' I knew my voice was frosty.

Eileen turned from the mirror, her eyes wide in astonishment. 'He didn't? Why not?'

'I'm not like you, Eileen. I can't, couldn't… I told him…'

'You didn't let him in?' Eileen seemed stunned. 'We thought…'

'No!' I was filled with rage, 'You and Alan. You didn't think at all. Or if you did, it was all about you. Did you really expect…?' But I saw from the expression on her Eileen's face that was exactly what she had supposed. 'You really thought I… Bob and I…' I was so angry I couldn't find the words to express my outrage. My best friend, had really thought that Bob and I would… 'Well, we didn't,' I said, wondering exactly where Bob had slept if the other couple had been in the boys' room all night.

Bob and Alan were already eating breakfast, a morning paper lying open on the table, when we joined them. I slid into my usual seat next to Bob. 'Morning,' I said, trying to sound cheerful. There was no reply. He didn't look up or stop eating. I wanted to ask what he'd done, where he'd gone, but didn't dare. He seemed different, unapproachable. What had happened to the man who'd kissed me by the seawall last night, who'd held me tightly through the film and who'd told me how beautiful I was?

'We should leave after breakfast,' Alan said, looking up. 'There's a train that'll get us in before lunchtime. I hope you two slept well.' He addressed his remark to Bob and me, winked, then gave Eileen a smug smile. She simpered in return. I cringed.

So, Bob hadn't said anything, and Alan assumed...? My blood boiled. I opened my mouth to set him straight, then closed it again. What good would it do? Bob might deny it. Wasn't that what men did? They stuck together and boasted of their conquests. There was no way he'd boast about being turned down, shut out, not when his best mate was...

I ate my breakfast quickly. It tasted like sawdust. I shook my head to Eileen's offer of tea. 'I'll just go up and pack,' I said, glancing at Bob out of the corner of my eye. His were focused on the copy of the *Daily Mirror*. He began talking to Alan, reading out the headline: *Britain and France mobilise*.

'It's coming,' he said, picking up his cup. 'We're right to be going home.'

He completely ignored me. It was as if I wasn't there. With a catch in my throat, tears not far from the surface, I walked out of the dining room with as much dignity as I could muster and took the stairs two at a time. I managed to stem the tears till I reached the bedroom, then threw myself onto the bed and let them flow. I cried for my lost love, for the war that was coming, for the future I'd hoped for. I knew Bob had finished with me – and it was *all my fault*. But I'd do the same again. And I couldn't help feeling a touch of pride that I'd retained my virtue. I'd been tempted and hadn't given in. I'd stood firm on my principles. I should be feeling righteous. Why then, did I feel so miserable?

Then I remembered the spey-wife's words: *You'll meet him, but it won't last.* I curled up and buried my head in the pillow, my heart breaking.

Ten

St Enoch station was in turmoil when we arrived back in Glasgow. Everyone seemed to be rushing hither and thither, and the news-stands proclaimed the rearmament we'd already seen in the morning paper.

While Alan and Eileen disappeared in the crush – he'd insisted on seeing her home to her door – Bob left with barely a goodbye. I gazed after him in despair, before making my own way to the tram stop and heading for home.

Once there, my parents and sisters greeted me as if I'd been gone forever and had been in danger from who knew what. The latest news had done more than shake them. I was immediately drawn into the bosom of my family. Father was already talking of joining the Home Guard – something they'd had in the last war for those men too old or infirm to fight – and Mother was busy looking out knitting patterns for socks, gloves, and helmets. The helmets were for the soldiers to wear under the army-issue hard-shelled helmets. No one asked about my week's holiday. I was glad.

'You'd think we were already at war,' Kate complained, as the family sat down to dinner, but we all ignored her and tried to behave as normally as possible.

We'd barely finished eating dinner when Nan rose to go.

'Where are you off to?' Father asked. 'Can't you spend one Saturday night with your family? We need to keep together at a time like this.'

'Colin's meeting me,' she replied. 'I need to see him. If…' She didn't need to say any more. We all realised what she meant. If there was to be a war, Colin would enlist with all the other young men of their acquaintance.

I shuddered. It was a strange feeling, like being in limbo, waiting for the inevitable, for the axe to fall, for war to be declared.

*

This morning the British Ambassador in Berlin handed the German Government a final Note stating that, unless we heard from them by 11 o'clock that they were prepared at once to withdraw their troops from Poland, a state of war would exist between us.

I have to tell you now that no such undertaking has been received, and that consequently this country is at war with Germany.

We huddled round the wireless at eleven o'clock on Sunday morning as our prime minister, Mr Chamberlain, uttered these fateful words, finishing with, *Now, may God bless you all. May He defend the right. It is the evil things that we shall be fighting against – brute force, bad faith, injustice, oppression and persecution – and against them I am certain that the right will prevail.*

We sat for a few seconds in silence when he finished speaking, then Father reached to turn it off. 'Well, that's it,' he said, his voice full of despair. 'I never thought I'd live to see another war. I'm just glad I have no sons to run off the way I did.' He shook his head. 'It's a bad day.'

Mother got up and went into the kitchen to put the kettle on. A cup of tea was her remedy for every problem, but I didn't see how it could help us today. Kate and I looked at each other, while Nan rose to fetch her coat.

'Where d'you think you're going?' Father thundered.

'Colin,' she said. 'Last night he said if it came to this, he'd enlist. I need to see him.' And she was off.

Mother brought in cups of tea, and we sat around not knowing what else to do, till Father got up and fetched in the gasmasks. We'd been issued them in July amid much laughter and joking about what we'd look like, along with dismay at their rubbery smell. It didn't seem so funny now with the possibility of poison gas from German bombers seemingly coming closer every minute.

Unlike some of our neighbours, Dad had refused to build an Anderson shelter, insisting our house could withstand anything the Jerries cared to throw at it. We'd laughed it off, never believing war would actually come. But it had. We were at war. In a few minutes everything had changed. Suddenly, the end of my romance was the least of my worries. What would this war mean for us, for my family?

'Father, what'll happen here? What will change?' Pragmatic Kate asked the question I'd been too scared to put into words.

Father pulled on his ear and seemed to think hard before replying. 'We're pretty close to the shipyards. I expect they'll be a target for their bombers.'

Kate and I looked at each other again. *Bombs on Clydeside?*

'As for you girls,' he continued. 'Well, most of the young men will go off to fight.'

I felt my stomach clench at the thought of Bob – and all the other young men I knew – in uniforms, being wounded, maybe even killed. Then I realised Father was still speaking.

'It'll be like last time. They'll need women to take the place of men in some jobs. Won't be the same need for your fancy hairdos,' he said to me.

'Our Kate will be well-placed with her business studies,' Mother said proudly, patting my sister's knee. 'There'll be jobs for girls like her. She'll be snapped up in no time.'

Kate grimaced at me, but it made me think. Maybe I should do something different. But first, I'd have to check what Lilian intended to do about the salon. Surely Father couldn't be right? Women would always want their hair done.

*

The rest of the day passed slowly. Eileen came round and we went out for a walk, but all we could talk about was the news of war. Her brothers were eager to enlist as soon as they could, one was keen on the navy, the other favoured the army. She couldn't stop talking about how Alan wanted to go too and what she'd do without him, wondering if he'd give her a ring before he went off.

Luckily, she was too full of her own worries to ask about what had happened between Bob and me. I managed to express my sympathy and keep mum about my own concerns. What was the end of a romance in the face of the imminent hostilities?

But when I returned home, the thought of Bob was uppermost in my mind. Maybe he'd change his mind – when he'd time to consider. Eileen had only mentioned his name once, and that was to say he and Alan had planned to enlist together, but that Bob might have to wait till the school would release him.

All I wanted to do was go to bed and curl up again, but Mother had made the usual Sunday roast dinner and Father wanted us all together to listen to the King who was to speak on the six o'clock news.

Nan rushed in, hair flying, her eyes red. 'He's done it. He's enlisted,' she sobbed, and threw herself into our mother's arms. I went over to comfort her too. That way, I could hide my own wretchedness by seeming to share hers. It wasn't that I didn't sympathise with her. I did. But she had her man, a ring on her finger and probably a wedding in the offing, while I… I sniffed thinking about my lost chance at love, sure I'd never love anyone as much, ever again. Bob had been my hero, my own Clark Gable. No one could match him.

Eleven

Bel couldn't believe her aunt had been so foolish. To have turned Bob Smith down again! How times had changed. Though, maybe if she hadn't been so keen to sleep with Callum all those years ago, her life would have turned out differently too.

She would never have thought she was pregnant; he'd never have been scared of commitment and might never have left her. But, she reasoned, it had been the seventies, and if she hadn't slept with him he could well have found someone else who would. And she'd be in exactly the same predicament as Aunt Isobel. Maybe times hadn't changed all that much.

She remembered those wild student days, the summers that seemed to go on forever, the long afternoons spent in an uncomfortable single bed in Callum's digs, the sound of a guitar from the boys upstairs and the strong aroma of curry rising up from the Indian restaurant below. They'd lived as if nothing would ever change. But it had. And by the time she knew for sure she wasn't pregnant, it was too late. Callum had gone. She'd learned that life can throw a curly one when you least expect it, but it had taken her experience with Pete in Australia to make her finally realise that the only person you can trust is yourself.

*

When Bel found herself standing at Mary's front door on Tuesday morning, she felt she'd gone back in time. Nothing seemed to have changed, and she was reminded of the many times she'd come here as a child, rung the bell and asked if Mary could come out to play. As teenagers, they'd sat in the upstairs window with Mary's record player, singing along to the latest pop songs and talking about the boys they didn't dare to date.

She remembered one summer evening in particular. Mary's parents had gone out and the two girls had taken the opportunity to dig out a packet of *Gauloises* cigarettes they'd bought secretly. They were smoking them, drinking cider and feeling very sophisticated when a group from Boy's High walked past. The boys stopped to lean against the wall and wave, and the girls nearly freaked out with excitement.

Bel was still reminiscing when the door opened and it took her a moment to come to terms with the present-day Mary when her mind was full of the teenage version of her friend.

'You made it,' Mary greeted her. 'Come on in.'

Bel followed her into the house, remarking as she went how little the place had changed from what she remembered.

'Yes,' Mary said. 'Mum and Dad didn't want to change anything and since they went. I… I guess I'm used to it like this.'

Bel sat down at the kitchen table while Mary made tea. She could see her friend had been busy that morning from the freshly baked scones sitting in the middle of the table and the sponge cake filled with jam and cream and topped with a light dusting of powdered sugar.

Mary joined Bel and poured the tea into two large floral china cups, then got up again and returned with sugar, milk, small bread and butter plates and dishes of butter and jam. 'Help yourself. I can't eat all of those on my own. One of the disadvantages of baking for one is that I tend to eat more.' She looked down at her girth with a regretful grin.

Bel followed her advice and enjoyed the first bite of a scone still warm from the oven. 'Mmm. Delicious,' she said, wiping a few crumbs from her lips.

'Dough School was good for something.' Mary smiled.

'What did you do when you left?' Bel asked.

'I got a few catering-type positions, then ended up like you – teaching. But you didn't stick with it? I remember your mum telling mine you were off to Australia. She thought it was only for two years. What happened?'

Bel hesitated and looked down, stroking the waxed tablecloth with her fingers. She finished her scone, took a sip of tea, then she made up her mind. They may not have seen each other for over forty years, may not even have kept in touch, but Mary was her best – her oldest – friend. She remembered how they'd shared all their childhood secrets, their teenage dreams, and regretted that their choices in life had forced them apart. It felt the most natural thing in the world to be sitting here with her old friend, almost as if they'd never been apart. She began to speak, the words pouring out of her.

'When I finished my teacher training, I just wanted to get away. I'd grown up in that house filled with women, all my relatives, and every one of them wanting to tell me what to do. It was hard being the only child in a house of adults.' She hesitated, then decided not to mention Callum. 'I knew if I took a teaching position here, I'd never leave. Then I saw the ad – *Come and Teach in the Sun*. It seemed like the answer to a prayer. It's not that I hated my folks, nothing as strong as that. I just felt stifled. I felt…' Bel closed her eyes for a moment, then opened them and spread her hands. 'I felt if I didn't get away then, I never would. I'd become part of the bricks and mortar.' She laughed. 'Seems silly now, but that's why I left.'

'No,' her friend replied. 'That's what happened to me, and to a lot of others like me.' She grimaced. 'But I didn't have your courage. And was that why you stayed away?'

'Not entirely. I discovered that, away from the claustrophobic atmosphere, away from everyone I knew, I could become a different person. I could spread my wings and become anyone I wanted.'

'And who did you become? I hear you call yourself Bel, now.' Mary leant her elbows on the table and grasped her cup in both hands.

'Oh,' Bel laughed. 'That was my attempt to stop people from calling me Izzy. Australians love to abbreviate names and Izzy wasn't what I wanted to be known as. I became Bel and the woman you see,' Bel added, wondering exactly what her friend did see. 'No that's too simplistic. I learned to fend for myself, to become independent. I discovered all the time I'd been straining against what I considered to be the tight bands and controlling forces of my family, I'd really been enveloped in a big security blanket. It wasn't always easy, but I learned to survive. And of course, the weather helped. It was like being on holiday seven days a week, twelve months of the year. I remember one day, lying by the pool, gazing up at the sky and thinking how it reminded me of a picture postcard.' She smiled and took another sip of her tea.

'Have a piece of cake, too,' Mary urged and, promising herself she'd walk it off later, Bel complied. 'So, you fell in love with Australia and didn't want to return when the two years were up?'

'With the country and a man.' Bel sighed, put down the cup she'd been holding and took a bite of the sponge. It tasted as light as it looked. 'Wow, this is yummy.'

'Yes, I heard you married out there. What…'

But Bel felt she'd said enough for one day. It was one thing to explain why she'd left Scotland, but the details of her marriage and subsequent divorce were matters she preferred to keep to herself.

It wasn't exactly true she'd fallen in love with the country and the man – at least, not in that order. Still reeling from being dumped by Callum, Bel had seen an escape to Australia as the opportunity for a fresh start. And it had been.

When she met Pete Sadler, he'd seemed like the answer to her unspoken prayer. Tall, handsome, with his own business and clearly smitten by her Scottish accent, he was a secure bolthole. So what, if there wasn't the passion she'd felt for Callum back in Glasgow. Look where that had got her. And by the time she'd realised that the handsome face was a front for a more insidious behaviour, she'd fallen in love with the sunshine, the open spaces and the clear skies, and the idea of going home to the close confines and poor weather of Glasgow was unthinkable.

'I have a question for you,' she said instead. 'Aunt Isobel mentioned she found the guy who's her solicitor – Mathew Reid – through you. How did that come about? And what does she mean by saying you helped her find him? It seems an odd way of putting it.'

'It was exactly like that. As you know, I pop in to see her regularly. I got into the habit of it even when she was able to get about for herself. I enjoyed hearing your news and it got me out of the house when Mum and Dad were so sick. Well, one day – it must have been soon after your own mum passed – I was telling her about the solicitor I was dealing with, the one my folks used. I suggested she might need one too – to manage her affairs – and she took down all the details. Don Reid was my parents' solicitor. Matthew is his nephew, When I said that, she seemed really excited.

'How odd. I wonder why?'

But Mary declined to speculate, instead asking, 'Have you met Matthew?'

Matthew? It seemed Mary either didn't know Matt or wasn't considered a friend. Bel didn't know why that gave her a small glow of satisfaction.

'Aunt Isobel insisted on introducing me. He *is* her solicitor, after all, and…'

'I suppose so.'

Bel was surprised to see a blush stain her friend's cheeks.

'He's the talk of the place, you know,' Mary said, confidingly. 'Since his wife died in such sad circumstances, and him never marrying again, and living out there all on his own.'

'His wife died?' Bel latched onto this information, disregarding the rest as mere gossip and perhaps the sad musings and misplaced hopes of a group of Mary's unmarried friends.

'Oh, it was such a tragedy! Didn't Isobel tell you?'

'No.' Bel was all ears, keen to find out more about the enigmatic Matt Reid, realising that her aunt hadn't said very much about him at all.

Mary was eager to put her in the picture. 'Well,' she said, helping herself to a second piece of sponge and offering the plate to Bel who shook her head. 'It all happened quite a few years ago, about five I think. The whole family were on holiday up north and Ailsa – his wife – had taken their granddaughter – Fiona, I think her name is – to do some shopping in Oban. You know what those roads can be like – one way tracks with sheep wandering everywhere. They were on their way back when it happened – a tourist car coming the other way. She never stood a chance.' Mary shook her head. 'It was dreadful. And the wee girl was badly injured too. They say she's never walked since.'

Bel felt the cogs falling into place – the reason for Fiona's wheelchair, Matt's reluctance to discuss it, and maybe even the motivation for his isolation. She was about to speak, express her sympathy for him, when Mary began to talk again.

'It's such a pity. A lovely man. A terrible waste. He'd make someone a wonderful husband.' She blushed again. 'And that place of his. No one seems to have seen it. Keeps very much to himself, he does.' She nodded as if to confirm her words.

Bel didn't know what to say. Mary's description of Matt Reid was at odds with her own experience. She'd found him enigmatic, taciturn even, but he'd shown no compunction about taking her to his home and had been friendly enough.

Taking in her friend's high colour, it suddenly occurred to Bel that when Mary referred to "they" and "people", she was talking about herself. Her old friend fancied Matt Reid!

When she got back to her aunt's, Isobel was napping in her favourite chair. Deciding not to disturb her, Bel made a cup of tea – she'd be swimming in the stuff soon, but it was better than the excuse for coffee that seemed to be prevalent here – and went to her room to read more of Isobel's story.

It was insightful to read about the beginning of the war. She knew very little about her parents' early years and, as a child and young woman, had expressed no interest in that part of their lives. She regretted it now.

What would she give to sit down and chat with her mum, find out how the blond choir member had become her dad, hear how they'd survived the war? But that was impossible now, so she had to make do with Isobel's memories. She settled down to read on, but her mind kept returning to the conversation with Mary.

She had to reassess her opinion of Matt. The poor man had gone through a lot; to lose his wife in the same accident that had crippled his granddaughter. No wonder he chose to hide away from the world, to devote himself to his home, garden, and family. She felt honoured to have been invited into his private sanctuary, but that may not have been his choice. Aunt Isobel seemed to have been behind his invitation as a means of showing Bel what was required to modify the Kelvin Drive house.

Bel shook her head in despair.

Twelve

'There was a call for you.' Isobel's voice reached Bel as soon as she opened the front door.

Bel and Mary had been to a movie at the Grosvenor cinema, and the night was so calm and beautiful, high clouds barely obscuring the moon, that they'd walked back across the bridge, reminiscing on their misspent youth and laughing at how seriously they'd taken everything back then. The cinema had been revamped and was a far cry from the one they remembered sneaking into for showings of X-rated films, hoping their heavy makeup would disguise their tender years.

Bel wondered who could be calling her. She'd spent the evening with the only person in Scotland who knew she was here, apart from her aunt.

'Young Matthew called. He'd like you to call him back.' Bel could see her aunt smiling, as she peered over her book. 'Good film?'

'Yes. The old Grosvenor's had quite a facelift.' Bel sat down, putting her feet up on a pouffe. 'We walked back, and Mary sets quite a pace,' she said. 'Matthew, you say? What did he want?' Bel was surprised at the warm glow she felt at the sound of his name, but immediately dismissed it as being caused by her exertion, although the walk back from the cinema had been fairly short.

'Why don't you call him and find out?'

'Now?' Bel checked the time. 'It's after ten. A bit late to be calling.'

'Nothing of the sort. If I know Matthew, he'll be waiting for your call. I told him you'd be back around now.'

Cursing silently, Bel hoisted herself out of the chair and made her way into the hallway where Isobel's phone sat on its table, a high-backed chair neatly placed beside it. She didn't want to give her aunt the satisfaction of listening to the call, but it would have been rude to have given in to her inclination and gone to the bedroom to use her mobile. Damn! She was so used to living alone, it was hard to make allowances for her elderly aunt. She supposed Isobel did have her best interests at heart, much as she'd struggled against her advice as a teenager.

'His number's by the phone,' Isobel called through the part-open door. Bel sighed, wishing she'd remembered to close it, as she pressed the required digits.

'Matt Reid.' The strangely familiar voice brought back the memory of the trip up the loch and his bright airy home.

She hesitated before replying. 'It's Bel, Bel Davison. I'm returning your call. Aunt Isobel said you wanted to speak with me.'

'Aye, I did. I was thinking you'd like to meet Andrew Forrest. He's the architect Isobel's contracted with.' When Bel didn't reply, he added, 'To plan the renovations. You'll remember…'

'I remember,' Bel said. This was all decidedly ghoulish. Her aunt was alive and well. Why was Matt determined to prepare Bel for her demise?

He seemed to sense her feelings. 'It's what she wants. You can ask her, if you don't believe me.'

'No, I do. It's just that…'

'I know. But we don't all get the chance to plan ahead – for when we're gone. And she wants to make sure it all happens just as she's planned it. Nothing left to chance.'

Bel sighed, knowing he was right. 'When had you in mind?'

'Tomorrow? I can pick you up at ten. He has his office in the city and we can maybe grab a bit of lunch afterwards?'

Bel wasn't sure about lunch, but decided not to argue. 'Okay. I'll see you then.'

She was lost in thought as she rejoined her aunt.

'It's fixed, then?' Isobel's question brought Bel back to the present.

'You knew why he was calling?'

'We spoke,' Isobel said, rather smugly, Bel thought. 'You'll like young Andrew. Has his head screwed on, that one. He designed Matthew's place up the loch, not that I've seen it.' Isobel's lips turned down.

'Would you like to?' Bel had no idea if and how this might be managed, but felt instinctively that it would please her aunt.

'Och, just the wishful thinking of an old woman,' Isobel dismissed the idea. But Bel didn't and made up her mind to broach it with Matt at the first opportunity.

Once in her bedroom again, Bel was keen to continue reading her aunt's diary to find out what had happened to Aunt Isobel and her mum back in the thirties. Curling up in bed, she turned on the bedside lamp and found the place she'd stopped last time.

Bel shivered as she read about war being declared. She knew how it had happened from the history books, but to read her aunt's account, to imagine the three sisters sitting with their parents in this very house, Chamberlain's words ringing in their ears, brought it alive. She laid down the papers thankful to be living in more peaceful times. What were *her* worries when compared to what they went through? At least she knew they'd survived. Her dad had too – or she wouldn't be here. She grinned. But what had happened to Bob Smith? Had he been killed? She slid down and closed her eyes. The next episode would keep for another night.

*

At ten o'clock on the dot, Bel heard a car draw up outside. Peering out the window, she was surprised to see not the low-slung sports car she'd expected, but a sleek silver hybrid. The figure that emerged looked like a stranger. This morning, Matt was dressed in a grey business suit with a white shirt and… was that an old-school-tie? Bel hid a smile and turned to her aunt. 'He's here.'

'I can hear as well as you. Who else would be driving up to the house at this time of the morning? Bring him in. I want a word before you go.'

Bel did her aunt's bidding reflecting, not for the first time, how easy it was to fall into old patterns. In this house, she sometimes felt like the sixteen-year-old who had dreamt of escaping.

And she had, she reminded herself. She was a grown woman with her own life on the other side of the world. This was merely an interlude to fulfil her aunt's wishes, till Isobel…

At that point, her musings always stopped. She didn't want to think about the reason for her visit and what would lead to her departure, despite being keen to return home.

'Good morning,' she said, opening the door to a smiling Matt.

'And a good morning to you. You're looking very elegant his morning, if I may say so.'

'Oh!' Bel looked down at the outfit she'd deemed suitable for a trip to the city and a visit to the architect. The pale blue pants with matching tunic top was a favourite of hers, one she often wore to the boutique and in which she felt comfortable. Just in time, she stopped herself from being self-deprecating and replying 'What, this old thing' Instead she merely said, 'Thanks. Aunt Isobel wants a word.'

Matt followed her and kissed Isobel on the cheek as before.

'Well, look at you,' Isobel said. 'Dressed to kill. You make a good pair.'

Matt turned and winked at Bel, making her feel uncomfortable.

'All set for Andrew, then?' Isobel asked.

'You wanted to speak to me?'

'Yes.' Isobel picked up a folder Bel hadn't noticed earlier. 'I wanted him to have another look at this stair-lift thing. Maybe a proper lift would be better. There's certainly room, if the building will take it.'

'I'll ask him, shall I?'

'Please.' Seemingly satisfied, Isobel leaned back into her chair.

'Is there anything you need before I go?' Bel asked.

'No, you'd better be away. But I want a full report when you get back, mind.'

Once in the car, Bel let go of the breath she'd been holding. Matt seemed to sense her relief.

'How are you two getting on?' he asked. 'I bet Isobel's not the easiest person to live with.'

'She's okay,' Bel said, determined to be loyal. 'It can't be easy for her, knowing…'

'But she won't go till she's ready. And the way she keeps changing these plans, that won't be for some time. You intend to stay till the end?' Bel saw Matt glance in her direction and raise one eyebrow.

'That's why I'm here.' But she knew she sounded churlish. 'I mean,' she added, 'I promised I would and I intend to keep that promise. Besides…' But she wasn't sure what else there was. Isobel was her only living relative apart from two distant cousins on her father's side who emailed her from time to time and were overseas right now. She had to do whatever it took to relieve her mind. *Surely Matt could see that?*

By the time they reached the city, Matt had briefed her on the man they were to meet. It seemed that, unlike Matt himself, "young Andrew" was indeed young. He'd designed Matt's house soon after he gained his degree and joined his father's business.

As the car slid into a parking spot outside a tall red sandstone building, Bel found she was looking forward to meeting the man who'd had the vision to develop such a unique structure and wondered what he had in store for the Kelvin Drive house. Although Bel had seen the plans, Isobel had been very tight-lipped about the nature of the modifications planned, merely saying that it would suit the future occupants.

'Wow, Glasgow has changed so much,' Bel said, gazing around her. 'You haven't been back since when?'

'Since Mum passed away – around thirty years ago now. But I didn't come into the city then. I haven't been here for over forty years.' Bel stepped out of the car and stood looking around just as a stiff wind blew up.

She raised her eyes to the grey sky and shivered. Despite the sun trying to shine through the clouds, it was a cool Scottish summer's day.

'Let's get you inside.' Matt locked the car and took Bel by the arm to lead her into the building, where they took a lift to the third floor. When they got out of the lift, a reception desk that wouldn't have been out of place in a five-star hotel was facing them. It seemed at odds with the building's exterior. Matt must have noticed Bel's look of surprise as he said, 'We're not stuck in the dark ages here, you know. We do keep up with the times – on the inside at least.

Before Bel had time to reply, a young man of around thirty with tousled red hair walked up to greet them. He was wearing large dark-rimmed glasses, his business shirt lifting out of a pair of worn jeans, and a tie hanging loosely from an unbuttoned collar. *So, this was "young Andrew".*

'Matt, good to see you. And this must be Isobel's niece from Australia.' He shook Matt's outstretched hand, then turned to greet Bel. 'You have the look of your aunt. She's a formidable woman to deal with – knows what she wants. Come through.' He led them through a glass door at the side of the reception desk and into a small conference room.

Once they were seated, and the inevitable cups of tea had been served, Andrew got down to business. 'You've seen Matt's place?'

Bel nodded.

'Well, Isobel hasn't, but she's made her wishes very clear and she tells me you're the one who'll be ensuring that all goes to plan. You'll be overseeing the renovations.'

'Overseeing?' Bel was stunned. That implied she'd be in Scotland. 'No, I don't think so. I live in Australia. I'm only visiting. I'm only here till…' There it was again, that veiled reference to her aunt's passing. She raised her eyes to meet Andrew's. 'Till she dies,' she said bluntly, while Matt cleared his throat.

'Hmm.' Andrew didn't seem to know how to respond.

'Can you explain the plans to Bel?' Matt asked.

'Certainly.' Andrew quickly recovered from the awkwardness of the situation and, opening a long shallow drawer, drew out several large sheets of paper. 'This is what the lower floor will look like,' he said, laying them on the table. Clearly comfortable with this task, he proceeded to explain how the existing house would be altered and modified to allow for wheelchairs and other pieces of equipment which might be required for the new residents.

By the time Andrew had finished explaining how he intended to modify both levels of the house, Bel was blown away with the detail.

'How amazing.' She leaned back and regarded the two men. 'But it looks very expensive. Does… Will there enough money?' She felt insensitive asking the question, but had to know.

Andrew paused and looked at Matt who replied, 'Yes. It seems your aunt has made some sound investments.' He coughed. 'I believe she received some bequests from her parents and some female relatives. They'd be your…?'

'Aunt and great-aunts,' Bel said slowly, remembering the various women who'd populated the old house as she was growing up. All had found a home with Bel's grandparents – what seemed like a throng of women who'd been the bane of her teenage years.

There was little else to discuss. Matt handed over the latest file from Isobel, charging Andrew with the task of further researching the matter of the lift. Then he and Bel made their farewells with Andrew indicating he looked forward to working with Bel, but not, hopefully, in the near future, and sending his best regards to Isobel.

'Now, how about a spot of lunch?' Matt asked, as they emerged into the fresh air, the street now busy with office workers seeking respite from their workplaces.

'Sounds good.' But Bel was still thinking about Andrew's impression she'd be staying in Glasgow for some time. Her trip was open-ended, but her life wasn't here. Aunt Isobel understood that, didn't she? Of course, she did. She'd said as much. So why had she given the architect the impression Bel would be staying around? He must have misunderstood.

Matt and Bel pushed their way through a crowded bar to a corner table. Surrounded by Scottish voices, Bel was surprised at how nostalgic she felt, remembering her first few years in Sydney when the very sound of her native tongue had sent her running in the opposite direction.

'What do you fancy?' Matt said, picking up a menu. 'How about I fetch in a beer while you decide?'

'Thanks.' Bel had the unfamiliar feeling she was being organised. It wasn't altogether unpleasant, but she didn't want to get used to it. She'd been her own person for too many years to give in to being cosseted. 'Just a half for me. I'm not used to drinking at lunchtime.

'A shandy then?'

'Fine.' When had she last had a shandy at lunchtime? These days a glass of Chardonnay with dinner was her usual tipple. The thought of a shandy – she could almost taste it – took her back years. Back to her student days when with a few friends, she'd sloped off to the pub at lunchtime – a lunchtime that often stretched into the early afternoon when only the closure of the pub around two or three o'clock signalled it was time to return to the reference library.

Perusing the menu, Bel realised Matt had deliberately chosen an eatery to demonstrate nouvelle Scottish fayre and, pleased to see none of the heavy traditional food she'd expected, settled on a roasted rocket and pear salad with Mull cheddar.

She laid the menu on the table and watched her companion weave his way through the other diners carrying two glasses. He was a fine figure of a man by anyone's standards, looming head and shoulders above those who were standing at the bar or waiting to secure a free table. No wonder, as Mary said, he caused a flutter in the hearts of Glasgow ladies of a certain age. He might be in his mid to late sixties, but he was still heart-throb material. A silver fox – wasn't that what men like him were called?

'Decided?' Matt placed the glasses on the table, the condensation creating pools of moisture on the wooden surface. That was one thing that had changed for the better. No more warm beer.

'The pear salad.'

'No wonder you're like a stick,' he said, then cursed quietly. 'Sorry. I'm not used to taking ladies to lunch. A pie and a pint at my local is more to my taste – and in male company. I've never… since…' He thrust a hand through his hair and took a gulp of beer. 'Ailsa was…'

'Your wife?' Bel asked in a low voice.

'Aye. She always said I was no good in company. And it's been a while since I made polite with a woman like yourself. But Isobel…'

'She does have a habit of getting us to do things for her, things we wouldn't think of doing otherwise,' Bel said ruefully, taking a sip of her drink.

'She's a fierce one, that's true. But maybe it's time I got out a bit more. Since you're only here for a short time, maybe I could show you…' His voice faltered and he stared down into his drink as if regretting his words.

Bel was saved from replying by the arrival of the waiter. They placed their orders, Matt choosing the Orkney sirloin steak, topped with blue cheese and served with peas and mashed potatoes. A real man's meal in Bel's opinion.

'So, what's your life like in Sydney?' Matt asked after a long pause.

'Good.' Did he really want to know or was he trying to *make polite* as he'd put it?

'Isobel tells me you're on your own there. No children or grandchildren?'

'No, Pete and I weren't lucky that way. Or maybe we were.' She smiled shortly. 'When I listen to the way some of my customers talk about their children, I often bless the fact that Pete and I weren't together long enough to bring another life into the world. But you have a... daughter is it?'

'And a son. Duncan's taken over the law practice, now I'm practically retired. He's a good lad. He and his wife have a boy. Jamie is just ten, and a wee terror.'

'You mentioned a Robbie and Fiona.'

'Aye, they're Elspeth's two. I see more of them. Elspeth's a teacher and she often brings them over in the school holidays and most weekends.' Bel noticed how his face lit up when he talked of his grandchildren. 'I think she believes her old man can't manage on his own. She likes to keep an eye on me – make sure I don't get up to mischief.' He laughed. 'She's just like her mother. She looks like her too...' His voice faded, and the smile left his face.

Bel bit her lip. She tried to remember how long ago Mary said it was since his wife died, but couldn't. 'Tell me about your grandchildren,' she said instead, and watched the fond smile return. For the next ten minutes or so, she was entertained by stories of the three children who were clearly the light of his life. No wonder he ignored the Glasgow ladies, Bel thought. His life was wrapped up in his family.

'So, you don't really have time to get lonely.' she said. But his reply was interrupted by the arrival of their meals.

'There are times,' he sighed, gazing down at his plate. Then he took a sip of his beer. 'Eat up,' he said, picking up his knife and fork and indicating Bel should do the same.

By the time they finished their meal, Matt seemed to have forgotten his lapse, but Bel hadn't. When he left to pay the bill, her eyes followed him thoughtfully. Maybe Matt Reid wasn't quite as self-sufficient as he seemed, or as he wanted everyone to think. Just for a moment, there had been a chink in the convivial armour he assumed, and through it she'd seen a man who was vulnerable, a man who still grieved for his wife, a man who had embraced the solitary life, but was sometimes lonely. It made him more human, more approachable, more likeable and she was filled with the desire to know more about the real man hidden behind his bluff exterior.

They were both silent on the trip across town. Bel was busy contemplating her new insight into her companion. She couldn't imagine what he was thinking, so it was a surprise when, as they pulled up outside the Kelvin Drive house, he turned to her and said, 'Well, what about it? Will you let me show you the new face of Glasgow?'

Unable to find a reason for refusing, and knowing her aunt would approve, Bel found herself agreeing.

'Good, I'll call you. Give my apologies to Isobel. Tell her I'll be in touch.' And, as soon as Bel stepped out of the car, he was off, leaving her gazing after the car and shaking her head.

'Is Matthew not with you?' Isobel greeted Bel as she walked into the hallway.

'No, he sends his apologies and will be in touch.'

'Did you offend him?' Isobel's voice sounded sharp.

'No, Aunt Isobel. Not at all. He wants to show me what he calls the New Glasgow.'

Isobel smiled. 'And I hope you agreed. That man's lonely, but scared to admit it.'

'I did agree.' Bel sat down beside her aunt, surprised the older woman was so perceptive and was already aware of what Bel had only come to realise during lunch.

'He's had a hard life,' Isobel continued. 'Lost his dad who he was close to, then his wife died in that terrible accident that left the granddaughter crippled.'

'Mary told me about that,' Bel said quietly.

'Did she now? She's had her eye on him for a while, along with a few others, but he's not been interested.'

Isobel sighed. 'Childhood sweethearts, they were, him and Ailsa. For a while it looked as if he wouldn't get over it. He was lost without her. But that daughter of his – Elspeth I think she's called – she brought him out of it, taking the little ones around and encouraging him to build that place of his. Stopped him moping around in the big house in Anniesland. And he's gradually left more and more of the business to the boy. I cannae mind his name.'

'Duncan,' Bel almost whispered.

'Aye. He told you?' Isobel's sharp eyes peered at her niece.

'He just mentioned them.'

'They kept him going. But it's time,' she said, almost to herself. 'Time for him to move on.'

Thirteen

Isobel – 1940

It was a dreadful year. Back in November the first bombs to be dropped on mainland Britain fell on the tiny island of Shetland to the north of Scotland. That shocked us. Why there? Why us? We'd all received instructions what to do in the event of an air raid, but hadn't really expected one. It really brought the war home to us in a way it hadn't been before.

Sure, we'd waved off many of our friends and brothers of friends. Jeannie's two brothers had gone in the first contingent and Nan's Colin had enlisted, but been sent north on Home Defence duties, whatever they might be. Early in the year there was another shock for us Scots – the first civilian death in March on Scapa Flow in Orkney where the grand fleet was anchored– only two months after over two million men between the ages of nineteen and twenty-seven were called up.

When Winston Churchill became Prime Minister in May, Father was pleased. 'Now we'll win this damned thing,' he said. 'Send that bastard back where he belongs.'

We knew he was referring to Hitler.

My life and that of my sisters didn't change much at first. Kate finished her business course and, instead of getting a clerical job in an office in the city as we'd expected, she found herself offered a position in an iron and steel works in Lanarkshire, and went off to board with our aunt and uncle there. It seemed there was a shortage of men to do the job, so she'd managed to leap up the career ladder and become the personal secretary to the boss.

It was strange in the house without her. She never said much, but when she did both Nan and I listened. She'd been the voice of reason.

Mother bought skeins of wool in shades of khaki and air-force blue and we spent each evening rolling it into balls and knitting socks, gloves and helmets for the men in the armed forces.

By the time Italy joined the war in June, no one was surprised, though we were shocked to the core when the Germans entered Paris in that same month. What surprised us at home was Nan's announcement one Sunday evening. Colin was on weekend leave and the pair had been to church as usual. They hadn't come straight home – I'd seen Father check his watch a few times and hoped he wasn't going to read the riot act to her when she did arrive. The war had made him even more edgy than usual.

She rushed in, her hat in one hand and pulling Colin after her with the other. The pair made their way to the fireplace and stood there, under the mirror, hand-in-hand looking for all the world like Hansel and Gretel lost in the forest. Except Colin was too tall for Hansel and Nan had a wide grin on her face. Colin looked very smart in his army uniform, but his shuffling feet were an indication of his nervousness.

'We want to get married,' Nan declared with a sideways glance at her beau.

'What's new?' Father said, turning back to his paper and drawing on his pipe, sending a sharp, spicy aroma into the room.

'I mean soon,' Nan added. 'We want to be married in case…'

I saw Colin's hand grip hers tightly and, for a moment, I wished it was me standing there with Bob Smith's hand gripping mine. Where had that thought come from? I'd only seen him once since we returned from Largs. Eileen and Alan had been in a rush to get married after war was declared and she'd asked me to stand up for her. As her best friend, I couldn't refuse, even though I knew Alan would have Bob by his side.

Dressed to kill in a navy crepe suit, the top inlaid with sequins forming the shape of leaves and the skirt with accordion pleats, I'd tried my best to remain calm throughout the ceremony, but the sight of the two men, both in the dress uniform of the Royal Air Force was almost too much for me. If Bob had been handsome before, the uniform only enhanced his good looks. He was positively glamourous. Clark Gable had nothing on him – even as Rhett Butler in what was now my favourite film, *Gone with the Wind*. I'd seen it four times and cried each time for what I'd lost.

Bob was polite after the ceremony, but he left the celebrations early, and I went home to cry myself to sleep and vow yet again to put him out of my mind forever.

Now it was Nan's turn and I was on her side, but knew Mother and Father wouldn't listen to me. I continued to knit and I listened while Father and Colin discussed the war.

Father's view was that, now Churchill was at the helm, it would all be over soon and the pair should wait till peacetime.

Mother followed her usual tack at such times and went off to make tea; as if a cup of tea would solve anything. But I guess for her it did. It gave her something to do. She nodded to me to join her in the kitchen, and sticking the needles through the glove I was knitting, I did so.

Having missed the discussion, I was surprised, when we returned, to find Colin and Father having a glass of whiskey together. Mother looked askance, but all our father said was, 'If the two of them are set on it, we should let them go ahead. The lad may be right, and if he's sent overseas our Nan'd never forgive me. But it'll need to be a small affair here in the house.'

That surprised me. Nan and I had always planned our weddings – from when we were tiny and used to dress up as brides, picking daisies and dandelions for our bouquets and marching up and down the garden singing *Here Comes the Bride*. A huge white wedding in our local church with the pews full of family and friends was obligatory. For her to agree to what some might see as a hole-in-the-corner affair was a clear sign of how much the war had changed our lives.

The wedding gave us something positive to focus on. Our minister agreed to perform the ceremony, and the only guests were to be family members plus Nan's friend, Jeannie. It was a far cry from what would have happened in peacetime, and what Nan had always declared she wanted for her big day. But she didn't seem to care.

'What if he goes overseas and gets himself killed?' she asked me one night as, lying in the darkness of our room, she confided that she and

Colin had "done it" on a weekend when she'd visited him in Crieff, and her landlady had left them alone and unsupervised. 'I don't think I could live without him,' she said. 'And what if I get pregnant? Our folks would never live it down.'

I must have muttered something in reply, but all I remember is turning over, face to the wall, and the tears running down my cheeks. I didn't know if I was crying for Nan or for my own lost chances.

The day came at last – a dim grey day with just a hint of sunlight peeking through the clouds. I was able to give the outfit I'd worn to Eileen's wedding another outing, while Nan had managed to find a green suit with fur trim. We wore matching hats that lay flat on the side of our heads and, of course, gloves. She'd decided against having two bridesmaids and Kate, who'd come back for the day, said she didn't mind. It saved her buying a fresh outfit. Clothes rationing didn't start till a year later, but the shops didn't have the same range of clothes as before and we were cautious about spending money on things we might only wear once.

Food rationing had begun, putting butter, sugar, and meat in short supply. Mother collected all our ration books and somehow managed to provide a decent meal for us after the ceremony which was short and sweet.

Besides his mother – his father had been killed in the first war – Colin's only relatives were a couple of aunts, an uncle and his cousin John who was his best man. His brothers had already been sent to the front.

John seemed like a nice fellow, shorter than his cousin, sandy-haired with freckles and an open expression on his face. He reminded me of Eileen's Alan. I imagined he was someone you could rely on and thought no more about him.

Typical of most weddings at that time, both men were in uniform. In this case, they wore the dress uniform of their regiment, the Cameronians – the Douglas tartan trews, neat khaki fitted jacket and the narrow cap with two trailing ribbons. Instead of flowers, which were difficult to come by, most gardens – ours included – having been dug up to grow vegetables, Nan carried a silver horseshoe covered with artificial flowers. Horseshoes were supposed to be for luck too, and with the thought of the two men heading off to the front any day, luck was certainly in order.

Despite the times, it was a lovely ceremony, and Nan and Colin were beaming with happiness. When it was over, and we'd finished the meal, I was helping my mother in the kitchen when I saw John hovering at the door.

'Can I have a word?' he asked, his face blushing.

I glanced about, but he seemed to be speaking to me. 'Me?' I asked, turning towards him, the plate I was washing dripping soapy water over the linoleum floor.

'I wonder,' he said, stammering a little. 'Would you like to take tea with me one day? I have a few more days' leave, before we go back up north.'

I put the plate down carefully and considered. It hadn't occurred to me I'd meet another fellow who'd want to take me out. John was no Bob – no Clark Gable lookalike – but he seemed like a nice lad, he was Colin's cousin, and he was going to war.

Was that enough? Maybe those feelings I'd had for Bob Smith were the work of the devil, tempting me into behaving badly. Maybe this was what love should be about. Maybe with John I could find a gentler sort of affection. 'I'd like that,' I said.

*

After a two-day honeymoon at the Crieff Hydro – a wedding present from Colin's Uncle James and Aunt Bee who appeared to have a few quid – which Nan said was out of this world, despite being close to the army camp, she moved in with Colin's mother in their flat in Hillhead. Colin was still posted up north, and Nan intended to visit as often as she could on weekends, when he wasn't on duty or involved in training.

It was okay for her – a new life as a married woman albeit one living with her mother-in-law instead of her husband. But it meant that now I was alone in the big bedroom that had once held three of us. I tried to enjoy having the whole room all to myself, but the truth was that I missed my sisters.

And now Eileen was married too. Although she was still living at home with her parents while Alan was posted, she wasn't so keen to go out in the evenings. I was still working at the salon which was managing to survive by providing women with the ever-popular rolls, waves, and pin curls. But good shampoos were becoming difficult to source and I was becoming bored.

Maybe that was why I agreed to continue seeing John when he came home for the odd weekend and why I wrote to him in between visits. It was nothing like the relationship I'd had with Bob. There was no trembling at the knees, no fear of not being good enough, no film star to compare him with.

But John was good company and often took me dancing to the Locarno. We talked and laughed, and it helped pass the time and take my mind off what was going on over there in Europe.

Fourteen

Bel – 2015

Bel wiped her eyes at the description of her parents' wedding. She'd seen the photo that had pride of place on her mother's bedside table, but it had never occurred to her the wedding took place right here, downstairs, in the room that was now her aunt's living room. No wonder Bel's mum had wanted her to have a big white church wedding.

She'd disappointed her, choosing instead to marry in what she'd imagined to be a romantic ceremony on a Sydney beach, only letting her mum know afterwards. How she now regretted her thoughtlessness.

She hadn't forgotten her aunt's desire to see Matt's house. So, next morning, when the two were chatting over yet another cup of tea, the sound of Betty's vacuuming in the background, Bel asked, 'If we can arrange it, would you feel well enough for a drive?'

Isobel, who had been a bit lethargic, immediately perked up. 'Where did you have in mind?'

'I've been thinking that, since it looks like I'm going to be here for some time, I should hire a car and...' She looked out at the bright blue sky in which there were only a few high clouds. 'We should take advantage of the good weather and make that visit to Matt's place up the loch. Would you like that?'

Isobel beamed. 'I most certainly would.'

'I can't think why he's never taken you up himself,' Bel muttered.

'Oh, he's offered many a time, but I've always said it'd be too much trouble. What would he be wanting to drive around an old woman like me for?'

'But I'm a different matter?' Bel chuckled at her aunt's embarrassed expression. 'Or do you want to get Matt and me together again?' she joked, surprised to see Isobel turn red.

'He's a nice man and he's been on his own for a long time. I'd like to see him with some feminine company before I go.'

'Less of this talking of you leaving. You're not going anywhere in a hurry – except up Loch Lomond. I'll ring and arrange a car today and call Matt too – check when he'll be home.'

In her usual organised fashion, Bel had a car arranged in no time and headed into the city to pick it up. On the way, she took the opportunity to call Matt, reasoning that she didn't want her aunt listening in to the call. He expressed delight at hearing from her, albeit surprised she'd managed to persuade Isobel to visit him. When they'd made arrangements for the following day with Matt offering to make lunch, Bel was puzzled to hear him hesitate, then ask, 'Where are you now?'

'Heading to Central Station to pick up a car.'

'Why don't I buy you lunch?'

'Again?' Bel couldn't help her response. Then, realising she may have sounded rude, she added, 'I mean, that would be nice, but you already…'

'I've had to come into the city this morning and was about to get a bite to eat myself. I could meet you at the station. There's a restaurant right there.'

'I remember, though it's probably changed a lot since I last visited it.'

'I'd say so. We can eat at Deli Central. They do a good soup and sandwich. I'll meet you at the entrance on Gordon Street. Twenty minutes?'

'You're on.' Bel smiled to herself for the rest of the trip as she gazed out the bus window at the changed city landscape. Matt Reid was proving to be an interesting character. According to Mary, he was a solitary man, still grieving for his wife, whereas Isobel saw him as someone in need of some feminine companionship. Bel? She was still undecided. She found him to be good company, a man who revealed more of himself each time they met. Getting to know him was a bit like peeling off the layers of an onion to reveal… She wasn't sure what she'd find when she got to the heart of him.

It was absurd, but she was discovering she wanted to know him better. Reminding herself, she was only here for a short time, and she wasn't interested in him as a *man*, Bel still couldn't dismiss a desire to learn more about what made him tick, what made him so… yes, fascinating.

Bel was still engaged in this line of thought when she stepped off the bus and made her way to the station. She saw Matt before he saw her and was able to observe him undetected. Today he was dressed in what appeared to be his uniform grey slacks and checked sports jacket. The wind had tousled his hair, giving him a dishevelled appearance and making Bel's fingers itch to smooth it.

She was shocked by this sudden urge. She hadn't felt the impulse to smooth or even touch a man's hair, never mind any other part of one, for years. Not since… Hell, she couldn't remember. That's how long ago it had been. She walked up and tapped him on the arm.

'Oh, hello!' Matt appeared startled. 'I didn't see you coming. I was lost in my thoughts. Let's go in.' He placed a hand on Bel's back and ushered her into the station and to the Deli.

The place was busy, but they managed to find a table backing onto one wall. Matt handed Bel a menu. She studied it keenly, glancing over at her companion from time to time and noting his intense expression, surely too intense for the menu.

Once they'd placed their orders, both opting for soup and baguettes with cheddar and roast vegetables, with Perrier for Bel and a beer for Matt, Bel asked, 'Is there something troubling you? You seem preoccupied.' Then she wondered if she'd been too presumptuous.

He seemed to consider, then make up his mind. 'You're pretty much a stranger, so maybe you can advise me.' He ran a hand through his hair in an obvious attempt to flatten it which didn't work, then started to speak.

'It's my step-mother. I'm to visit her this afternoon. She's around the same age as your aunt, maybe a few years younger. Unlike Isobel, she's been in a nursing home for years and suffers from dementia. The odd thing is, she's now started to talk about Dad as if… as if he didn't love her… as if he always yearned for someone else. I expect it's my mum she's talking about. Annie – my step mother – and I never got on. She and Dad married when I was in my teens and I left home as soon as I could. It wasn't a happy marriage. I always had the suspicion she'd tricked him into it somehow. It was a godsend when Uncle Don took an interest in me. He's my mother's brother and had no children of his own.'

'So?' Bel couldn't see what the problem was.

Matt started playing with his fork, drawing lines on the tablecloth with the tines. 'It's beginning to worry me. She thinks I'm Dad and keeps haranguing me about it.'

'Do you visit her often?'

He shrugged. 'There's no one else. But it's difficult.'

'Would you like me to come with you?' Now why on earth had she said that? She barely knew the man. What would he think of her? 'I do have some experience with older women,' she said, haltingly. 'And maybe having a stranger there would help.'

She saw his eyes lighten with something like relief. 'Would you? Oh no, it's too much to ask. Elspeth came for a bit, but Annie took against her and it made the visits even more difficult.'

'No worries. Today?'

Matt seemed to rally at Bel's offer, and they agreed that once she'd picked up the car, she'd follow him to the nursing home.

That settled, they enjoyed a leisurely lunch, sharing student memories of Glasgow. They discovered that they'd attended Glasgow University around the same time, Bel's first year coinciding with Matt's final one. They spent several minutes trying to work out if they'd attended the same parties, only to conclude that they'd moved in very different circles. Although establishing they'd both attended the same Daft Friday event – the annual December celebration at the university union – they had no friends in common.

Talking of the past made Bel think of her own heady student days and remember Callum, the boy who'd broken her heart back then. The break-up that changed her life.

When they'd finally finished lunch, Matt left Bel to organise her car, arranging to meet her outside his office and warning her of the one-way system which had been implemented since she'd lived there.

*

Bel followed Matt's car to the city outskirts. Her hire car was a smaller and lighter model than she drove back home, so it took her some time to become accustomed to it, but she managed to keep Matt's vehicle in sight as he weaved in and out of the traffic.

Finally, they both pulled up in front of what had obviously once been a large family home set in beautiful grounds. A gardener was tending to one of the extensive flower beds which was a riot of vibrant colour.

'These places have either been turned into hotels or nursing homes,' Matt said, as they walked towards the imposing entrance and climbed the steps.

Once inside however, there was no mistaking the building's purpose. A smell of urine overlaid with disinfectant and polish pervaded the atmosphere, and several uniformed women in rubber-soled shoes were pushing wheelchairs or assisting more mobile residents.

'Here to see Annie?' asked one, as Matt and Bel paused inside the entrance. 'She's in the television room.'

'Through this way.' Matt led the way to a large room at the back of the building. Its tall, narrow windows looked out onto a paved courtyard and a tennis court. Bel could see a few people sitting in wheelchairs, apparently enjoying the view of a couple of younger figures, perhaps staff, knocking a ball to each other. But those inside were displaying no interest in the view. All were ensconced in armchairs facing a large television screen showing a tennis game in process.

To Bel, this seemed incongruous, given the game going on outside. But, on closer examination, she noticed that few of the old people were actually paying attention to the television program. She also noted that the empty chairs had name-cards stuck to them, presumably indicating the owners of the chairs. This seemed unbearably sad. She was so glad her aunt had remained sufficiently independent to live in her own home.

'That's Annie.' Matt indicated the chair farthest from the door and next to the window where a frail woman in a blue and white dress was staring blindly into space. 'She may not recognise me today, but let's try.' Matt sighed, and Bel followed him into the room and across to his stepmother.

'Annie?' he said. 'It's Matt, and I've brought a friend to visit today.'

'Hello, Annie. I'm Bel.' Bel bent over and held out her hand to the woman, who stared at her silently with wild eyes, before emitting a shriek.

'That woman! You've brought that woman to see me!' Annie's hands started to wave furiously in the air as if to drive Bel away.

Bel backed off, unsure what to do.

Annie continued to shout obscenities and thrash her arms around. One of the carers started to run towards her.

'I'll wait outside,' Bel mouthed to an obviously distressed Matt.

When he joined her, Matt drew his fingers through his hair, then put his hands in his pockets, 'I'm sorry I subjected you that. She's not usually so aggressive. I don't know what happened.'

'It seemed to be my presence that set her off. For some reason, she didn't like my being here. Sorry. Not one of my better ideas.'

'No.' Matt looked down at his feet, then raised his eyes to meet Bel's with a sheepish grin. 'I think I owe you a drink after that. I hope it hasn't put you off me. I *would* like to get to know you better and not all of my family are like Annie. I can be more than an odd old Scottish solicitor, you know.'

Bel's heart leapt at this – the first indication Matt had any interest in her apart from seeing her as Isobel's niece and the heir to her aunt's estate. She wasn't sure why, and didn't take time to analyse her feelings. 'I'm bringing Aunt Isobel to visit you tomorrow, remember. So you'll have to continue being the odd solicitor for a bit longer. Though I wouldn't call you odd exactly.' She glanced at him, head on one side. 'Maybe enigmatic is a more apt word.'

'Enigmatic? Hmm.'

By this time, they'd reached their cars. Bel held out her hand to shake his, only to feel an arm go around her shoulders and find herself subjected to a brief peck on the cheek.

'See you tomorrow, then,' he said, before getting into his car and driving off.

Bel touched a hand to her cheek, a faint smile hovering on her lips. Was this the same peck Isobel received on a regular basis or had Matt meant something more? Chastising herself for being a silly old woman who should know better than to be swayed by the charm of the first man to touch his lips to her cheek in years, Bel got into her own car and followed Matt down the long driveway.

Fifteen

Bel – 2015

'So this is it?' Isobel gazed at the tall glass-fronted building with its muted bricks blending into its surroundings. 'It's not…'

'Not exactly the croft or bothy you imagined?' Bel chuckled. 'He's done well to combine a modern building with the adjoining landscape.

'Young Andrew's done well, you mean? I doubt Matthew could have managed all this on his own.'

'And here was me imagining you thought he was a miracle worker.'

'Maybe on some counts, but he's no architect. It's a fine house he has here. Now, are you going to help me out of this car of yours or keep me sitting here all day?'

Bel hastily got out of the car and, going around to the passenger side, took her aunt's cane, then offered her arm to help the older woman out.

Suddenly the door of the house opened and a whirling white dervish emerged barking furiously, followed more slowly by a smiling Matt.

'Welcome,' he said, opening the gate and greeting both women with a peck on the cheek.

Definitely nothing special, thought Bel, revising her opinion of his earlier peck with an unexpected tinge of disappointment.

'So, this is where you've been hiding?' Isobel pointed her stick at the house. 'There's an awful lot of glass. I don't think I could be doing with being that exposed.' She shuddered.

'My only neighbours are the sheep and they don't bother me and Hamish too much,' Matt replied, gesturing to the wide expanse of muir and hillside that surrounded the place. 'But come on in and see the rest.'

The two women followed him inside where Isobel grudgingly complimented Matt on the design and asked pertinent questions about the special modifications to suit his granddaughter's needs.

'See,' she said to Bel. 'Young Andrew knows his business. We chose well, Matthew and I. Though the Kelvin Drive renovation will be a sight different, he'll be using some of the same techniques. Yes.' She nodded. 'It's going to work just fine.'

'I thought we'd eat outside,' Matt said. 'There's a grand view of the loch and Ben Lomond, and it's a pity not to take the benefit of such a great day.'

Once outside where the sunlight was spilling onto the paved courtyard, Bel and her aunt settled themselves in a couple of cane chairs. They were able to enjoy the warmth of the sun in this sheltered spot while Matt disappeared into the kitchen to fetch what he described as a bachelor's poor attempt at lunch.

'I'm not accustomed to entertaining ladies,' he said, returning with a tray on which were three plates heaped with cold chicken salad. 'When Elspeth visits she usually brings a basket of food too. I guess she still thinks her old dad can't cope on his own.'

'How long has it been now?' Isobel asked in a gentler voice than Bel had heard her use.

'Five years.'

All three were silent for a moment.

Matt seemed to recover first. 'I manage pretty well for the most part. I don't need much when I'm here on my own and Hamish makes sure I don't forget mealtimes.'

'Aye, he's a canny wee dog. And you say your Toby is the same breed?' Isobel turned to Bel.

'They could be twins, but my Toby's a few years older. He's had time to become a bit more sedate,' she said as Hamish, as if understanding he was the topic of conversation, began running around in circles and panting furiously.

'This looks delicious,' Bel said, when Matt sat down to join them, while Hamish, having exhausted himself, finally settled at his master's feet.

They'd finished the meal, and Bel was drinking a welcome cup of coffee as the trio enjoyed a companionable silence. She was considering how peaceful it was sitting here. Gazing at the yellow of the gorse mingling with the white and purple of the heather and the blue water of the loch, she could understand why Matt had chosen to build in this remote spot. Here, one could forget there was a busy world out there and enjoy the serenity of the surroundings. For a brief moment, she envisioned how her life would be, here in Scotland, in the country she'd been so quick to abandon for the excitement of a new life in the sun.

Suddenly Hamish's ears pricked up and he began to bark.

'What…?' Matt began, then all three heard the sound of a car draw up and stop.

'Are you expecting more visitors?' Isobel asked.

'No. The only…' Matt began, but was interrupted by a cheerful voice calling out from inside the house, the sound of running feet and the hiss of rubber wheels on slate. 'It's Elspeth and the bairns,' he said, rising to his feet only a moment before a boy looking like a much younger version of Matt burst through the doorway.

'Hi Grandad. Surprise!' he yelled, then stopped as his eyes took in the two women. 'Oh!'

He was followed more slowly by a young girl in a wheelchair, her blonde hair tied back in a ponytail, and a tall woman with short reddish-blonde hair carrying a cakebox.

'Hi Dad, I saw the strange car. We've brought…,' she began, her voice faltered as she took in the two women. 'Who…?'

'This is Isobel MacDonald and her niece Bel Davison,' Matt said, half-rising and turning red.

As if he'd been caught out in a misdemeanour.

'Isobel's a long-time client of mine, and Bel's all the way from Australia. This is Elspeth, my daughter,' he added.

'Australia?' The little girl's voice was eager. 'We've been studying that in school. Do you really live there? Do you have kangaroos and koalas?'

'Don't be stupid, Fi,' the boy said. 'They're only in zoos or in the outback, aren't they?' he asked Bel.

'Not exactly. They also live in lots of places near the coast, but you're right that there aren't too many in the city where I live.'

The girl, who Bel had identified as Fiona, looked downcast while her brother beamed. 'See?' he said in a superior voice.

'That's enough, Robbie,' his mother said sharply. 'I'm sure your grandfather's visitors don't want to hear you two arguing.' But, although she spoke to the children, Bel was conscious of Elspeth regarding her with narrowed eyes.

Bel rose. 'We should probably be going. It was good of you to invite us to lunch, Matt. Aunt Isobel was keen to see Andrew's work. I'm sure she now feels even more confident in his abilities.' She knew her tone had become formal. There was something in Elspeth's expression that seemed to be warning her off.

'You don't need to rush away,' Matt said.

But Isobel was already reaching for her stick and hoisting herself out of the chair. 'No, lad. We've taken up enough of your time. You'll be wanting to spend a while with the bairns, now they're here. Nice to meet you, Elspeth. Your dad often mentions you.'

'If you're sure?' Matt rose.

'Can you come and tell me all about Australia some other time?' Fiona asked Bel. 'I've never met anyone from there before.'

Bel shot a glance at Matt and noted him nod slightly before replying, 'I'll have to check with your grandad about that.' She saw Elspeth's lips tighten. *What was her problem?*

Matt helped Isobel through the house and into Bel's car. 'I'm sorry our afternoon was interrupted,' he said. 'Bad timing. It's school holidays, but I wasn't expecting Elspeth to show up today. She usually calls first.'

'It's nice you have family that drop in,' Isobel said. 'They seem like nice children.'

'They are, but....' Matt pushed back a lock of hair that had fallen over his forehead. 'I hope... I mean...' His eyes met Bel's and he cleared his throat. 'That drink I promised. I meant it. I'll call you, shall I?'

'Do that.' Bel felt a warm glow at his words. She hadn't forgotten the promised drink, but thought he might have had second thoughts.

'The wee boy's a lot like Matt,' Bel said, as they drove off.

'Aye, that dark hair and the eyes. It runs in the family. I never imagined...' Isobel seemed to be lost in thought.

It wasn't till they were driving through the outskirts of Glasgow that she spoke again. 'That Elspeth has a protective streak. She'll not let much get past her. She's had Matthew to herself for too long.'

Bel didn't reply. She had no idea what her aunt meant.

Isobel didn't explain, but when they'd reached home, and Isobel was settled in her usual chair, she brought up the subject again. 'He'll have trouble with that one,' she said.

'Who?' Bel was puzzled.

'Young Matthew and that daughter of his. She's been ruling the roost since her mother died and she won't give up easily.'

'Give up? What do you mean? She seemed a nice enough woman, though not at all like Matt.'

'No, she takes after her mother – in looks and personality. Ailsa had that reddish-blonde colouring too. What I mean is that Elspeth took over her father's life when her mother died. It was natural, I suppose, as the only daughter. They were able to share their grief and, as long as young Matthew was stuck out there on his own, she could organise him as much as she wanted. But if he decides to move on, find another female companion, take another wife even…' Isobel shook her head. 'She won't like that one little bit.'

Bel was surprised to feel a sense of disappointment at the idea of Matt with another woman, though she wasn't sure why. She'd never entertained any thoughts in that direction herself, had she? So why did the image of a strange woman – maybe one who was younger and blonde like his wife had been – fill her with dismay?

'Has he his sights on anyone?' she asked in an attempt to dismiss her unwelcome thoughts.

'Maybe,' Isobel said smugly.

Bel lifted an eyebrow, but her aunt wouldn't be drawn, only saying, 'I could do with a cup of tea now we're home.'

Deciding it was no business of hers, but still feeling as if she'd lost something she hadn't known she had or wanted, Bel went through to the kitchen to make tea.

*

Next time Matt called, it was to Bel's mobile and she was walking in the park taking advantage of some unexpected sunshine and reminiscing about the many hours whiled away here as a student. Back then, Kelvingrove Park had been a popular venue for walking on summer dates given the long hours of daylight. Not much had changed since then, and Bel suspected not much had changed since Aunt Isobel's day either. It was strange to think of her aunt as a young woman rejecting the advances of her boyfriend or what she'd have called her fellow or her beau.

People had changed though. There weren't too many girls who'd act coy or have moral scruples these days – or even in Bel's youth when the only fear had been of getting pregnant.

She was lost in thought when her mobile rang, bringing her back to the present with a start. She saw Matt's number on the face and smiled.

'Hello, Matt.'

'Hello there. I hope I haven't caught you at an awkward time.'

'No. I've just been reliving my misspent youth in Kelvingrove Park.'

'Oh, yes. Memories. I guess we all wandered around there at one time or another. About that drink...'

'You don't need to feel obligated.' For some reason, Bel felt a trifle shy. She wanted to be sure he wasn't doing this out of any sense of duty to her aunt. She still harboured a niggling suspicion that Isobel had her own agenda when it came to Matt and her niece.

There was silence at the other end, then, 'I'm too old and ugly to do anything I don't want to. So, drinks. Are you on?'

Bel couldn't help herself, she laughed out loud. 'I'm on. What did you have in mind?'

'It seems a pity to waste these lovely evenings, so what about I pick you up and we drive up the Loch to a favourite watering hole of mine?'

This wasn't what Bel had expected. She'd anticipated meeting him in town and having a drink surrounded by a crowd of other people, much like their lunches. This suggestion meant he'd have to take the trouble of driving into town to pick her up, then bringing her home again.

'I could meet you there.'

'And forego the opportunity for another drive in my wee buggy?'

Laughing again at this description of his expensive model sports car, Bel replied, 'How could I refuse?' and they made arrangements for the following evening.

*

The next evening was a perfect Scottish summer evening, the sort that didn't often come around. The air was balmy with very little breeze, and Bel began to look forward to driving into the country in the open-topped car, and to seeing Matt again. Now she'd managed to dismiss the notion he was only being nice to her in an attempt to curry favour with her aunt, she could relax and accept that she *did* enjoy his company.

While reminding herself she was only here for a short time, only as long as her aunt needed her, she decided there was no reason she couldn't enjoy a bit of male company during her visit. And he *was* good company, as well as being the best-looking sixty-something male she'd met either here or back home.

When she was with Matt, his presence rekindled feelings Bel thought gone forever and there was some pleasure in the realisation that her body could still respond to a man in this way.

'You're looking good,' Isobel said, when Bel appeared dressed casually in her favourite style – a pair of tailored pants matched with a long tunic. Tonight, they were in a pale lilac and she'd thrown a long scarf in a deeper shade around her neck ready to cover her hair if the breeze should become too strong while driving.

'Thanks. It's not too much?'

'I think he's worth the effort. Mind you're nice to him. He's a good man and he hasn't had it easy these last years.'

Bel was saved from the caustic reply which came to her lips by the arrival of the man himself.

'Away and let him in,' Isobel said and, biting her tongue, Bel did just that.

'You're looking very elegant again,' Matt greeted her, giving her the peck on the cheek she was becoming accustomed to – the one she'd persuaded herself meant nothing. It was only his way of being polite, but it did prompt the hint of a tremor in her. She quickly suppressed it as he then greeted her aunt in what appeared to be exactly the same way, making Bel wonder if this was his standard greeting for women of a certain age. She giggled inwardly at putting herself in that category, but she'd never see sixty again so she supposed she did belong in that group.

Matt soon had her settled in his car and, on his advice, she'd wrapped the scarf around her head, allowing the ends to blow in the wind and experiencing an unexpected sense of exhilaration. They chatted easily on the way and, before Bel realised it, drew up in the car park of an older-style hotel opposite the loch.

'We're here,' Matt announced.

Bel rearranged her scarf and gazed around. It was a still evening and there was the gentle buzzing of insects. The roar of a jet ski in the distance broke into the otherwise hushed evening air which held an elusive scent from the past. She stood still for a moment, breathing in the atmosphere before allowing Matt to take her arm and lead her inside the traditionally- styled white building.

Being a weekday evening, there were only a few couples seated at the round tables near the window. Matt seated Bel on a tartan-covered sofa in front of a low table. 'Wine?'

'Yes, please. Red, tonight, I think.'

While he went to the bar to order, Bel leant back in her seat and considered her feelings for this man who'd appeared in her life so unexpectedly and had taken over her thoughts. His whole demeanour was so different from all the men she'd been involved with. He seemed unaware – even uncaring – of the effect he might have on people. It was refreshing. A small voice inside her was tempting her to… what?

Before she could finish that thought, Matt returned carrying a goblet of wine and a small glass of whiskey.

'They have a fine malt here,' he said, as he placed both glasses on the table and joined her on the sofa, leaving only a small space between them. It was a little too close for comfort for Bel but, since she was sitting at the edge of the sofa, there was nowhere for her to move to. She picked up her wine and took a gulp to calm the butterflies in her stomach.

'Everything okay?'

'Fine.' Bel forced a smile, then relaxed. What was she afraid of? She was no foolish young virgin, not like her aunt had been. The thought of Isobel with her moral scruples brought a real smile to her lips.

'That's better,' Matt said. 'For a moment, I thought you were going to bail on me. I wanted to apologise for Elspeth.'

Bel was puzzled. What did Elspeth have to do with them? Then she remembered Isobel's not so subtle remarks.

Matt picked up a beer mat and began to balance it on its edge and twirl it, before letting it fall flat again. 'She… she sort of took over when Ailsa passed away. I was a wreck, and if it hadn't been for her…' He dragged a hand through his hair. 'It was her suggestion I get away from the house in Anniesland. I think that's what saved me. I got caught up in the building. Between her and young Andrew, I got through the worst of the grief.'

'And your son?' Bel asked.

'Duncan? He was closest to his mum and reacted by throwing himself into his work. As I withdrew from the business, he took over more and more of my clients.'

'But not Aunt Isobel.'

'No. She's special.' He rubbed his chin. 'We've always had a unique relationship. She's treated me a bit like the son she never had. I'm not sure why.'

'And she's always said I was the daughter she never had.' Bel grinned. 'So, we're like her substitute children – brother and sister.'

'I don't think of you as a sister.'

Bel didn't know how to respond to that, so she buried her nose in her wine glass, almost choking as she tipped it up, and spilling a few drops on her tunic.

'Let me.' Matt drew out a handkerchief and started to dab at the stain.

'No.' Bel pushed his hand away. 'Best I get some hot water on it.' She stood up unsteadily and looked around wildly.

'Ladies is over there.' Matt pointed to the far corner of the bar.

Once inside the toilet, Bel soaked the spot where the wine had left its mark, managing to dilute it sufficiently to remove the worst of the stain. Then she stood, hands on the edge of the sink and stared into the mirror. What had happened out there? The man had made a perfectly innocuous comment and she'd freaked out like a sixteen-year-old. She put both hands to her inflamed cheeks and admitted to herself what she'd subconsciously known all along. She was attracted to Matt Reid.

Sixteen

Isobel – 1941

My boredom with my job was soon resolved. Early in 1941, there was a directive for all unmarried women between the ages of twenty and thirty to register for war work. This meant I could leave the salon without feeling guilty.

My new role was in the Rolls Royce factory in Hillington where I worked on the milling machine making parts for aircraft. We worked long shifts – sometimes from six in the morning till six at night, or six at night till six in the morning. It was hard work and pretty tiring, but the other women were a cheery bunch, and the management often put on entertainment for us in the evenings.

Then the war came to Scotland.

In March, we experienced what came to be called the Clydebank Blitz. We knew the town of Clydebank would be a target for the German bombers because of the ships and munitions being produced there. Over two nights the whole town was almost destroyed and we heard and felt the blasts right here in Glasgow. When we next saw Kate, she told us it had been just as bad where she was in Lanarkshire.

She also told us she was dating a Polish soldier, but that's another story, and she's not here to tell it – poor Kate died young. After the invasion of Poland, a large number of Poles arrived in Scotland and set up bases there. It appeared that Kate's fellow was part of the Polish Recruitment Bureau based in Carluke, just up the road from where she was staying.

Since we didn't have an Anderson shelter, when the sirens sounded and our neighbours dashed out to their back yards carrying their gas masks and little brown cases of personal papers, we huddled in the cupboard under the stairs and clung to each other, hoping against hope the bombs would miss us.

We spent two nights crouched in the tiny space, our only light a small torch. We'd come to recognise the sound of the German planes – different from those of our own aircraft – and we held our breath listening to the drone of the aircraft in the distance and the roar as they came closer, only to be terrified by the shriek of the bombs which screamed as they fell.

We were lucky, but not everyone in Glasgow had been so lucky. Several houses in Maryhill were destroyed including that of the grandmother of Nan's friend, Jeannie.

After that, Father wanted Nan to come home. But she reckoned she was as safe in Hillhead as she'd be in Kelvin Drive and she'd promised Colin to be company for his mother. She resolved to become involved in war work too, finding a job in another Rolls Royce munitions factory in Alexandra Parade in what used to be the Senior Service cigarette factory. After a couple of years at Hillington, I joined her there.

But that was later. These early war years were filled with more social life than I'd been used to. Apart from John's visits, I was now part of the close-knit group of women I met through working in the factory. We all got on well and, when we weren't working or too exhausted to do anything but sleep, we hit the town.

The city was full of servicemen on leave who were keen to put the war behind them for an evening with a girl. There were plenty of dance spots to go to. At weekends, we mostly went to the Locarno on Sauchiehall Street which became a favourite of mine. During the week, when we were off in the afternoons we loved to visit other places like Greens Playhouse where they had afternoon dancing. You could say we danced away the war years as we tried to emulate our new heroes Fred Astaire and Ginger Rogers and forget that our dance partners might not be alive in a week's time.

Later, when America joined the war, many of the soldiers were GI's and rumour had it that they had a plentiful supply of nylons and chocolate. I never found out as I ensured I only danced with *our own boys*.

They were heady times which were brought to a sudden end by the news that both John and Nan's Colin were to be posted overseas.

*

Glasgow seemed strange. It had become a city of women and children, though many of the children had been evacuated due to the danger from the bombs. Air raids were a common occurrence by now, but the gaiety of evenings out dancing and trips to the pictures continued unabated.

All of Britain was suffering, and when September third came around, we'd been at war for two whole years.

Then, in December, the country was shocked by the news that Japan had bombed Pearl Harbour. Father thought it was a good sign. 'The Americans will have to come into the war now,' he said. 'It won't be long before it's over.'

Nan, Kate and I weren't so sure. We remembered his prediction when Churchill had taken office and here we were, still with mounting lists of casualties. So far, both Colin and John had escaped death, but I knew worry kept Nan awake at night and I did manage to spare a thought for John, when my social life permitted. One of Eileen's brothers had been killed at Dunkirk a year earlier, and, although Alan had made it home, he'd been wounded. We lived from day to day, never sure if the next would be our last.

I was shocked by how this mindset affected many of my contemporaries. They seemed to have thrown good sense and morals to the winds in their desire to comfort the brave men they met. Not me! If I hadn't succumbed to Bob's urging, why would I let down my guard for a stranger I met on the dance floor?

I was glad I could tell my dance partners I had a boyfriend at the front, even though I knew there was no passion in what I felt for John. I knew in my heart I'd never feel for another man what I'd felt for Bob. But I wrote to John regularly and even visited his mother, spending many Sunday afternoons drinking tea with her and her sister, poring over pictures of John as a child and younger man, and talking of *after the war*. It was a phrase on everyone's lips – how everything would change, be better. As if with the cessation of hostilities, a beautiful glow would envelop us and make everyone happy.

But we knew this couldn't be the case. By now we were following the war avidly in the newspapers. Every day lists of the dead and wounded were published. I stopped reading them. It caused too much anguish to read the names of boys I'd been to school with, sons of neighbours, and brothers and husbands of friends. It may have been heartless, but I found it easier to just get on with my life, live day to day and hope for the best. I wasn't alone in this view. Many of my workmates felt exactly the same way, and this is what enabled us to get through each day.

It was therefore a shock, when I arrived at John's mother's house one Sunday to find the blinds drawn. I knew immediately, and my heart sank. John was gone! I may not have loved him in a passionate way, but I did harbour a strong affection for the man. He was modest and kind – good husband material many would say. My hand shook as I rang the doorbell, realising that, in the back of my mind, I'd thought that maybe – if he asked – I might say yes. That hope was now dowsed as thoroughly as the hoses extinguished the fires from the bombing.

'Isobel. How good of you to come. You won't have heard...' His aunt answered the door, her eyes red with weeping. 'Come away in. Jess is in the kitchen. We got the telegram yesterday.'

I wanted to run in the other direction. I wasn't good with other people's grief. I found myself ushered into a musty, darkened room. I could barely make out the hunched figure of John's mother sitting in the corner, but I could hear her sobbing.

'It's Isobel,' said his aunt.

'Oh, my dear. You must be devastated too,' she said, weeping. 'He had such plans for you both.'

My eyes began to moisten, more in shame than grief. I'd been wrong to give John cause to hope. Although nothing had been said, and there had been no agreement between us, I'd known how he felt. He hadn't been one to try to take advantage of the war, to push for a commitment. He'd been content to wait, and that had suited me. I suppose I'd seen him as second best – a back-up if all else failed. Now I regretted leading him on; my tears were genuine.

'You made him happy,' his mother said, wiping her eyes. 'I already looked on you as my daughter-in-law. I know John was planning on buying the ring on his next leave. I'm so sorry, my dear.'

Buying the ring? I'd had no idea. I didn't know what to say, so I said nothing. Somehow, I got through the afternoon, but when I left, although the sun was shining, it was as though a large cloud obscured it. With John's death, something had smashed into pieces. I'd been personally affected by this evil war. It was no longer something we talked about, read about. It had reached out and touched me.

I caught the tram home and walked along the road in a dream. I'd lost my safety net. My mood must have shown in my expression, because when I walked in the house my mother asked, 'What's the matter?' Then her face changed. 'It's John, isn't it? Oh, Isobel!' She opened her arms. I fell into them, and the tears which had started earlier began to fall in earnest.

'Oh, Mother,' I wailed. 'He... he was going to buy me a ring.' That was all I could think of. I didn't even know if I wanted a ring from John. But the fact he'd intended to buy me one, to ask me to marry him, meant someone had loved me, someone had wanted to spend the rest of his life with me. And that life had been snuffed out like a candle.

'How did...'

'I don't know. I didn't ask. What does it matter? He's gone now.'

My mother straightened. 'We need to call Nan,' she said. 'Her Colin and John...' She didn't need to finish her sentence. I knew what she was going to say. They were in the same regiment. Maybe Colin had been killed too, and Nan was too distraught to let us know. She went to the phone.

I trailed upstairs to the room I now slept in alone and I threw myself on the bed, feeling empty. If John could be killed, no one was safe. I supposed I'd known that already, but it hadn't sunk in. I lay there thinking of John on his last leave. He'd been so full of fun, so cheerful. To think of all that exuberance gone was difficult to contemplate.

Then my thoughts turned – as they often did – to my first love – to Bob Smith. I remembered how he'd looked at Eileen and Alan's wedding – so handsome in the uniform of the Royal Air Force. Eileen never mentioned him these days, though I was sure she'd say if he'd been shot down. She would, wouldn't she? I felt a jolt of alarm in the pit of my stomach at the thought he might be dead too and began to cry again.

It was only then I accepted what I'd really known all along – the hope that, when this dreadful war was over, when our world was back to normal, Bob would seek me out, we'd make up and he'd ask me to marry him. It was Bob I wanted to marry, not John or any other fellow. My tears dried. I went to the bathroom and washed my face, then headed downstairs.

'Nan's fine,' Mother greeted me. I looked at her askance. 'Colin,' she said. 'There's been no word, so that's good, isn't it?'

I remembered. I'd been so wrapped up in myself, in my own hopes and fears, I'd completely forgotten Mother's concern over my sister's husband. 'Yes, that's good,' I said.

Seventeen

Isobel - 1946

At last the war was over, and the men were returning. Eileen and Nan had greeted their husbands with the excitement that was their due. They were all busily searching for accommodation in post-war Glasgow as the men readjusted to life in what was called civvy street. Both Colin and Alan were lucky their former bosses took them back, but I did wonder what happened to the women who'd filled their jobs during the war.

It didn't take Nan and Colin long to find a flat off Byres Road, not far from his mother. With the housing shortage after the war, several new towns were being built, and Nan had been worried they might have to move out of the city. But, fortunately for them, Colin's mother heard of an old woman who'd died, and they were able to snare her flat before anyone else discovered it was vacant.

I barely knew my sister as she turned into a real housewife. At the end of the war, she'd returned to her job at the Co-op and she and Colin seemed happy enough. Though, when we met up, I noticed a big change in him. The cheerful joking young fellow who'd gone off to war with such enthusiasm, had returned a morose creature with mood swings. But Nan loved him and was willing to cater to his every whim. They came to visit every Sunday after church. Colin had joined the choir again, and Nan was hoping that would help turn him back into the happy man she'd known before the war.

I hadn't seen Eileen for a few weeks when I received a call out of the blue inviting me to dinner in their new flat in Anniesland. She said it would be just us as Alan was going out and that she had something to tell me. Since she and Alan had only recently been reunited, I assumed she was going to say she was expecting like almost every other wife in town.

During the meal, which was frugal as rationing was still in place, we chatted about the changes wrought by the men's return and what it would mean for those of us who'd been engaged in war work or had taken on men's jobs for the duration.

'What will you do?' Eileen asked. 'I'll have Alan's wage coming in, so I don't need to worry so much. Will you go back to the salon?'

'No,' I said, though the thought had crossed my mind, albeit briefly. 'Kate saw a shop for rent in Byres Road and we're thinking of taking it and setting up a dress shop.' I took a deep breath. 'Now that things are getting back to normal, women will be thinking of buying pretty clothes again, so...'

'You thought you'd cash in? What a good idea!'

'We plan to start small since there's still clothes rationing. We'll have blouses, jumpers, cardigans and skirts, stockings when we can get them, then when the rationing finishes we can branch out into dresses and evening wear if it goes well. We thought we'd call it Plain and Fancy,' I said in a rush. 'What do you think?'

'I think you've hit on a good plan.'

'Now I've told you my news, what about yours?' I asked, preparing to offer my congratulations and be bored with baby talk for the rest of the evening.

Eileen looked down at the tablecloth and fiddled with her knife and fork before replying. When she raised her eyes to meet mine, I saw they were filled with what looked like pity. 'It's Bob,' she said. 'Bob Smith. He's getting married on Saturday.'

I felt my body grow cold as a chill found its way from my toes up to my head. It was as if I was floating on a cloud of icy cotton wool. No! This couldn't be happening. Bob couldn't marry someone else. I heard her words through a fog of despair. I still loved him. I never thought he'd gone from my life for good. I'd been waiting for him to come back. Now that he was demobbed, I'd hoped he'd come looking for me and I'd have the fairy-tale ending I'd dreamed of.

'Oh!' was all I could say. I knew if I tried to speak I'd break down. But I needn't have worried, Eileen was babbling on.

'Mhairi's a teacher,' she said. 'Bob went back to the school when he came out of the Air Force and she'd just joined the staff. Twisted him round her little finger, Alan says. It's his buck's night. That's where Alan is.' She stopped suddenly. 'Are you all right?'

'Ye...es.' I felt as if I was returning from a long journey and that nothing would ever be the same again. 'I have a bit of a headache,' I lied, though perhaps it wasn't really a lie as my head did feel a bit odd. 'Maybe a glass of water?'

As Eileen went to the kitchen to fetch it, I surreptitiously wiped my eyes. I pushed my hankie back into my pocket, took a couple of deep breaths and managed to paste a smile on my face before she returned. 'Thanks.' I gulped greedily from the glass. 'I think I'd better go home.'

*

I don't know how I made it home. As soon as the front door closed behind me, I rushed upstairs and flung myself on the bed. I couldn't stem my tears. Until now, I hadn't realised how much I'd been counting on Bob coming back to me, begging me to return to where we'd been before the war. I hadn't expected him to remain faithful all these years – he was a man after all, and I knew they had *needs*. But I'd hoped...

I'd been living in a fool's paradise. I'd conveniently forgotten I was the one who'd rejected him, who'd refused his advances. I'd ignored the fact I hadn't heard from him all through the war – and that I'd been involved with another man. I'd always harboured the hope that when the war was over, everything would return to normal. And, for me, normal meant that Bob and I would get together again.

His imminent nuptials put paid to that idea. He was lost to me forever.

'What's the matter with you?' Kate, who'd returned home at the cessation of hostilities and the return of men to the factory, pushed open the door and threw her hat on the bed. 'Your eyes are all red. Have you been crying?'

I quickly sat up and rubbed my eyes making them redder than ever.

'Are you all right, Izzy?' Kate joined me on my bed and put her arms around my shoulders. Her sympathy was too much. I began to cry again.

'He's getting married,' I wailed, unable to keep it to myself. Soon everyone would know anyway.

'Who is?' Then Kate's eyes widened. 'You mean… that fellow you were sweet on before the war? What was his name again?'

'Bob,' I sobbed, 'Bob Smith.'

'But that was *years* ago. You didn't think…?' Her eyes met mine and I could see in them the realisation that it was exactly what I had thought. 'Oh, poor Izzy!' she said, drawing me closer and rocking me like a baby.

We sat like that till we heard the front door open and close.

'The parents are back,' she said. 'We should go down. They'll be wondering what's wrong.'

'You go,' I said, sniffing. 'I'll wash my face first. Don't let on, will you?'

'Not a word,' she said and disappeared.

By the time I joined the family downstairs, I found them discussing some new arrangements. It seemed that a couple of elderly female relatives, distant cousins of Mother's, women whose husbands had been killed in the first war, had been bombed and had been living in interim accommodation. They'd now outstayed their welcome in their temporary homes. Mother was all for offering them space in our house. Father was being cautious.

'What if…,' he began, before putting up all sorts of objections, but we knew Mother would get her way. Her final comment, 'They're family,' settled the matter, and Kate and I were detailed to prepare two of the spare rooms upstairs for their arrival.

I'd always thought the house was like a big empty shell and quite looked forward to our new boarders. The discussions about where they'd sleep and how we'd arrange meals took my mind off my own worries for a bit. This at least was something I could take action on.

*

The other thing to take my mind off Bob Smith's marriage was the shop Kate and I were setting up – Plain and Fancy. This was to be a completely new venture for me, but Kate's experience at the Co-op stood us in good stead. It wasn't long before we were unpacking our first load of stock and getting set up to open.

While Kate had the business know-how, I came into my own when we were selecting the fashion items and in arranging the window display, for which I discovered I had a talent. It was a thrilling moment when we stood outside the window of our very own shop and we clasped each other in excitement.

On opening day, we couldn't wait for our first customer to arrive. We stood behind the counter with bated breath. What if no one came? We'd sunk our meagre savings into this venture. It had to work.

But we needn't have worried. Kate had predicted correctly. The timing was right. From the first trill of the doorbell signalling the arrival of a customer, we didn't stop. And after that first day, we were busier than we could ever have imagined.

'If this continues we may need to take on an assistant,' Kate joked. But we knew neither of us wanted to share Plain and Fancy with a stranger.

Life at home continued much the same. Our new residents mucked in with the chores and the house seemed to run smoother than ever. I was too busy to spend time moping and when I did spare a thought for my lost love, there was always something more pressing to attend to allow the thought to take root.

*

1950

One Saturday, Nan dropped into the shop unexpectedly. She started browsing our knitting patterns which were kept in a large book on the counter.

'Something for yourself or Colin?' I asked, moving round to look over her shoulder.

She blushed, and I noticed she was examining patterns for matinee jackets.

'Who…?' I began, then noticed a big grin on her face. I threw my arms around her and called out to Kate, 'Our Nan's expecting!'

'Shh.' Nan peered round the shop but, discovering she was the only customer, began to bubble with her news. 'I've just found out and you two are the first to know. I'll tell Col tonight. We've been trying for so long that we thought…' Her voice dried up, but we knew what she meant. The war had changed so many of our menfolk. For those women who didn't fall pregnant immediately their men returned, it was a real concern that whatever had happened *over there* might have rendered them incapable of fathering a child.

We helped her choose a pattern and some wool, opting for white and lemon till the baby was born, though Nan had hesitated over the pink in the hope she was carrying a girl. 'I don't know anything about boys,' she said when we remonstrated with her and suggested Col might want a son to carry on his name.

On Sunday, there was a celebration at home. The news of a baby was a breath of optimism after the horrors of the war years. Even Col seemed to be feeling hopeful about the future. For Nan's sake, we hoped this was a good sign. Mother cooked a special roast beef dinner and Father went as far as to open his precious whisky for Col and him, while we women sipped a small glass of sherry.

'You'll need to take good care of yourself now,' Mother told Nan, 'and make sure that man of yours looks after you properly.'

'He does, Mother.' Nan, threw a loving glance toward where Col and our father were discussing the fate of their favourite football team. 'I know he seems different since he came back, but he *did* come back. So many didn't. And underneath, he's still my Col. He's not as strong as he used to be, but he'd do anything for me and he's over the moon about the baby.'

Colin must have sensed we were talking about him because he looked over and as his eyes met Nan's, I saw them exchange the sort of look I'd have given my eye teeth to exchange with a man. The sort of exchange I doubted I'd ever experience now.

When they were about to leave, Colin dropped the clanger. He took Nan's hand, smiled at her and turned to face the rest of us. 'Nan and I have some other news,' he said. 'Once the bairn's born, Nan'll have to stay home.' He hesitated and cleared his throat as if knowing his next words wouldn't be welcome. 'We'll need a bit more than what I'm earning at the store, so…' I saw his hand grip Nan's tightly. 'I've been asking around and it seems there are jobs going in the pits in Fife.'

There was a stunned silence. Our family had lived in Glasgow for generations, Colin's too. To think of the young couple moving away, especially now there was a baby in the offing – our parents' first and only grandchild – was too awful to contemplate.

Father was first to find his tongue. 'It's a long way, lad. You have a good job here, and a place near us and your own mother. Surely the two of you would be better placed to stay where you are? And if you need a bit of help…'

'We've talked about this, Father, and decided it's best for us. Col can make a lot more money, and I can stay home with this one.' Nan stroked her still-flat stomach.

'I'm sure they're doing it for the best,' Mother said to Father, but I could see she was about to burst into tears at the thought of her only grandchild living so far away. 'What does your mother have to say about it, Colin?'

Colin looked at his feet. 'We haven't told her yet, Mrs MacDonald. We'll be going over to Hillhead after we leave here.'

'It'll be a shock to her too, son. But I suppose we'll all get over it. Needs must, eh?' Mother managed to smile at Nan and him. 'Well, we mustn't be keeping you if you're dropping in there on your way home.'

The pair left with lots of hugs and well wishes, but once Mother had closed the door behind them it was a different matter. Father started to rail on about the need for unions to make sure the men returning from the war had a living wage, and wonder why Colin couldn't have looked for a job nearer home in the shipyards, while Mother finally gave way to tears. Kate and I rallied round saying it wasn't too bad, that they weren't going off next week, and maybe it would never happen.

But we knew Colin had made up his mind and sooner or later, we'd be saying goodbye to our wee sister.

Eighteen

Bel – 2015

Bel was sitting on her bed, replaying the evening in her mind. She felt like a love-struck teenager, though love was probably not the right word. Her feelings seemed more akin to lust. Not that she intended to do anything about it. Apart from that odd remark about not thinking of her as a sister – which could mean anything – Matt's behaviour and comments had been most circumspect. He hadn't said or done anything to make her think he saw her as anything more than the niece of a client who'd become a good friend.

She was grateful her Aunt Isobel had already gone to bed when she returned, and had crept in as quietly as she could, knowing her aunt was a light sleeper. The last thing she wanted was to give an account of her evening when Isobel would no doubt want to know how she and Matt were *getting on*.

Bel tried to analyse exactly when her feelings towards Matt had begun to change, when they'd transformed from wanting to avoid any close contact to the jolt of desire she'd experienced in the hotel. She shook her head in amazement that she could still feel this way at her age. Fortunately, Matt hadn't appeared to notice. Apart from a gruff, 'Are you okay?' when she returned from the ladies, he'd carried on the conversation as if nothing was amiss.

At least, over the years, Bel had had plenty of experience in hiding her feelings. Her brief marriage had taught her that. She'd become expert in putting *a brave face* on things and knew how to hide her emotions. She suspected Matt was the opposite.

Her impression of him was that what you saw was what you got. He was a man who'd eschew subterfuge. This was why his apparent pleasure in her company stunned her. From all she'd heard of him, he'd shunned women for the past five years. Why should she imagine she'd be the one to bring him out of his self-imposed solitude – a sixty-five-year-old woman from Australia?

Unable to sleep, Bel decided to read more of the Isobel saga and, after changing into her nightdress and fetching a cup of cocoa from the kitchen, she propped herself up in bed and drew the sheaf of papers towards her.

Bel sipped the warm drink and smiled as she read about the announcement that her mum was pregnant. So, she'd wanted a girl? The warm glow that filled Bel had little to do with the cocoa drink. It was lovely to read – all these years later – how delighted everyone had been to hear she was on the way.

But she frowned when she came to the part that they planned to go to Fife. Why so far away? And back then, when families didn't have cars, it must have been devastating for the prospective grandparents on both sides. Bel didn't remember her dad's mother. She'd died while Bel was little, but she did remember how loving her mother's parents had been.

She laid down the page she was reading and gazed into space trying to imagine what it must have been like for a young couple making a fresh start after the years of war. Gradually her eyes began to close.

But her dreams were not of her family, or of the war years, but of the dark-haired, dark-eyed man with whom she'd spent the evening.

*

Bel entered the kitchen warily next morning, expecting a full interrogation on her evening with Matt but, to her surprise, her aunt wasn't sitting in her usual spot. Worried, Bel went through to the front bedroom and tapped gently on the door.

'Aunt Isobel. Are you okay?' She carefully turned the handle and pushed the door open.

Isobel was sitting up in bed hunched over, her eyes closed and a bloodstained handkerchief in her hand.

Bel rushed over. 'Oh, Aunt Isobel. What's happened?' A shaft of fear shot through her. Her aunt couldn't be… She wasn't ready for this. But before Bel had time to dismiss the selfish thought, Isobel opened her eyes and seemed to grasp the handkerchief more firmly.

'I'll be fine. I'm not dead yet. I'll be here to bother you for a bit longer.'

Bel sighed with relief and perched on the edge of the bed. 'You gave me such a fright. But you're not well. Should I call the doctor?'

'I just had a bit of a spell. I haven't been well for months.' Isobel tried to laugh, but it ended in a hacking cough. 'There's not much William Ramage can do for me, but call him if you like. It's time you met him anyway.' She fell back against the pillow and exhaled noisily. 'I think I might stay here today.'

'Can I get you anything?'

'I might be able to manage a cup of tea… and maybe a soft-boiled egg. My mother always made us soft-boiled eggs when we were sick.'

'Coming right up.' Bel stroked a lock of hair away from her aunt's face and patted the hand grasping the handkerchief.

*

Once in the kitchen, Bel had to grip the edge of the sink before doing anything else. She knew her aunt was sick. That's why she was here. And Isobel was setting everything in place for when she was no longer alive. This relapse shouldn't come as a shock. But it did.

Bel had managed to put her aunt's ill health to the back of her mind as she went gallivanting around with Mary and Matt and took herself off down memory lane.

To be fair, Isobel had encouraged her. But no more, Bel decided. Her place was at her aunt's side. She'd never forgive herself if anything happened while she was out enjoying herself.

She found the doctor's number on a pad beside the phone – the same place she'd found Matt's earlier – and arranged for him to visit later that morning. Then she busied herself making the tea and egg Isobel had asked for. While she waited for the water to boil, she managed to make herself a slice of toast and swallow it down. It wouldn't help Isobel if she fell ill herself.

When the doorbell rang around nine, Bel rushed to answer it, only to find the door open by itself. She'd forgotten it was Betty's morning to clean. The small woman bustled in and headed for the kitchen,

'You're in a hurry today,' she said as she stepped past Bel.

'It's Aunt Isobel. She's…'

'Having one of her bad days, is she? Your visit's fair perked her up, but it's no surprise if she's taken a turn for the worse. She told me…' Betty buttoned her lip as if she'd spoken out of turn.

'She says she'll stay in bed today. I've called the doctor.' Then Bel realised what Betty had said.

'Has she been like this before? Since I've been here, she hasn't…'

'Doctor Ramage can't do much. It's her sickness. She knows she hasn't long. That's why she sent for you, my dear.' Despite her unemotional words, Betty's eyes reflected her compassion for Bel's concern.

By this time, they were in the kitchen and Bel sat down with a thump. 'I know, Betty. At least I thought I did. But she's been so well. And she even managed that trip out to Matt's.' Bel thought back and realised that her aunt had looked a bit pale ever since. 'Was it too much for her? Have I helped make her worse?'

'Dinnae fash yourself. She loved it. Told me all about it, she did. But you can't stop time. She knows that and has tried to keep well as long as she can to enjoy your being here. But none of us live forever, and her time will come sooner rather than later. You have to accept that.'

Bel knew she was right, but was amazed at how realistic Betty was about Isobel's imminent death. Her astonishment must have shown on her face.

'We've talked about it,' Betty said. 'She's not afraid.' She seemed about to add more, but the bell rang again.

'That'll be the doctor now.' Bel went to the door where a man in his thirties wearing a grey suit and carrying a small case was waiting.

'Doctor Ramage?'

'That's me. You must be Bel, the niece from Australia. Isobel's had another of her turns, has she? In here?' He gestured to the open door of the bedroom and walked in.

Bel followed to hear him greet her aunt in a cheerful voice.

'Hello there, Isobel. You've been malingering again, have you? Let's have a look at you.' He turned to Bel. 'You can leave us if you like.'

'William here might like a cup of tea when he's done with me,' Isobel said in a hoarse whisper.

'Right,' said Bel, hesitating in the doorway for a moment before returning to the kitchen where Betty already had the kettle on.

'He'll be wanting his tea, Bel. And he enjoys a wee bit of shortbread with it.'

Bel shook her head in disbelief. Her aunt was seriously ill, dying maybe, and the doctor's tea and shortbread seemed to be taking priority.

'Sit yourself down. There's nothing you can do, and your aunt would be that upset if he didn't get his usual. He'll be through soon, and you can ask all you want about her. She'll rally again. You'll see.' Betty nodded to herself and proceeded to set out a couple of cups and saucers and a plate of shortbread fingers. 'You'll be having a cup with him, yourself.'

It wasn't a question, and Bel nodded resignedly and pulled a chair out from the table. She'd really have liked to be in her aunt's room to hear what Doctor Ramage had to say, but clearly she wasn't welcome there.

Betty timed it well and was pouring the tea when the doctor popped his head into the kitchen. Bel stood up immediately 'Is...?'

'Thanks, Betty,' he said, then his eyes met Bel's worried ones. 'Your aunt will get over this attack in a day or so. But I'm afraid there will be more like it. She doesn't intend to go into hospital, doesn't want anything to prolong her life, so we just have to make her as comfortable as we can while these attacks last.' He helped himself to two spoonsful of sugar and stirred his tea. 'It's hard to watch, I know. You'll probably find by tonight, she'll be feeling a little stronger and may even want to get up tomorrow.'

'And if she does?'

'If she feels up to it. She's the best judge as to what she's capable of. She was telling me you'd both taken a wee drive the other day.'

'Was that what brought this on?' Bel was feeling guilty again.

'No, no. She's had a few attacks like this in the past, and I warned her they'd probably increase. She's a determined lady. Let her do what she wants. She won't go till she's ready. Believe me. I've seen a lot of these old dears. They can hang on till, it seems, they're suddenly able to let go. Someone or something happens, and they feel it's time. There's no telling when that'll be for Isobel. Your presence here has been a tonic for her. Kept her going for longer than I'd predicted.'

'Oh!' Bel took a sip of her own tea and watched William Ramage help himself to a piece of shortbread. She wanted to ask him for more information, wanted to know how long… but the words wouldn't come. She couldn't ask how much longer her aunt would live, so she drank her tea instead.

When he'd finished and praised Betty for the tea and shortbread, Doctor Ramage rose to leave. At the door he said, 'I'll pop in next week, shall I? That might set your mind at rest. I know it's not easy watching someone die but, rest assured, she's not in pain. She just has these bouts when her breathing becomes very laboured. Most of the time she can handle it. I gave her a small sedative, so she'll sleep for a bit and, as I said, she should feel a bit stronger when she wakens. I know there's no point in telling you not to worry, but it won't help your aunt and it's better for her to have someone cheerful around her. So, no going around her with a sad face or walking on eggshells. Just act normally. That's what she wants of you and that's what'll help her most. Promise?'

'Promise,' Bel said, feeling like a small child. But, as she turned back into the house, she knew it was a promise she'd find difficult to keep. The sight of her aunt in such distress had shaken her, and it was difficult to accept it would happen again and again until Isobel's body gave up for good.

Back in the kitchen, Betty had begun her cleaning routine. 'I hope you're not going to be under my feet all morning,' she said gruffly, the slight break in her voice telling Bel the woman was more upset than she let on. She must be. As Isobel had told Bel, Betty had been coming here for years. While not exactly friends, they'd seen a lot together, and Betty would be just as distressed as Bel when Isobel passed away – perhaps more so. In typical Scots fashion, she was able to hide her feelings behind a brusque facade.

'I'll be in my room,' Bel said.

But when she got there, she stood for minutes just gazing out of the window, blind to the view. Memories came flooding back. The time she and Mary had pretended they couldn't hear when Aunt Isobel had wanted to take them to the cinema; the way she'd always been eager to leave her aunt's company; the arguments; how she'd admired her aunt's dress sense; the way she'd often watched her aunt style her hair, vowing to have a bun just like hers when she grew up. Bel touched her short head of hair – that hadn't happened. Short hair was much more practical in Sydney's summer heat and humidity, and she'd never had time to fuss with longer hair.

She finally sighed and turned on her iPad. Maybe it would take her mind off her aunt's illness if she checked out her emails and got in contact with people back home. She'd only been here a few weeks, but already Sydney seemed very far away. She smiled ruefully. It *was* very far away, about as far away as you could get. And, oddly, Glasgow was feeling much more real to her as time went on. The longer she stayed here, the less important her life in Sydney seemed to be.

She began to read her emails. There were a few from Jan reporting on the shop takings. She smiled to see that Isabella continued to be as popular as ever despite Jan reporting that the papers were full of companies going under due to the growth in online shopping. It seemed that the ladies on Sydney's North Shore still preferred the personal service the boutique offered.

She finished a lengthy reply to Jan, thanking her for her continued good work and the regular reports and providing a little of her own news, with no mention of Matt Reid. She'd just pressed *send*, when a new email popped up from an unknown address.

Wary it might be spam, Bel studied the first line, then realised it was from a well-known firm of solicitors in Sydney, so decided to open it. She read it carefully, then let out a whistle of surprise. It was an offer to purchase Isabella and the amount they were offering was way beyond anything Bel might have expected.

Her immediate reaction was *absolutely not*. It seemed a large developer wanted to buy the line of shops where Isabella stood to replace it with a block of units with cafes and small shops at ground level. That meant her store wasn't the only target. Bel sighed. She had enough on her plate without this worry. Then she brightened. Isabella wasn't the only target, and she couldn't imagine the neighbouring shops being willing to sell out either.

Interrupted by another ring of the doorbell Bel sighed, closed the email, and went to answer the door.

'It's only me.' Mary stood there smiling, her face falling when she noted Bel's look of surprise. 'I've brought Isobel's library books.' She held up a bag. 'I know it's not my usual day. Did she forget?'

'Oh. We're all at sixes and sevens. Aunt Isobel's had a bad night and she's having a sleep. But come on in. It's Betty's day, but I'm sure I can offer you a cup of something.'

'Tea'll be fine,' Mary said, following Bel through the hallway where the sound of a vacuum in the living room told Bel that Betty had finished in the kitchen. She glanced at the closed door as she passed her aunt's bedroom. Isobel would still be asleep. There was no sense in disturbing her.

'What have you been up to?' Mary asked, when they were both seated with their tea and pieces of gingerbread Bel had unearthed from the pantry. 'You'll never guess what I heard?' she continued without waiting for a reply. 'Mr Matthew Reid has been seen out with a *lady friend*.' She uttered the last two words as if he'd been engaged in an obscene act in public.

'Oh?' Bel asked, sipping her tea and wondering if she was the lady friend in question or if Matt had a collection of *lady friends*. She had no intention of revealing her meetings – could they be called dates? – to her old friend.

'Yes,' Mary went on. 'Bold as brass, having lunch, right there in Central Station. Not afraid anyone would see him either.'

Bel bit her lip and held back a smile. 'Well, fancy that. But why is it so shocking that the man should have lunch with a friend?'

'It…,' Mary stammered. 'It's out of character for him. He's always kept to himself, ignored us women, even.' She drew herself up and Bel had to hide a smile at the outraged expression on her friend's face. 'It's just not right.'

'But surely he has the right to see whoever he pleases? He's not answerable to your social circle.' She fell silent, wondering if she'd said too much, but Mary didn't appear to notice.

'We've done our best to see he's included in all our invitations,' her friend continued. 'He ignored every single one of them. Ever since Ailsa passed away. We tried to take pity on a lonely man. And now, how does he repay us? By cavorting around town with a stranger!'

Bel was lost for words. But she was certain of one thing. Mary was the last person she could confide in. She realised this with a sense of disappointment. For once in her life, Bel wanted another woman to confide in, and her old friend would have been perfect. Maybe Jan, back in Australia, would be the one who could offer advice. She'd had a rough trot herself recently and had managed to come out reasonably unscathed.

'More tea?' Bel gestured to Mary's empty cup.

'No. I'd better be getting on. I'll leave Isobel's books here, shall I? Maybe you can let me know when she feels well enough for visitors?'

'I'll do that. I'm sure she'll love to see you.'

They'd barely reached the front door, when the bell pealed again.

'It's like Paddy's Market here today,' Bel sighed, opening the door to see Matt standing there with a bunch of flowers and wide smile on his face.

His expression changed when he saw Mary. Bel looked from one to the other, not sure who looked most surprised. Matt's jaw dropped and Mary started to simper, not an attractive look in someone of her age.

'You heard Aunt Isobel was having a bad day,' she said quickly. 'How kind of you to drop by. Mary was just leaving.' The two jostled each other in the open doorway as Bel ushered Mary out and Matt in. She closed the door behind her friend and exhaled loudly.

'What was that about? The flowers are for you. Did Isobel take ill?'

'She had a bad night and we had the doctor this morning. She'd sleeping now. Mary popped in and…'

'You'd better sit down and tell me what's up.' Matt took Bel by the arm and led her to the kitchen. The warmth of his touch helped diminish the tension she'd been feeling ever since she found her aunt earlier that morning. She suddenly felt dizzy and stumbled as they reached the kitchen table. She grasped the back of a chair for support.

'You're not going to collapse on me, are you? I didn't take you for one of those women who…'

'No. I'll be right in a minute. It's been quite a morning.'

'Is that young Matthew's voice I heard?'

Bel looked round to see Betty coming in carrying the vacuum cleaner. She'd forgotten all about the woman who'd kept her distance during Mary's visit.

'I'll just put this away and I'll be making some tea. I see you already had a cup with that Mary Anderson.' She sniffed. 'And I'll put these in a vase.' Betty nodded toward the flowers Matt had laid on the table. 'You don't look too well, Bel. Sit yourself down. Hot, sweet tea is what you want.'

'She's right,' Matt murmured, as Betty left, the cord of the vacuum trailing after her like a tail. 'What happened?'

'Nothing. Everything. This morning…' Bel waved a hand in the air, unable to explain why she'd suddenly felt faint.

'It'll all seem better after a cup of tea,' Betty bustled in, put the kettle on and began to set out two cups and saucers. 'But would you not be better in the front room? I'm done in there now.'

'I think Betty wants us to get out from under her feet,' Matt said. 'Do you feel up to moving?'

Bel tested herself, then pushed herself up. 'Sure.' She didn't want another cup of tea – this would be her third in as many hours – and she wasn't sure what to say to Matt. She needn't have worried. As soon as they were seated in the living room, in the chairs on both sides of the window, Matt broached the subject.

'Know Mary Anderson well, do you?'

'We were childhood friends, best friends, right into our teenage years. Then lost contact as we went our separate ways. She just lives along the road and seems to have kept up with Aunt Isobel. How do you know her?'

Matt didn't answer immediately, but steepled his hands and leant his chin on his fingers. Then he looked up with a sigh. 'You've been gone a long time, Bel. You may have forgotten how like a small town some parts of Glasgow can be. Mary… she's one of a group of women who… Damn, there's no nice way of saying this. They're a group of harpies who try to get their claws into every single man in their orbit. They pretend concern, sympathy even, but they're out looking for husbands – for some it's their second or third. I experienced it when Ailsa died and I've kept my distance ever since.

'Your friend Mary's not the worst of them. I probably have more time for her than the others. Her folks were clients of my uncle and she recommended the firm to Isobel. But as I said, I try to keep my distance, letting young Duncan deal with her these days.' He thrust a hand through his hair. 'God knows, I'll never be the answer to any of their prayers, but it doesn't seem to stop them.'

By the time he'd finished talking, Bel was laughing.

'Well may you laugh,' he said. 'You've not had to sneak round corners at church socials, slide out of the office when one of them comes in simpering and asking if she can see 'the other Mr Reid'. It seems that, in the circles your friend moves, any single man or widower over the age of fifty is fair game.' He paused, then began to laugh along with Bel.

'I suppose there *is* something funny in my imagining every woman *of a certain age* in this neck of the woods is after my ancient body. That's not really what I wanted to suggest. It just sometimes seems that way. That's why you were such a breath of fresh air. Why...'

Bel's eyes met his, and she blushed at what she thought she saw in them. Through the laughter, the twinkling, there was a warmth, a hint of something that...

'Mary was telling me we'd been seen eating lunch,' she said.

'Seen eating lunch? My God! Is that a crime these days?'

Bel looked down and stroked the edge of her shirt. 'She said it was... unusual... for you to be seen with one of the fair sex.' She glanced up again to see Matt's eyes still full of laughter.

'She actually said that?'

'Well, I think what she said was that you were seen *cavorting around town with a stranger*. Clearly, they didn't know who I was. Unless you make a habit of cavorting around the centre of Glasgow with strange women?' She grinned.

'*Cavorting*, is it? Well, well. If I'd known we were being spied on, I might have given them something to talk about. But enough about me.' He became more serious. 'You said Isobel had a bad turn. How is she?'

'Doctor Ramage said she should feel better later today, but...' Bel's mouth turned down. 'There's nothing he can do. She doesn't...' Her eyes began to fill with tears.

'No. She's determined about that.' Matt took one of Bel's hands in both of his. 'It'll be okay. You'll see.'

'It's just...' Bel wasn't sure how to frame the words. 'Damn-it!' She wiped her eyes with the back of her free hand. 'We were never close.

As a child, I got angry a lot… with her. I'm not sure why. She was always good to me, treated me like her own daughter, the one she'd never had. And I… I pushed her away. Now we're the only two left and…'

She felt a warm pressure on her hand.

'It's okay,' Matt said. 'I'm sure she understands. She's not the easiest person to get along with. I always get the feeling she's had a hard life, that there's something in her past she regrets.' He sighed. 'Maybe I'm just being a fanciful old man.'

'And she'd hate to think we were talking about her like this.'

'She would that.'

'Tea!' Betty pushed open the door and entered carrying a tray. 'Your stomachs will be thinking your throats have been cut waiting for this. I popped in to see how Isobel was going, just in case she fancied a cup too. But she's sound asleep. Best thing she could do.'

Bel and Matt looked up, startled.

'Oh, Betty. We'd…' But she realised she couldn't tell Betty they'd forgotten all about the promised tea. 'We've been talking and didn't notice the time.'

'No wonder with so much going on here this morning.' Betty set down the tray. 'Now just let me know if you're wanting anything else,' she said, directing her words to Matt before leaving and closing the door.

'You're clearly a favourite with Betty, too,' Bel said, helping herself to one of the cups and a piece of buttered gingerbread.

'What can I say? My charm knows no bounds.' Matt's amused expression contradicted his words.

'Why did you call round?' Bel suddenly remembered Matt had arrived with a bunch of flowers, unaware of her aunt's turn for the worse.

'Ah! I was hoping I could persuade you to risk another outing with me. There's still a lot of the new Glasgow you haven't explored and….' He paused, clearly seeing Bel's expression. 'Maybe when Isobel has recovered from this attack?'

'Maybe, though I'm loath to leave her now I've seen for myself how quickly she can go downhill. I *did* come here to be with her, not to be gallivanting around the countryside, or the city for that matter.'

'Sure thing. Well, if you change your mind, the offer's open. I thought you might even fancy a hill walk. It's the best time of year for it.'

'That sounds nice, but I'll have to say no. For now, anyway. Maybe…' Bel felt torn. The thought of a hill walk was much more appealing than sightseeing in the city. Although Glasgow had changed during her absence, it still held too many memories.

But she'd enjoyed the two trips out of town, and the thought of walking across the muir and in the hills behind Matt's house did have a lot of appeal. She could almost feel the wind in her hair, the heather underfoot and hear the cry of the wild birds. On the other hand, she'd made a commitment to her aunt, one she didn't take lightly.

'Okay. Let me know how Isobel goes on.' Matt rose to take his leave and Bel followed him to the front door. She was sorry to see him go. He was good company, had a sense of humour similar to her own, and had managed to take her mind off the sight of Aunt Isobel as she'd been that morning – hunched over and clearly very ill.

'Thanks for dropping by.' Bel held out a hand to shake his, surprised when his arm reached around her shoulders to give her a hug. His lips lightly touched her cheek.

'Take care,' he said, and was gone, his little car driving off down the road with a roar, the tyres screeching as it turned the corner and out of sight.

Bel turned back into the house, feeling hollow, as if something was missing. She peeked into her aunt's room. Isobel was still sleeping peacefully. The sounds of vacuuming, overlaid with out-of-tune singing coming from upstairs told her Betty was still hard at work.

At a loss for something to do, Bel wandered around the living room, picking up and laying down photographs and ornaments, till she chastised herself for being so dejected. She couldn't understand why. It wasn't only her aunt's sickness, it was… Matt Reid. Damn the man! She couldn't get his face out of her head. He'd come to see her, brought her flowers, and she'd told him she was too concerned about her aunt to see him again.

Nineteen

Nan's baby was a little girl and I was thrilled to discover she'd called her after me – another Isobel. I hoped my namesake would have more luck than I'd had. As I held her at the christening, I looked down on the innocent little face and felt a sense of ownership. This Isobel would be the daughter I'd never have. She was so tiny, so dainty and her hair was dark like mine, though Mother assured us it was her baby hair and would soon fall out.

Nan and Colin were still living in Glasgow, so we were able to spend time with my sister and the baby. But their plans hadn't changed. Colin already had a job lined up, along with a house, and Nan was thrilled at the thought of having her own back garden.

The day came when they were off. Nan, Colin, and wee Isobel got into the car Colin had bought on the promise of his new job. We were all there to wave them off and, despite Nan's tears, and Colin's promises to bring her back often, we knew life would never be the same again. Nan's daughter would grow up on the other side of the country, away from her family.

'It's a sad day,' Father sighed as we watched the car disappear down the street.

'They'll be back,' Mother predicted. 'And it was good of the lad to bring them round before they left.' But once we were back inside she began to wilt. 'It's the thought of that wee bairn growing up so far away. She willnae ken us.'

I hugged Mother and glanced at Kate over her head. 'You still have Kate and me,' I said. 'We're not going anywhere. Not now we have a shop to run.'

'Aye.' Father sighed again. 'And I dinnae ken why the two of you think you can make money from women's fripperies.'

'Now, Geordie. The girls are doing their best. It's a fine thing they've got going. They're their own bosses. Isn't that something?'

'Hmm.' Father didn't offer any further comment. He picked up his paper and immersed himself in the sports pages.

'Dinnae pay him any attention,' Mother said. 'But it's a pity oor Nan's going so far away. She could maybe have helped you out a bit.'

'Mmm.' That had been our plan, one we hadn't mentioned to Nan, but which Kate and I had discussed in the dark, on nights when we couldn't sleep. Now we'd have to manage on our own or employ a stranger.

*

Plain and Fancy was fast becoming the go-to spot on Byres Road for women's garments and what we called notions – sewing thread, buttons, fasteners and the like. We found women would come in for their bits and pieces for sewing, then come back to buy a blouse or a cardigan. It was a slow process, but we were gradually making a name for ourselves and now that clothes rationing was over, women were enjoying renewing their wardrobes after the spartan years of the war.

Nan and her bairn may have moved away, but the letters flew back and forth. We kept abreast of Isobel's first tooth, her first steps and, when I was able to get away for a couple of days, Mother and I travelled across the country to see them for ourselves.

*

'There they are!' As the train chugged to a stop, Mother pointed to the young woman standing on the platform carrying a baby. We fetched our cases down from the rack, and opened the door.

Before I could step down, Mother was already hugging my sister and exclaiming how Isobel had grown. 'And just look at her hair,' she said. 'She's going to take after you, Isobel.'

'Mmm.' I wasn't sure it was a good thing. I wouldn't wish my looks on anyone, least of all this tiny morsel. I drew closer and peeked down at the little face, almost hidden by a woollen cap. She wasn't like me at all, apart from her dark hair. She was pretty, with her tiny nose and rosebud mouth. 'I don't think she looks like anyone but herself.'

'You looked just like that at her age.' Mother turned to me with a smile. 'Wait till she's a bit older and you'll see the likeness.'

'Maybe Mother's right.' Nan was always the one to try to settle any family disputes. 'She certainly didn't get her dark hair from either Colin or me. Did you, my wee lamb?' She gazed down fondly at the child.

I picked up our cases, and Mother took hold of our large shopping bag. She'd insisted on packing a couple of sultana loaves she'd baked and there were several cardigans for Isobel plus some books and toys Kate and I had picked up at the markets. 'Have we far to go?'

'A short bus ride,' Nan said. 'Wait till you see the house. It's not much, but it's home, and Col has been working hard to get the garden into shape.'

When we got off the bus, we walked a few blocks, ending up at a row of miners' cottages – single-level homes opening directly onto the pavement. Although they had a mean look about them, they were sturdily built and every doorstep had been carefully outlined in white showing the pride the housewives took in appearances. As we went in the door behind Nan, I also noticed the shining brass of the doorbell, and heard Mother grunt her approval. Old habits die hard, and Nan had learnt well, as we all had, growing up to undertake chores under Mother's careful guidance.

Nan put the bairn down in a playpen that took up most of the living room, and showed us round. It didn't take long. The house comprised a living room, kitchen, bathroom, bedroom and a front room that doubled as Isobel's bedroom judging from the cot sitting under the window. It was a far cry from the spacious house in Kelvin Drive, but Nan seemed happy playing house here with Colin and her wee girl.

Mother must have had the same thought. 'Hmm. I suppose you have to start somewhere.' She drew a finger across the window sill, then checked it for dust.

Nan and I exchanged a smile.

'It's lovely, Nan,' I said. 'Will Colin be home soon?'

'Not till after five when his shift ends. I thought we could have a bite to eat, then maybe take Bel to the park. I can make some sandwiches.'

'That'll be good, dear. But not the park for me. You two young ones go and I'll just have a lie down.'

That suited me. It would give Nan and me a chance to talk by ourselves, for me to find out if she really was happy here, in this tiny house, so far away from home.

After a lunch of egg and lettuce sandwiches, washed down with lashings of tea, Mother settled herself on the sofa in the front room, while Nan and I set off for the park with young Isobel in her pram.

'I'm glad to have the chance to talk to you like this,' Nan said, as she wheeled the pram carefully along, wee Isobel chortling and waving to everyone we passed.

'She's a cheerful soul.' I picked up the small blue dog she'd thrown from the pram for the umpteenth time. 'What did you want to talk about? Is everything okay with you and Colin? Are you really happy here?' I looked around at the great stacks belching smoke, smelt the ever-present stench from the brickworks, and wondered how anyone could live here, never mind like it.

Nan's eyes widened. 'Happy? Of course, I'm happy. Why wouldn't I be? I have everything I've always wanted. I have Colin and this one.' She clucked at her daughter who grinned back and waved the toy dog at her. 'No, it's you I wanted to talk about.'

'Me?' I stopped and stared at her. 'What about me?'

'It's about time you found yourself someone, too. You're not still mooning over that Bob fellow, are you? He's married, Izzy. He chose someone else. You need to get over him.' She put a hand on my arm. 'I want to see you happy.'

'I am happy. Kate and I have the shop and...'

Nan shook her head. 'That's not what I mean. You need someone to care for, to care for you – and a child of your own.' I saw her eyes linger on her daughter and felt a tug of envy.

'I'm fine.' But she was right. I hadn't forgotten my first love. I doubted I ever would. I'd convinced myself I'd put it behind me, that I didn't care anymore. But it only took Nan's words to bring it all back.

'We should be getting back. It looks like rain.'

I looked up and, sure enough, the sky was darkening. We turned to make our way home, barely speaking as Nan wheeled the pram quickly, and I thought about what she'd said and the memories her words had evoked. Was I never going to be free of them?

By the time we got back, Mother was stirring. I offered to help feed and bathe my namesake and revelled in the touch of her soft baby skin on my cheek as I held her close, and the sweet smell of her after-bath body. It would be nice to have one of my own, but the only man I wanted was taken, and I'd be damned if I'd settle for second best.

Twenty

Bel – 2015

Doctor Ramage proved correct. Isobel rallied in the early evening and managed a bowl of the chicken soup Betty had made before leaving.

'I'll be fine,' she said, as Bel hovered over her, worried about a relapse. 'Seems my time hasn't come yet. Did I hear young Matthew here earlier?'

'I thought you were asleep.'

'Aye, I was. But that contraption of his makes a terrible racket. I did hear it, didn't I? What did he want?'

Bel busied herself tidying up the bedside table. 'He brought some flowers and…'

'Flowers?' Isobel perked up. 'Not for me, I'll be bound. You've won a heart there. Hmm?'

'They were for me, but I don't know about winning a heart.' Bel blushed, feeling uncomfortable. 'He's polite – a gentleman.'

'Not too much of a gentleman, I hope.' Isobel coughed violently, and Bel removed her tray until the bout was over. 'I…' she began. 'You'll have read… I might have expected too much of a man. I may have been wrong.' She gazed into space, while Bel wondered how she should respond.

'Times were different back then,' she said at last.

'For some of us.' Isobel seemed about to say something else, but instead, reached for the tray again. 'I can manage. You go away through and have your own dinner. I'm still a bit sleepy. Might even get a good night's sleep.' A suggestion of Isobel's old self shone through as her lips turned up in the semblance of a smile.

'If you're sure?' Bel was loath to leave her aunt. But she knew that, as long as the old lady was alive, she'd be dishing out orders and striving to retain her independence. She sighed and headed for the kitchen where her own dinner was waiting.

Picking at the unappetising casserole she'd defrosted, and wishing she'd chosen to have a bowl of the chicken soup, Bel considered Matt's visit that morning. What did it mean? Did it mean anything? Questions whirled around in her head till she felt dizzy. She chastised herself. She was too old for this.

Her eyes fell on the flowers he'd brought, which Betty had arranged in a vase and placed on the dresser. It had been kind of him – a nice gesture. It had been years since she'd last received flowers from a man. It had made her feel... What exactly? Cherished was the word that came to mind. She chuckled. What an old-fashioned expression! But he was an unusual man, unlike any she'd ever met.

She laid down her fork in surprise at this revelation, then gave herself a mental shake. She wasn't here in Scotland to moon over a man, no matter how unusual or attractive he might be – and Matt *was* attractive. She'd come to be with Aunt Isobel in her last days and that had to be her focus. According to Isobel's saga, Bel had held a special place in her aunt's heart right from the time she was born. Bel had never appreciated just how much she'd meant to her aunt, whose attentions had frustrated her as a child and teenager. Now she felt guilty for the way she'd ignored Isobel, argued with her opinions and dismissed her as being totally out of touch with Bel and her friends. Now she'd learnt something about Isobel's younger days, she was developing more of an understanding of her aunt. Isobel hadn't had an easy life.

*

Next morning, Bel was shocked to find her aunt sitting at the kitchen table as usual. Her expression must have given her away.

'You can't get rid of me that easily,' Isobel said with a chuckle. 'I've confounded Ramage again. I bet he told you I'd be laid up for days.'

'Well…'

'I knew it,' Bel's aunt crowed. 'It was just a wee spell yesterday, not the one that's going to see me off.'

'You seemed pretty sick to me. I was worried.'

'No sense in worrying about me. What's to be will be, and one of these days, my time will come. But not yet. Not today. Now what are you up to today? Seeing young Matthew again?'

'No! I intend to stay with you. What if…' Bel grew cold at the thought that her aunt could have another of these attacks and any one of them might be her last.

'That's good of you, my dear. But these things are unpredictable. I could pop off tonight or last like this for months.'

Bel felt her aunt's eyes on her, evoking memories of a younger Isobel who'd brook no nonsense.

'I don't want you hanging around the house like a wet week, waiting for me to pop my clogs. Not when there's a fine young man looking to squire you around.'

Bel smiled at the thought of Matt *squiring* her around. The phrase had a touch of a Georgette Heyer romance novel about it, and the last time she'd read one of those had been in this house. She must have been all of fourteen at the time, dreaming of a Prince Charming coming to sweep her off her feet. Well, Callum had been no Prince Charming, neither had Pete or any of the men she'd met since. She'd long ago come to the conclusion that no such person existed. They lived in the realm of the romance novel along with soulmates and other such figments of their authors' imaginations. Aunt Isobel's tale was a case in point, and even her mother's love story had a sad ending.

'Well?' Isobel's voice was impatient, and Bel realised her aunt was waiting for an answer.

'Not today. I think I'll stay here. Mary dropped in your library books yesterday. I might see if one of them appeals to me.'

'Oh! I missed her. I'm sorry. She's good to an old woman, and I often suspect she has a lonely time of it herself, all alone in that big old house. Maybe you two could go out again.'

'Maybe,' Bel agreed, but she wasn't keen. The pair had probably just about got to the end of their shared memories and now their lives were so far apart they had little in common and less to talk about. Especially if Mary had hopes where Matt was concerned. As if reading her mind, Isobel's next words took Bel by surprise.

'I think the poor girl may have harboured the notion that Matthew might look in her direction. She wouldn't be the only one. Since Ailsa passed there have been a wheen of them waiting in line. But he does seem to have taken a shine to you,' Isobel concluded with a smug smile. 'Did he not want to take you out somewhere? He didn't come all this way to deliver a bunch of flowers, did he?'

Surprised to have Matthew's estimation of Mary and her friends so thoroughly confirmed by her aunt, Bel answered without thinking. 'He wants to show me the new Glasgow and mentioned a hill walk. But I told him I couldn't go anywhere while you were ill.'

'Bless you. But I'll be "ill" as you call it for the rest of my days, and you can't spend all your time here watching my every breath. I can't promise I won't take my last gasp while you're out gadding about, but I'll do my best. How's that sound?'

Bel couldn't hide her smile. Aunt Isobel was so matter-of-fact about her death. She wondered when the old woman had reached this degree of acceptance of her fate. It must be odd to know that your days were numbered and to be unafraid of that final moment. So much so that you could joke about it.

'Now, the sun's shining today. Why don't you give the lad a call and tell him you're ready to go?'

Bel tried to think of a good reason to refuse, but couldn't and an hour later she was ready to be picked up by an apparently delighted Matt.

Before she could go downstairs, she heard the door open and Matt greeting Isobel in his usual enthusiastic fashion, followed by Isobel's warm-hearted reply. Not for the first time, Bel thought that, if she was the daughter her aunt had never had, then Matt might well be the son, so fond of him did she appear to be.

She hurried downstairs to be greeted by Matt's wide grin, a grin that made his eyes crinkle at the corners.

'You auld fraud,' he said, giving Isobel his usual peck on the cheek while she waved him away with a shaky hand.

'You two young things away and enjoy yourself. I'll be fine here. And I'll still be here when you get back,' she added with a sly grin. 'I don't intend to meet my maker today.'

Bel shuddered at her aunt's good-humoured reference to her imminent demise, but recognised the usual Scots dark sense of humour which had been absent from her life for the last forty years. 'Are you sure? We can do this another day.'

'Away you go. Don't keep the man waiting.'

Matt was standing patiently, hands in pockets and a smile on his face. 'Shall we?' he asked.

With a last worried glance at her aunt, Bel joined Matt in the doorway and allowed him to lead her out and settle her in the car.

'Where are we off to?' Bel twisted round to face Matt who was already starting the car.

'I thought we'd do the touristy thing. You've been gone a long time and, as you've already noticed, the city has changed a lot. We'll start with the Clyde Arc, take in the Armadillo and have lunch on the Clyde Waterfront. The dirty old river has taken on a new lease of life with apartments, retail outlets and restaurants. You won't recognise it.'

'The Armadillo?' Bel asked with a laugh. 'What on earth…?'

'It's an event centre on the Clyde, an auditorium on Finnieston Street. It's been compared to the Sydney Opera House.'

'You're joking.'

'No. Really. It's something to do with the shape. It…'

'Wait a minute.' It was as if a light suddenly went off in Bel's brain. 'Is it that white shell-like building they use in the introduction to the *Taggart* series on TV?'

'It is.'

'Oh! I've often wondered about that. I didn't recognise the building. I'd love to see the real thing.'

'And you shall.' Matt put the car into gear and they drove off.

*

'Wow! We could almost be on Sydney Harbour.' Bel slid into a seat on the edge of a concrete deck which stretched out into the river, amazed at the transformation of her home town. 'I'd read about the sandstone buildings being cleaned, and the changes to the city centre surprised me, but this…' She gestured across the river.

'So, not the backward place you remember, eh?'

'I didn't…' A flush crept across Bel's cheeks. She saw Matt roll his eyes. 'Well, maybe. You have to make allowances for us colonials.'

'Is that how you see yourself?'

Bel considered for a moment before replying. 'I guess so. I've spent most of my life in Australia. Although…' She hesitated. This trip was bringing back memories she'd thought were gone forever. 'I'll always have a soft spot for Scotland and Glasgow. And the Glasgow I remember – the one I was so eager to leave – seems to have vanished. Some spots are the same – the University, Kelvingrove Park, the house I grew up in…' She gave an involuntary shudder.

'What is it about that house? I've noticed you seem to be a different person when you get away from it.'

Bel gazed blindly out at the murky waters of the Clyde and the new white bridge spanning it as she tried to formulate her answer. She cleared her throat and avoided Matt's eyes. 'I don't really know. Sometimes it's as if it closes in around me, leaves me gasping for air. I can't explain it.' She laughed awkwardly. 'I'm just a silly old woman. Don't pay any attention to me.'

'No.' Matt leant forward. 'I think I understand. When I lost Ailsa, I couldn't bear to be in the house.' He looked down at his hands. 'It was full of memories, full of her. It… it was oppressive.' He raised his eyes to meet Bel's again. 'I sold it as soon as I could. Duncan didn't understand. It was the family home. He wanted me to keep it – like a shrine, I suppose.' He dragged a hand through his hair and leant back. 'But Elspeth did and encouraged me to sell up. Best thing I ever did. And now…'

'Now you have your wonderful place on the loch.' Daringly, and without thinking, Bel placed a hand on Matt's. Her eyes misted over, and she felt an ache in her throat. He really did understand. A house could be like a living thing, and sometimes you had to walk away to retain your sanity.

'So, you left and now you're back.'

'But only temporarily. As soon as I'm not needed I'll be off again.' For the first time, Bel found she could refer to her aunt's death without feeling guilty.

'I'll miss you.' Matt's voice was so low, Bel almost missed the words.

She withdrew her hand. Had he really said that? He'd miss her? She'd be glad to be shot of the place again, to be back where she belonged. Or would she? Bel looked across the table, her eyes meeting those deep pools of chocolate brown once more and she felt a tinge of regret. 'I'll miss you, too.'

Twenty-one

Bel – 2015

It was raining again. How could Bel have forgotten? She'd become so accustomed to Sydney weather, she'd conveniently pushed the damp Scottish weather of her childhood to the back of her mind. She peered out the window, before deciding that there was a glimmer of weak sunlight trying to make its way through the clouds.

'It's only a bit of a drizzle,' Isobel told her as they ate breakfast together. 'Not enough to stop you and Matt.'

'Hmm.' Bel wasn't so sure. When the hill walk had been mooted, Isobel had been quick to assure the pair she was quite capable of managing on her own for the day, especially as it was one of Betty's days to "do". But Bel had imagined sunshine or, at the very least, high clouds. She wasn't so sure about walking across the heather in rain.

'You'll be fine. Look, it's beginning to clear.' Isobel pointed to the faint glimmer of sunshine Bel had noticed earlier. 'You'd better wrap up warmly. It'll likely be cool out there on the muir with the wind coming off the water.'

Bel forbore to tell her aunt she wasn't a child or even a teenager anymore, and had been looking after herself for over forty years. But good sense prevailed. She knew Isobel was only showing her love and concern, even though her words reminded Bel of a time she preferred to forget.

Bel slung her bag over one shoulder and picked up the anorak she'd purchased especially for the occasion, before heading downstairs. 'I'll be off now.' She popped her head into the living room where her aunt was buried in the paper.

'Another one gone,' Isobel said, looking up. 'I don't know why I bother to read the obituaries any more. There are hardly any of us left. It'll be mine next,' she predicted soulfully, but chuckled when Bel grimaced. 'Away you go. That young fellow will be champing at the bit waiting for you, and Betty'll be here before you get to the end of the road. You dinnae need to worry about me.'

Bel enjoyed the drive out to the loch, remembering her earlier trip, when she'd had the wind in her hair. She was glad to leave the city behind her and head out into the countryside. Winding the window down, she breathed in the damp morning air. It felt gentle on her skin as it kissed her cheeks. She turned on the car radio, surfing the wavelengths till she found one playing old favourites, then sang along to tunes from the seventies.

When she stopped the car at the house, a now familiar little white ball of fur hurtled down the driveway, barking furiously. Matt had a good early warning system in Hamish.

'Good morning.' Matt appeared in the doorway, wearing a pair of faded jeans and green marled sweater, the turned-up collar of a white shirt peeking out at the neckline. 'You made it?'

'Good morning to you.' Bel didn't consider his question deserved a reply.

Well, aren't you a sight for sore eyes?' he said. 'It's going to be a grand day. I'm glad to see you've got the proper attire, though...' His gaze fell to Bel's feet clad in a pair of trainers. 'These might get ruined. The ground's still pretty wet from the rain.'

'They're old. It won't matter,' Bel said, eager to be off, and feeling frustrated at both her aunt and Matt treating her as if she was incapable of dressing properly for a day out.

'How about something to sustain us before we leave?' Matt opened the door wider to allow Bel to enter, and she was almost bowled over by an excited Hamish as she walked through the house and into the kitchen. The sun was already shining in through the windows, confirming Isobel's forecast of a good day.

'Coffee?'

'Sounds just the thing.'

Matt busied himself with the coffee machine and produced some fingers of shortbread to go with the coffee, feeding a broken piece to a grateful Hamish. 'So,' he said, when they'd drained their cups, 'ready for a stiff climb?'

Bel's eyes widened and she felt her body tense. A stiff climb? She'd envisaged a casual stroll. She wasn't unfit. She did exercise regularly back home, but she *was* sixty-five and hardly up to a stiff climb.

Matt obviously noticed her surprise. 'Only joking, but there are a few places where we'll be going uphill. Doesn't worry you, does it?'

Bel felt his gaze on her, and unconsciously straightened her shoulders. She met his eyes to see the twinkle she found so attractive 'I'll be right. Should we be setting off?'

Matt picked up a small backpack, Bel hadn't noticed earlier. 'I've packed a bite of lunch for us. Means we won't have to rush back. Mind if Hamish comes along?'

At the sound of his name, Hamish began running around in circles, and Bel laughed. But her amusement was tinged by a hint of sadness. The little dog reminded her so much of her own Toby.

They finally set off, the sun beginning to beat down on them. Bel sniffed in the hauntingly familiar fresh scents of the heather, thyme, and gorse as she avoided the clumps of their more spiky cousin the thistle. It felt good to be outside in the company of this man and his dog. The conversation flowed easily, but much of the time they were content to walk in silence, enjoying the glorious day and the scenery.

As Matt had threatened, their route took in a few mild climbs, but nothing Bel couldn't deal with. Nevertheless, she was glad when Matt called a halt for lunch.

Bel gratefully dropped to the ground, tucking her feet up under her and taking in the view of the loch, now far below them. The ground between her and the water appeared to be a carpet of green, yellow and purple. She stretched her arms in the air. It felt good to be alive.

'Enjoying it?' Matt was opening the backpack and removing packets of sandwiches, a couple of hard-boiled eggs, two apples and two cans of *IRN-BRU.*

'Gosh. You have been busy. And I haven't tasted *IRN-BRU* for years. I loved it as a child – and the ads.'

'I know.' Matt chuckled. *'If there was any more iron you'd rust.'*

They laughed at the shared memory.

'It's not much, but it should keep us going,' Matt said. 'We'll go up a bit further, then head for home.' He filled a plastic bowl with water for Hamish and put down a sausage for the wee fellow.

'Do you come up here often?' Bel asked, when the sandwiches were finished and she was about to bite into her apple.

Matt gazed down at the view, He drew up his knees and wrapped his arms around them. 'Pretty often. I like the solitude, the sense of being at one with nature. I can think up here, away from everything and everyone.' He reached out to take Bel's free hand.

At his touch, Bel's heartrate rocketed and she felt a distinct tingle of something like... *passion*? She shivered.

His hand tightened and the pair sat in silence enjoying the peace and a sense of harmony with nature.

Suddenly, Matt dropped his arm, stretched out his legs and turned to Bel. 'Shall we get going again?'

'Sure.' Bel prepared to set off, helping Matt pick up their debris, a warmth radiating through her at the thought that he'd chosen to share this spot, this special spot, with her. Did that mean something or was she being foolish? Matt was so easy to be with. In his company, she felt like a teenager again. Not the mixed-up, rebellious teenager she'd once been, but the one she'd always wanted to be.

'Ready?' Matt's voice interrupted her thoughts. 'We'd best turn now if we want to beat that storm,' he said, pointing to dark clouds forming overhead.

It was easier going down, but as the sky darkened, they began to move more quickly, and Bel forgot to be cautious where she placed her feet. She was hurrying in Matt's wake, the little dog, running alongside, when she tripped. Feeling herself fall, she tried without success to regain her balance. Losing her breath, she landed in a heap, her right ankle twisted beneath her. She gasped with shock as she saw Matt's figure moving further and further away. 'Help!' she called breathlessly. 'Matt!'

Hamish heard her first and ran back barking. At the sound, Matt turned and seeing Bel's plight, hurried back too.

'I'm sorry,' Bel said. 'I tried to get up, but... It's my ankle.'

'Let me.' Matt put his hands under Bel's arms and gently helped her rise. 'Don't try to put your weight on it. If we go slowly we can make it. It's not far now.'

Together, they hobbled down the rest of the track and across to the house, where Matt deposited Bel on the sofa.

'Don't move.'

While Matt disappeared into the kitchen, Bel sank into the soft cushions, her ankle throbbing with pain. She could see it was swollen and was wondering if she should try to loosen her trainer when she heard the fridge door open and close.

Matt returned with a bag of frozen peas. 'Let me.' He sat beside her and began to unlace her trainer and gently ease it off her damaged foot. Then he placed the frozen pack on her ankle. 'It's supposed to help,' he said with a wry smile. I'm not much good at this.' He rubbed the back of his neck.

'A cup of tea would be good.'

'Of course.' Seemingly glad to be given some guidance, Matt disappeared in the direction of the kitchen again and, apparently pleased to have company, Hamish jumped up to join Bel, carefully avoiding the injured foot.

For a moment, Bel was overcome by dizziness and closed her eyes. What a blow. The day had been going so well and now this! How was she to get home with a crook ankle? It would be difficult to drive – maybe impossible. If she could get it strapped up, she could maybe hobble, but where to? Maybe Matt could drive her back to Glasgow? But she'd be no use to Aunt Isobel like this. She leant her head back on the arm of the sofa in an attempt to still her reeling thoughts.

'Tea up, and I put three spoonsful of sugar in. You had a shock,' Matt added, when Bel opened her mouth to object. He sat on a nearby chair, holding his own cup in both hands and shook his head. 'What are we going to do with you?'

'I can't stay here.' Bel didn't know what made her say that. There had been no suggestion she stay, no indication of what might happen next. But she knew how much Matt valued his solitary existence and didn't want him to feel any sort of obligation, to feel he should... There she was again, she thought, making completely unwarranted assumptions about her companion.

'I think you should.'

Bel gasped and put a hand to her throat, the cup in her other hand beginning to tilt dangerously.

'You'd better drink your tea before you spill it all over yourself.'

Bel did, and Matt retrieved the empty cup.

'I should… stay here?' She couldn't believe that's what he meant.

'Well, you're not going to get far with that ankle and I have a spare room. Unless you think it improper?' He smiled, and Bel was lost.

'But…'

'Who'll look after you back in Glasgow? Isobel?'

This was so close to what Bel had been thinking, she gulped. 'No, I…'

'It'll be a few days before you can put any weight on it. You'll need to keep it up till then Best you stay here. I can let Isobel know and drive you back when you feel able.'

Bel found herself agreeing. There was something comforting about someone taking charge, making the decision for her. She'd been on her own for so long. While she felt she should be the one to call her aunt, she forced herself to relax while she heard Matt's voice on the phone in the background.

'If I didn't know better, I'd swear she was pleased at the news,' he said on his return. 'You two *are* getting on okay, aren't you?'

'Yes.' Bel wrinkled her brow. Although she'd suspected her aunt of trying to throw her and Matt together, surely there was no way she'd take pleasure in Bel's injury?

The storm finally broke while Matt was heating up a dish of lasagne he said his daughter had brought over. It appeared she despaired of his cooking ability, so kept him supplied with home-cooked dishes on her regular visits. 'I can do a few things,' he said defensively. 'I can boil an egg, make an omelette, fix a salad, cook a steak…' His repertoire seemed to fizzle out, and they both laughed.

Sitting on the sofa, Bel had a clear view of the storm's approach through the huge window. She watched, fascinated, as the sky turned from grey to purple to black and the trees in the yard began to shake as the wind blew up, thunder raged and flashes of lightning streaked across the sky. It was like watching it happen on a wide-screen television. Bel and Matt were cocooned in the house while the squall raged outside.

'Glad we're not on the road?' Matt handed Bel a glass of red wine and joined her to appreciate the spectacle. Hamish had crawled under the coffee table at the first clap of thunder and looked to remain there.

'I'd rather watch it from here.'

'How's the ankle?'

'Still a bit sore, getting stiff now. Thanks for strapping it up. I should probably try to move it.' Bel wiggled her toes and winced. 'Ow! Maybe not just yet.'

Dinner over, Matt helped Bel to her room by placing his arm around her waist and hers around his shoulders.

'This is you.' Matt gradually released his hold on her and let her drop down onto the bed. 'Will you be okay? I'm right next door if you need anything…'

There was a pause as if he didn't know what to say, then he bent over and kissed Bel's forehead. His lips remained there for a moment longer than she deemed necessary, then he straightened. 'Right… Well… See you in the morning.' He turned out the light and left, closing the door behind him.

Bel lay there in the darkness, wondering if she could manage to undress, then decided it would be too much effort. She touched the spot Matt had kissed and contemplated the sensations which had flooded her at his touch. She remembered the time he'd given her a peck on the cheek and her subsequent disappointment. But this had been a kiss – a definite kiss – and his lips had lingered.

She was sleeping in Matt's house. He was right next door. She was feeling an attraction she hadn't felt for such a long time. And it seemed as if he might be feeling something too.

Bel fell asleep with a smile on her face

*

When she awoke next morning Bel's whole body was stiff. She tried to stretch, and her injured ankle immediately forced a groan to escape her lips. She rubbed her eyes and looked around the room. Like the rest of the house, it was sparsely furnished. Alongside the bed there was only a small bedside table and a low chair. There was a door opposite the bed, through which Bel could see a wash basin and the edge of what appeared to be a shower. Having slept in her clothes she'd dearly love a shower.

She was just trying to figure out how she could manage to manoeuvre herself across the room when there was a knock at the door.

'Are you awake?'

Bel moistened her lips to formulate a reply, wondering what on earth she must look like, when Matt spoke again.

'Would you like a coffee? I have one here.'

Bel sighed. There was no escaping the fact that she probably looked a mess. Usually unconcerned about her appearance, she wanted to look her best for this man. 'Sounds lovely.'

The door opened and a smiling Matt appeared bearing the promised cup of restorative caffeine. Bel pushed herself up against the pillows and took it gratefully, surprised when Matt didn't immediately leave, but stood gazing down at her with an unfathomable expression on his face.

'Is there something you wanted?'

Matt seemed to collect himself. 'Did you sleep well?'

'Reasonably well.' In fact, she'd been dead to the world as soon as her head hit the pillow.

'I expect you'll want a shower.' Matt seemed to think about this for a moment. 'I have a walking stick. Would that help you…'

Bel almost laughed at his awkwardness, grateful nevertheless that he'd come up with a solution.

'That sounds wonderful.'

He looked awkward. 'And… if you'd like a change of clothes… there's a track suit… it may be a bit big, but…'

Bel felt her spirits lift. She'd slept in these clothes and didn't relish the idea of wearing them for however many days she'd be here. 'Thanks. Maybe I could wash these?'

'I can do that. I'm not completely useless.' He hesitated. 'I'll fetch that stick and tracksuit now, shall I?'

When he'd left, Bel sipped her drink then, daringly, swung her feet over the edge of the bed and reached for her bag which Matt had placed on the bedside table. After drawing a comb through her hair, she felt more presentable and ready to face the day. By the time Matt returned with the promised stick and fresh clothes, she was beginning to feel more like her old self.

'The stick belonged to my dad,' he said. 'In his later years, he had trouble with his hips. It's the only thing of his I kept. May need it myself one of these days.' He handed it to Bel and dropped the track suit on the bed. 'I'll leave you to get on, then.' He left again, this time closing the door behind him.

Bel sat there for a few moments. Matt had given no indication of being anything other than a polite host with an unexpected – and perhaps unwanted – guest. Maybe she'd imagined more tender feelings the night before. Maybe she'd read much more into his kiss than he'd intended. Rebuking herself, she gradually slid off the bed and, with the aid of the walking stick, slowly hobbled into the bathroom.

*

Leaning heavily on the stick, and feeling not unlike her aunt, Bel slowly walked into the sun-filled room where Matt was busy in the kitchen. Managing to make it to the sofa with some effort, she sank into its cushions with relief.

'Ready for another coffee and a bite to eat?'

'Yes, please.' Bel realised she was hungry. 'I'm sorry I…'

Matt ignored her comment. 'I have scrambled eggs and toast on the way. Okay for you?'

'Sounds delicious.' Bel decided to give in to being looked after. She never got sick, apart from the odd cold, and was accustomed to looking after herself. It was such a new experience for her. She should make the most of it, but accepting help wasn't easy for her. She was more like her aunt than she'd realised. At that moment, Hamish jumped up to join her and she forgot her qualms as she fondled the dog's ears and stroked his soft coat.

After breakfast, which they ate from trays on their laps, Matt slipped on a tweed jacket. 'I'm afraid I have to go out for a bit. I have an appointment with an old client. It's local, so I shouldn't be gone for long. Will you manage on your own? There's the paper and…' He looked around as if to see what more he could offer her.

'I'm not completely incapacitated,' Bel said, then, considering she may have been unnecessarily sharp, added, 'I'll be fine. I'll have Hamish to keep me company. Off you go and do what you have to do.'

Bel read the paper, then started on the crossword. She remembered how she'd loved the challenge of the *Herald* crossword all those years ago, but as life became busier crosswords had disappeared from her life.

She must have dozed off, because she was brought back to consciousness by the sound of a sharp voice.

'What are you doing here?'

Bel opened her eyes and blinked as Hamish scrabbled to get down from her lap where the paper still lay open at the crossword. Standing in the doorway was a woman Bel recognised as Matt's daughter, and she didn't look happy.

'It's the lady from Australia!' This voice came from behind the woman and a small figure propelled her wheelchair towards the sofa. 'It's Grandad's friend, Mum. Where is he?' Her eyes searched the room for evidence of Matt.

'Hello, Fiona... and... It's Elspeth, isn't it?' Bel felt at a distinct disadvantage, lying there with her foot propped up, no doubt looking as if she belonged there. She tried to push herself into a more upright position.

'I know who you are. You're that woman Dad had here before with the older lady. He said she was a client. What are you doing here now? And where's Dad?' Elspeth added without waiting for a reply.

'He's visiting a client.' Bel decided to answer the second question first. 'And I'm here because... we went for a hill walk yesterday, and I twisted my ankle. Your dad was kind enough to...'

'You've been here all night?' Elspeth's voice was outraged. If Matt and Bel had been caught in *flagrante delicto*, she couldn't have sounded more appalled.

A protective daughter. Bel was wondering how to provide an explanation that would satisfy the woman when the sound of a car pulling up made both women turn toward the door. Matt came breezing in.

'Elspeth, I didn't expect you today.'

'Obviously!' His daughter's tone was scathing, but Fiona wheeled her chair towards him.

'Hi Gramps!'

Matt bent down to give the girl a hug. 'No Robbie today?' He raised one eyebrow in his daughter's direction.

'He's at a birthday party, so I talked Mum into us coming here instead, and…'

'You were out, and this *woman*…'

She said it as if it was a dirty word. Maybe to her it was. Bel's presence had clearly upset her, and she wasn't going to let it go easily.

'I've been seeing auld Jimmie Barton in the village. Did you call?' He glanced towards Bel who shook her head. She might not have answered the phone if it had rung, but she'd definitely have heard it.

'Do I need to make an appointment to see you now? Fiona was keen to visit and we just hopped into the car. But it seems you have another *visitor*.'

The word seemed to lie between them as Matt dragged a hand through his hair. Bel could see the tips of his ears turn red. 'Bel… We went walking yesterday, and she turned her ankle. It seemed sensible for her to stay till she can put her weight on it again.'

Elspeth's lips tightened. 'She said.'

'Well, then. I brought home a pizza for lunch. There's some salad in the fridge. It should be enough for four.'

For the first time, Bel noticed the box Matt had dropped on the kitchen bench.

'I'll fix it.' Elspeth moved into the kitchen and took charge, making it very clear that she was accustomed to being there and considered Bel to be an interloper who had no place in this house or in her father's life.

While she fussed around clashing plates and banging cupboard and fridge doors, Matt joined Bel and Fiona, who had wheeled herself close to the sofa.

'Tell me about Australia,' the girl said. 'You promised.'

'Not now, Fi.' Matt patted Bel's hand. 'How was your morning before…' He nodded in the direction of the kitchen.

'Good. I almost finished the crossword.' She held up the paper, folded open at the page. 'Then I think I must have fallen asleep.' She smiled at the tender look in Matt's eyes which told her he didn't share his daughter's opinion of her.

'I like crosswords too,' Fiona said.

'Maybe you can help me finish this one then?' Bel said, handing it over.

Fiona puzzled for a bit then her tongue appeared between her teeth as she filled in the solution to five down which had been baffling Bel. 'Easy peasy – silent majority. You've got three across wrong. It should be augur.'

'You're way better than me. I used to be good at them, but I'm out of practice.'

'Told you she was sharp,' Matt said proudly, only to be interrupted by a call from Elspeth.

'Where shall we eat?'

'Oh, can we sit outside?' Fiona pleaded, then turned to Bel. 'Can you get out there? It's not far and it's so nice in the sun.'

'Good plan, Fi. I can help Bel out. We won't have too many more days like this.'

Matt hoisted Bel up and, with the aid of the walking stick, she made it out to one of the cane chairs, while a disapproving Elspeth ferried out plates and bowls of food.

Thanks to Fiona, they made it through the meal without further discord from Elspeth, who answered in words of one syllable when spoken to. Fiona used the meal and her mother's silence to hector Bel with questions about life in Australia and proved herself to be already pretty familiar with the country.

'We studied it at school,' she said in response to Bel's praise of her knowledge, 'but it was mostly about sheep farms and places like the Sydney Opera House, not about what it's like to actually live there. I never knew there were so many beaches. I'm going to go there one day.' She lapsed into silence as if considering how that could be accomplished.

'And how long do you intend to stay at Dad's?' Elspeth asked, focussing her attention on Bel.

Matt didn't give Bel a chance to reply. 'She'll stay as long as necessary. There's no sense in her returning to her aunt's where she has to manage stairs and care for a sick woman.'

'Hmph. Who's caring for your aunt while you're here?'

'She doesn't need daily care. She's actually quite independent. But I'm with her because...' Bel's voice dropped.

'Isobel is terminally ill,' Matt finished for her. 'Bel's in Scotland until she's no longer needed.'

'You'll be going back then?' Elspeth gave a slow smile.

'My home's in Sydney. That's where my house and business is, and my little dog.' Bel turned to Fiona. 'I have a little dog, just like Hamish, but my Toby's a few years older. I have a friend looking after him – and my business – while I'm here,' she said to Elspeth. That seemed to satisfy Matt's daughter, who began to collect the dirty dishes and carry them into the kitchen.

'I can do that, Elspeth.' Matt rose and took the stack of plates from her hands. 'You stay here and talk with Bel.' He winked at Bel as he walked off.

Searching for a topic of conversation that wouldn't be controversial, Bel began to talk about her aunt's plans for the house in Kelvin Drive. 'Not everyone is as lucky as you, Fiona, with a loving family to take care of you,' she finished, smiling at the girl who'd been hanging on her every word.

'And you're to be involved in this too?' Elspeth seemed to mellow slightly on hearing about the proposal.

Bel sighed. 'Aunt Isobel wants me to oversee it, but I'll need to get home. I expect your dad will be more involved. He's her solicitor and has been privy to all her plans. I'm just the one who'll be making sure her wishes are carried out.'

'And you're not… you don't disagree with her decision? The house would bring you a tidy sum.'

'Lord no!' Bel laughed. 'I don't need her money. Sorry, that didn't come out the way I intended. What I mean is that I'm comfortable where I am. I have a good life and…' she glanced at Fiona, 'I've always supported children with a disability back home. One of my favourite charities is Youngcare. It's based in Queensland and they do great work in supporting young people with high care needs.'

'Oh!' Elspeth appeared to be digesting this information.

'Can I help?'

The two women turned to look at Fiona who was smiling eagerly.

'Can I be involved? When you're setting this house up. I know what people like me want – the sort of things they need to make them feel at home, to make them feel normal. It's not as difficult as you might think.'

'Oh, Fiona. I don't know…' her mother said.

'Well, I'd certainly be glad of your help,' Bel said, 'and maybe my aunt would like to meet you – properly.'

'Was that the lady with you last time? The older one? Can I, Mum?'

Elspeth hesitated. 'Maybe. But Bel will have to ask her aunt first, make sure she agrees.'

This was the first time Elspeth had actually used Bel's name. It had taken her daughter's innate good sense to force her mother to remember her manners.

'You two getting on okay?' Matt emerged from the house, a tea towel in his hands. 'Anyone for coffee?'

'Thanks, but we must be going.' Elspeth pushed back her chair. 'Bel's been telling us about the plans for her aunt's house. It all sounds very interesting.'

Matt raised his eyebrows in Bel's direction, a faint smile on his face. 'Right. I'll see you out. Be back to help you inside,' he said to Bel as the three left her to sit and contemplate the dramatic change in the young woman's attitude. It didn't change the fact that she disapproved of Bel's friendship with Matt, but did go part of the way in establishing some common ground.

*

'I'm sorry about Elspeth.'

Matt and Bel were sitting side-by-side on the sofa, Bel's foot supported by the large pouffe. 'That's okay. I think she finally realised I'm not the threat she imagined. I…' Bel stopped, surprised to feel Matt's finger on her lips.

'Shh. I know what she imagined. Since Ailsa died, Elspeth has taken over my life – and I've allowed it to happen. She's monitored my comings and goings, judged my friends, brought me food and generally tried to make herself indispensable. Until now, it hasn't been a problem. She almost went to pieces when her mother died and taking on Ailsa's role seemed to help her.' He grimaced. 'I should have stopped it long ago, but I had no reason to, and…' he paused and pulled on his ear, 'if I'm honest with myself, I quite enjoyed it. But now…' He took a deep breath. 'Now I've met someone I'm interested in, my daughter's overly concerned attitude has the potential to make life difficult.'

Matt exhaled as if he'd come to the end of a difficult revelation. Bel noticed his ears turning red again and his eyes flickering in every direction except hers.

The flutter that had begun in her stomach with the touch of his finger became a full-blown shockwave. 'Someone you're interested in?' Her heart raced as she waited for his reply.

'This isn't easy for me, Bel.' Matt's voice lingered over her name as if he was stroking it. 'I'm out of practice.' He exhaled loudly. 'Too old for this sort of thing. But since meeting you, I've felt... stirrings... of something I never thought I'd feel again.'

Bel clasped her hands tightly in her lap, so tightly that her nails dug into the flesh of her palms. Matt's words – tantamount to a declaration – were unexpected, but not unwelcome. She looked into his eyes, those deep brown eyes that had disturbed her dreams more than once.

'Me too.'

Twenty-two

Isobel – 1955

The years passed quickly and, as we'd expected, wee Isobel grew up without us. Nan brought her to see us each Christmas, but Col's shift work made it difficult for her to come more often. That and the cost of travelling across the country.

She always seemed cheerful when we saw her, and her letters were full of the child's exploits and how happy she and Colin were. But reading between the lines, I knew they were finding it difficult to make ends meet. Nan's last letter had mentioned how Isobel would be starting school after the summer, and that she'd be looking for work she could do in school hours.

That dark February evening is stuck in my mind. The rain was pelting down. We'd lit the fire in the front room, drawn the curtains and were just settling down to listen to *Hancock's Half Hour* on the wireless when the phone rang.

'Who the devil's ringing us at this time of night?' Father wanted to know. It wasn't really late, but he hated to be interrupted during one of his favourite programs.

Mother was about to get up, but I said, 'I'll go,' and made my way into the draughty hall. I was hoping it was a wrong number, and I could get back into the warmth of the front room soon.

I could barely hear my sister's tearful voice. 'It's Col…' Her voice broke and I strained to hear what she was saying, but could only hear crackling on the line.

My stomach contracted as I remembered how my brother-in-law had never been the same since returning from the war. What had happened now? My sister's silence was frightening me.

'Nan? Are you still there?'

There was some background noise, then I heard Nan's voice again. 'I'm at the hospital. There was an accident. He…'

'Where's Isobel?' Nan must have thought me uncaring, but all I could think of was my beloved niece.

'She… she's with a neighbour. The doctors say… they don't know… Oh, Izzy, what am I going to do?'

I pictured my sister and niece, all alone so far away, in what was to me, almost a foreign country, with Colin in hospital and no one to turn to. I spoke without thinking. 'I'll catch the first train in the morning. Is there anything you need?' Even as I said it, I knew it was a daft thing to say. Nan was devastated. She needed her husband. She needed her family. 'Will you be all right till I get there?'

'I… I think so. I need to get home to Isobel, but…' Her voice was flat.

I sensed her dilemma – a sick husband right there in the hospital and wee Isobel waiting at home, wondering where her mum and dad were.

'Go home and try to get a good night's sleep. There's probably not much you can do there. How badly hurt is Col?'

'I don't know. They say he was crushed. He's still unconscious. I've been sitting with him since I got here.' Her voice broke again.

My throat ached. I didn't know what to say. 'I'll be there tomorrow,' I said again. I hung up and sat looking at the phone before returning to join the others.

'You were a long time,' Mother said.

'Will you wheesht, woman,' Father said. 'I'm listening to this.'

Then they seemed to notice my sombre expression.

Mum started to rise, her ball of wool falling to the floor. 'What's wrong?'

'That was our Nan. It's Col…'

'Oh, my. Turn that off, Geordie. Our Nan's in trouble. Is it that lung disease?'

'An accident, Nan said. I told her I'd catch the train in the morning.

You'll manage without me for the day, Kate?' I turned to my sister, who nodded.

Mother looked flustered. 'What happened? Do you think we should all go? Maybe…'

'I don't know any more. Nan was that upset. She could barely speak. Let me go on my own tomorrow. I can look after Isobel, see how things are and let you know.'

Reluctantly, they agreed, and Father turned up the sound of the wireless again, but I didn't hear a word of the rest of the program. I was too busy thinking about Nan. This would never have happened if they'd stayed in Glasgow. And if Col had become ill here – and needed hospital – we'd all be able to support her, plus Col's… Oh, heck! I'd forgotten all about Mrs. Davison, Colin's mother. I wondered if Nan had called her too, if I should, if… It was all too hard and not my place. I rose. 'I'm off to bed. I'll have an early start tomorrow.'

*

When I peered out the window at the crack of dawn next morning, I saw that the rain had stopped, but there had been a frost overnight, leaving the roads and pavements glistening with icy slicks. There would be no running to catch the bus to the station this morning. I'd need to leave in plenty of time and tread carefully.

'I made you some sandwiches for the trip.' Mum nodded to the paper bag lying on the table as she dished up my porridge. 'You'll be needing something to keep you going. Get that down you for now. It'll stick to your ribs.'

'Thanks.' Despite the seriousness of the day, I smiled at the familiar phrase. I'd eaten so much porridge in my life, my ribs must be well and truly packed with it. But I did enjoy it with lashings of salt and cream, and I'd only have the pack of sandwiches for lunch and heaven knows what when I finally got to Nan's.

There was more than a hint of ice in the air and I could feel it bite my nose as I walked carefully to the bus stop, pleased to see a bus already on its way. At this time in the morning it was filled with men in their work overalls, with only a few smartly dressed women like myself.

Since we'd opened our shop, both Kate and I prided ourselves on dressing in fashion. This morning I was wearing my new black wool coat with the fur collar over my best tweed suit, and had pulled my black cloche hat down over my hair. Head bent, I burrowed my chin into the soft fur to protect myself from the piercing wind.

I reached St Enoch's station just as my train was about to leave and managed to find an empty compartment. Sinking into the rough fabric seat with a sigh, I hoped Nan had managed to get some sleep. Last night I'd prayed for the first time in ages. I'd prayed for Colin's recovery, for my sister and her bairn, and for my own future. I hadn't given up hope of finding someone, even though I still harboured memories of one Clark Gable lookalike. I closed my eyes and must have dozed off, because when I opened them again the train was crossing the Forth Bridge, its red steel columns hurtling past the window.

Blinking to bring myself properly awake, I opened the sandwiches Mother had prepared and finished them just as the train pulled into Nan's station. This time there was no Nan to meet me, and the wind seemed even sharper than the one I'd left in Glasgow as I fought my way to the bus stop.

The bus deposited me a couple of blocks from my sister's house and, bending my head, I leaned into the breeze as I walked the now familiar last few yards to Nan's house. My sister's pallid face told me all I wanted to know. I drew her into a tight hug before shrugging off my coat and tossing my hat onto the table.

'I rang the hospital from next door,' Nan said, her eyes red and puffy. 'They said there had been no change overnight. Oh, Izzy! What if… He didn't look like my Col, lying there surrounded by tubes and bandages. It was as if he was already…' Her chin trembled and her shoulders drooped.

'Auntie Izzy.'

I turned to see my niece tugging at my skirt. 'Oh, you wee darling!' I picked her up only to discover how heavy she'd become, and pressed my face against hers. She struggled to get down again, and I let her slide to the floor, 'Have you had anything to eat?' I asked Nan.

'I couldn't stomach anything. Isobel had her breakfast and I made some tea.' Nan looked around as if she wasn't sure where she was. 'I need to get to the hospital.'

A half-empty cup sat on the table alongside an empty bowl. 'Sit down. I'll make a fresh pot and you can tell me what happened. You need to keep up your strength. You're no good to Col – or Isobel – if you get sick too.' I filled the kettle and found some milk and a chocolate biscuit for my niece who was content to enjoy these before slipping off to work on a jigsaw puzzle. When the tea was masked, I made some toast to accompany it and sat opposite Nan.

'Now tell me what happened.'

She slumped in her chair and rubbed at her eyes with a sodden hankie. 'Col… he hasn't been well all week – his lungs get bad in this weather. I wanted him to stay home, but he wouldn't hear of it. I think he was worried they'd dock his pay if he was off sick again.' She sniffed and wiped her nose, then paused and took a deep breath before continuing. 'So he went in, and about four o'clock there was a knock at the door.' She paused again and gazed into space as if reliving the moment. 'It was Iain – one of his pals. He said there'd been an accident and I should get down to the pit right away. I didn't even take off my pinny. Aggie next door came out to see what was up and offered to take Isobel in for a bit.' She drew a deep breath again. 'I went straight to the hospital with him, then I rang you.'

'Was it a big accident? Were others hurt?'

'No. Just my Col. They'd made him up to foreman. He was that proud. The shift was about over when what they call a sling chain connected to a drum shaft broke. It fell into a concrete drum pit and crushed him against a wall. I can't bear to think about it; my Col lying there all crushed and bleeding.'

I went around the table and hugged my sister again, stroking her hair and rubbing her back. But I felt helpless. This was something I couldn't fix. I didn't even know what to say to her.

Nan struggled from my grasp. 'I need to get going. Will you be okay with this one?' She nodded towards Isobel who was still happily engrossed in her puzzle.

'We'll be fine. You take care of yourself, mind. Can you let me know if…' I didn't know whether I meant if Colin improved or if the worst happened, but Nan seemed to understand.

'I can ring Aggie. She's a good neighbour. Her Tommy's down the pit too. She'll pass it on if there's anything…' Her voice died away.

After fussing a bit Nan left, and I began tidying up. Clearly my sister hadn't been herself since she heard the news. The sink was full of dishes, the beds unmade and the bedroom was a mess of clothes as if Nan had taken them all out of the wardrobe and thrown them down.

When I'd finished, it was time for lunch, and my niece wandered into the kitchen, her thumb in her mouth. 'Mummy?' she asked, her bottom lip trembling.

'She's with your daddy right now,' I said. I picked Isobel up and hugged her, hoping my voice sounded cheerier than I felt. 'I thought we might have some lunch, then go to the park.'

'Oh yes!'

The promise of a trip to the park seemed to satisfy the wee one, so I busied myself checking the cupboards and, finding several tins of baked beans, decided beans on toast would make a good lunch for us. There had been no word from Nan, so I could only assume there was no change.

I had just donned my coat and beret again, and was helping Isobel into her warm coat and hat, when there was a knock at the door. Startled, I answered it to find a blonde woman a few years older than me, standing there in a wrap-around apron, her arms folded to keep herself warm. She seemed surprised to see me.

'Oh! I was wondering if Nan wanted me to have the bairn for a bit again today. Is she not here?'

'I'm her sister – Isobel. I came over from Glasgow this morning. Nan's at the hospital. You'll be Aggie?'

'Aye.' The woman looked past me to where Isobel was standing holding her woollen dog by one leg, her thumb in her mouth again. 'It's a terrible thing.' She shook her head. 'That pit has taken so many of our men. I hope...'

I didn't wait to hear what she hoped or didn't hope. 'We're just off to the park. Isobel likes the swings.'

'That she does.' Aggie seemed to realise I wasn't one to gossip and turned away. 'I'll be away in, then. If...'

'Nan said she'd ring you if there was any change,' I said, remembering Nan's words.

'I'll be sure to let you know if she does,' she said, and walked away muttering about poor pit maintenance.

I had a nice time at the park with young Isobel, pushing her on the swings and even managing to laugh as she urged, 'Up, up!' But it soon began to turn dark and we headed for home. I wondered when Nan would get back and realised I wouldn't get back to Glasgow that night, maybe not the next either. I'd stay as long as my sister needed me.

When we got to the house, there was a note on the door from Aggie. I knocked at her door, my heart in my mouth. Was there news?

This time the door was opened by a young lad of around sixteen. When he saw us he yelled, 'Mum,' then said, 'Hello young one,' to Isobel who seemed to know him. When Aggie came to the door, she ushered us inside and insisted we sit down at a table that was already set for their family meal.

'Nan rang?' I asked.

'A few minutes ago. You just missed her. No change she said. She'll be back late and wondered if you could stay. She said she'll ring again later. If you have to get back, I can…'

'No. I'll stay. If I could maybe make a call to let our family know?'

'Of course. The phone's in the hall. Will you have a cup of something?'

'Thanks.' I dialled the familiar number and filled Mother in on my plans and Colin's condition, then, leaving a few coins for the call on the hall table, went back to the kitchen where Isobel and the boy were playing tiddlywinks. She had her coat off and was looking quite at home as she pressed on the coloured discs trying to make them jump into the pot.

'She's fine with Donald. He likes the wee lass. You look as if you need a cup of tea.' I took a seat, realising I hadn't had a minute to relax since I got off the train. It had been a long day and it wasn't over yet. I had no idea when Nan would return and Isobel had to be fed, bathed and put to bed. Although I'd visited several times and was familiar with my niece whom I loved like a daughter, I'd never had to take care of her, never been with her without Nan's capable presence.

Over tea, I discovered Aggie was a non-stop talker. In a short space of time I learnt more than I wanted or needed to know about the perils of going down the pit. Aggie's man had been there all his working life, but she wanted better things for their only son. 'He'll be taking his Highers,' she said proudly. 'Maybe we'll even see him go to university. Such a shame about your sister's man. It's what we all dread happening, but it's a living.' She sighed.

I wondered how they could all exist that way, with the men risking death every day. Was it worth it? For the umpteenth time, I wished Nan and Col had stayed in Glasgow. They'd have been safe there. Though I guessed the lung disease Col had developed in the war would get him one day wherever they lived.

Isobel had been in bed and asleep for hours by the time Nan returned home. I'd enjoyed bathing her, pouring water over her slippery body, tucking her up in bed and reading her a story from her favourite *Uncle Arthur's Bedtime Stories*. I had the wireless on, but I wasn't listening to it. I was worrying about what was happening at the hospital when the door opened and Nan came in on a rush of cold air. She was as white as a sheet.

I stood up and helped her off with her coat. 'Is…?'

'No change. The doctors say if he doesn't rally soon….' She fell into my arms sobbing as if her heart would break. 'He can't… mustn't…' she muttered so softly I could barely hear her.

I patted her back, helpless in the face of such abject misery. I'd had my own troubles to bear – when I lost Bob Smith, when I heard he'd married, but my unhappiness had been nothing compared to this outpouring of grief. The love between my sister and her husband had been a wonder to me. Surely it couldn't end like this?

'Sorry.' Nan's red-rimmed eyes met mine as she began to rock back and forth. 'I can't believe… He's lying there so still. It's as if he's already…' She shivered, clutching her arms around her body.

I hugged her firmly as if I could hug away the terror in her mind.

'Isobel?' she asked, as if suddenly remembering.

'Asleep. Can I get you anything? Do you have any whisky in the house?' I thought it unlikely, but what Nan needed right now was a good stiff drink.

'I think there's some left over from Ne'erday. In the pantry.'

I helped Nan into a chair and fetched a couple of glasses and a half-full bottle of *Johnny Walker*, deciding to join her in a wee dram.

'We were keeping it for a special occasion,' Nan said, her voice breaking as she sipped the fiery liquid, shuddering as it made its way down.

We sat in silence for a few moments, before I rose. 'You should get to bed. Try to sleep. The whisky will help. And you'll be going to the hospital again tomorrow?' It wasn't really a question. I knew my sister. She'd sit at Col's side until there was some change. I hoped it would be for the better, but felt that the longer he remained unconscious the worse it would be. I realised I should be prepared for the worst and, if it did happen and Col died, Nan couldn't stay here on her own with the bairn.

*

Colin remained in a coma for seven days. They were the longest seven days I can remember. Each day followed the same pattern. I would try to persuade Nan to eat breakfast before she left for the hospital. Then I'd spend the day with my niece who, while unaware of what was going on, often asked where her mum was, and I'd try to comfort her with this tale and that.

Nan would arrive back late after Isobel was in bed and would sit staring into space, twisting her hands or pulling on her hair. She rarely spoke. It was as if she'd withdrawn into a world I couldn't enter, a world that contained her and Col. Even little Isobel failed to draw any response from her.

I worried about my sister.

Then, after seven days of this, she arrived home in the middle of the afternoon. Isobel and I had just returned from the park and on the way home we'd stopped at a street stall where I'd bought my niece a windmill. Wee Isobel rushed at her mother waving the toy and yelling, 'See what Auntie Izzy bought me? See how it goes?'

But Nan turned away from her daughter. Her face was gaunt, her eyes even puffier than before. 'He's gone,' she said in a flat voice. She slumped into the nearest chair and dropped her head into her hands.

'Come here, pet.' I drew Isobel away from her mum and, taking her into the other room, set her down with a box of crayons and a colouring book, before returning to my sister who was sobbing uncontrollably. Not knowing what to do, I sat opposite Nan while she cried her heart out. When the room began to get dark, I cooked some eggs for Isobel and me and took our plates through to the other room, telling my niece we'd have a picnic.

By the time I came through from putting Isobel to bed, Nan had pulled herself together enough to take off her coat, but was gazing into the distance as if seeing something I couldn't.

'I can't go on without him, Izzy. He was my whole life.'

'You have to. There's wee Isobel. Col wouldn't want you to let her down, to let *him* down. Now would he?' I held my breath waiting for her reply.

She sighed and picked up a watch I hadn't noticed lying on the table. 'This was his. They gave it to me. The doctors.' She raised her eyes to meet mine. 'Where *is* Isobel? I need to tell her. How can I tell her?'

'She's in bed. There's no need to do anything tonight. Would you like me to go next door and call Mother?'

'Would you? I don't think I could talk to them.'

I made her a cup of tea laced with more of the whisky and made sure she drank it before I left. Aggie next door went quiet when she heard the news. All she said was, 'It's a sad day. You'll be wanting to use the phone?'

Mother was shocked to hear of Col's death. I suppose she'd assumed he'd recover and everything would return to normal. 'We'll be there tomorrow,' she said. 'Your father and me. We'll book in somewhere. There'll no be room at Nan's for us all, will there?'

'Mother says they'll be here tomorrow,' I said to Nan when I returned to find her sitting where I'd left her, as if turned to stone, her fingers clutching Col's watch. She didn't give any indication she'd heard me, so I helped her up and into the bedroom.

'I'll be fine now.' She shook off my hands.

'See you in the morning, then.'

I couldn't sleep. Col was dead. What would Nan do? I was relieved our parents would arrive in the morning. It would share the load.

*

Next morning, Nan rose before me, but when I entered the kitchen, she was wandering around like a lost soul while Isobel ran around with the windmill we'd bought the day before.

'I'll make some breakfast,' I said, taking a packet of cornflakes from the cupboard and sniffing the milk to check it was still fresh.

'My puir wee lassie.' It was almost lunchtime when Mother hurried in to envelop Nan in a warm hug, while Father stood helplessly by.

'It's sad it's come to this,' he said, removing his hat and hanging his coat on a hook on the back door. 'Has…' he nodded towards Nan, 'anything been arranged?'

I shook my head, knowing he was referring to the funeral. This seemed to energise him. He sat down at the table and pulled a sheet of paper from one pocket and a pencil from another. I almost smiled. Father and his lists. He always had to have something to do. He'd be in his element arranging for Col's funeral, and it would take the pressure off Nan.'

'I spoke with Jean Davison. She's not well enough to take the trip. But to lose her son like this. It's hit her hard. We need to dae oor best for the lad.'

'How can I help?' I joined Father at the table, leaving Mother to deal with Nan's listlessness and to fuss over her granddaughter who was delighted to have a new audience.

By lunchtime, everything had been organised – we'd visit the hospital in the afternoon, and the funeral would take place in two days' time. Father had gone into town to meet with the undertaker and make all the arrangements.

'You'll be coming home, of course. You and Isobel,' Mother said when we were sitting over a cup of tea that evening. 'We've plenty of room and you'll be with family. There's nothing for you here now.' The unspoken words – *now that Colin's dead* – fell between us like a stone in a pond, the ripples reaching into the corners of the room. Nan nodded, seemingly unconcerned about her future, while I speculated what that might mean for me.

It would be good to have my sister home again, and to have wee Isobel growing up right there in our house. Despite the reasons for this, I couldn't hide a buzz of pleasure. It would really be as if she was my daughter, the daughter I'd never have.

Twenty-three

Bel – 2015

They sat in silence.

For Bel, it was like being a teenager again without the accompanying adolescent angst. Part of her was thrilled that – at her age – she'd attracted the attention and interest of a man like Matt, one who was obviously sought after by the ladies of his social circle. Another part of her was aghast. What was she doing? How could this come to anything? And did she want it to? Her life was on the other side of the world. There was no way their two lives could do anything more than intersect briefly. Could that be enough?

Matt stroked her cheek. He placed a finger under her chin, turned her head toward him and their lips met. This kiss was unlike the times his lips had pecked her cheek, touched her lips briefly or lingered on her forehead. This kiss was full of the supressed passion of a man who had been starved of love for a long time. An answering ache in Bel met his and they clung together, everything else forgotten.

They drew apart at the sound of a car pulling up and Hamish barking furiously.

'Damn! Who is it now?'

Matt smoothed his ruffled hair and headed for the door, while Bel regained her breath and tried to settle herself more sedately among the sofa cushions.

When Matt returned, he was accompanied by a younger version

of himself – a tall young man in his thirties with close-cropped black hair wearing jeans and an open-necked checked shirt. 'This is Duncan. Duncan – Bel, a friend. Bel twisted her ankle when we were out walking yesterday, so she's stuck here for a bit.'

'Right.' Duncan looked from Matt to Bel and back again. 'Right,' he repeated. 'There's no need to make excuses, Dad. It's time you found someone to keep you on the straight and narrow.' He winked. 'Pleased to meet you, Bel.'

'Hello, Duncan. Likewise. Sorry I can't get up.' She gestured to her foot, still propped up on the pouffe.

'What brings you here? Has your sister been talking to you?'

'Elspeth? Haven't heard from her in weeks. I'm on my way up to Crianlarich and thought I'd drop in to pick up the file on the Drummond case. You said you'd look over it for me.'

'Sure. It's in the office. If you'll excuse us for a few minutes, Bel? Come through and I'll fill you in, son.'

When the pair had gone, Bel gazed out of the picture window and contemplated the difference between Matt's two children with respect to her presence in their dad's house – and life. While his daughter regarded her as a threat – even a rival for Matt's time and affection – Duncan seemed to look on her as the answer to his unspoken prayers. In fact, she was neither. She was merely a… distraction? She liked that. Whatever there was – or might be – between her and Matt could only be a temporary distraction for both of them, albeit a pleasant one.

Having settled that to her satisfaction, she leaned her head back against the soft cushions of the sofa and closed her eyes. She must have dozed off, because the next thing she knew was the gentle pressure of lips on hers and a murmured voice.

'Where were we?'

Bel's eyes flew open at once. 'Your son?' She looked around wildly. It was one thing for Duncan to approve of Bel's presence, but it was quite a different matter to be caught canoodling. *Where had that term come from? Had she been influenced by her reading of Isobel's story?*

'Gone. You looked so peaceful lying there, he didn't want to disturb you.' Matt caressed Bel's forehead and stroked a strand of hair back from her eyes.

His face was so close Bel could see the tiny crow's feet at the corners of his eyes, these eyes she wanted to drown in. His son had those eyes too. Her hand reached up to touch Matt's cheek, feeling its roughness against her fingers. It was a long time since she'd touched a man like this. She'd forgotten the sheer pleasure of it. Matt groaned and a spiral of desire uncoiled in Bel's stomach. She wanted this man.

'This is no good.' Matt extricated himself and stood up. 'I'm too old to make love on a sofa. Maybe we should slip into somewhere more comfortable. Or am I moving too fast for you? It's been a long time.'

'You said.'

'So?'

'Love in the afternoon?' Bel realised she was using delaying tactics, but was enjoying the anticipation. Then she noticed Matt's strained expression and relented. 'You may have to help me.'

'No trouble.' He bent to slip one arm below Bel's knees, placed the other around her shoulders and, with an instruction for her to, 'Grab hold of me,' lifted her from the sofa and carried a laughing Bel to his bedroom.

*

The sun was low in the sky when the two finally disentangled themselves and lay side-by-side, spent and breathless.

'Wow!' Matt leaned over Bel with a smile, his fingers caressing her naked breasts. 'You're beautiful. I've been wanting to do this ever since I first saw you.'

'Surely not?'

'Well, since that first time you came out here. I wanted to pick you up, carry you away and ravish you. But I supposed you'd think I was mad.'

'Very likely.' Bel stifled a giggle. 'At our age…' But his finger was on her lips again, muffling what she was about to say.

'What's age? I don't feel any older than I did at seventeen, though I wish I'd known then what I know now. It's as the old saws say. *Youth is wasted on the young.* What if we'd met back then? I wonder…'

'But you met your wife. You *were* happy, weren't you?' Bel propped herself up on the pillows as best she could and fixed her gaze on Matt.

'Of course. I had a good marriage and two wonderful children, even if one is overprotective of her old dad. But we were around uni at the same time. It's surprising we didn't bump into each other. We didn't, did we?' He furrowed his brow.

'I'd have remembered.' But would she? Back then, she'd been caught up in her relationship with Callum which had taken her into the Art School crowd with their wild parties and lost weekends. She'd had no eyes for anyone else and no time for the more conservative students around the uni. Much of those years had passed in a haze for Bel, a haze from which she'd been rudely awakened by the threat of an unwanted pregnancy.

'We're here now. Let's just enjoy that.' Matt laid his head on Bel's lap and her fingers unconsciously began to tangle themselves in his hair.

When they finally crawled out of bed, it was quite dark, the glow of the moon shining through the window and sending a beam of light across the grey slate floor of the main room. As Matt turned on the light, a small white figure erupted from the corner of the room and rushed towards them.

'Steady, Hamish.' Matt stopped to pat the little creature while Bel slowly made her way back to the sofa. Hopefully this damn ankle would feel stronger in the morning. She'd been here long enough, though it did have its advantages. She gazed at Matt's back while he filled his pet's bowls. He'd made love with the energy of a man half his age, taken Bel to heights she'd never experienced, a level of ecstasy she'd thought lost forever.

She examined Matt from her vantage point on the sofa. What was it about him that attracted her so much? Granted, he'd kept in shape – there wasn't an ounce of spare flesh on him. His hair was still thick and the white strands only served to enhance his fine features – his wide forehead, straight nose and deep brown eyes. But it wasn't only his looks. As Bel got to know him better, the enigmatic, taciturn Scotsman had become someone she could trust, someone she felt comfortable with, someone she could love? That might be going too far. One unexpected roll in the hay, memorable, even unforgettable, but that was all.

When Isobel died, she'd return to Australia and the memory of this interlude would be something she'd treasure, something to be taken out on those lonely nights when life became overwhelming, when the thought of growing old alone became too much to bear. She felt the hairs lift on the back of her neck at the idea that, like Isobel, she would be alone in her twilight years.

'How does steak and salad sound?' Matt's voice brought her back to the present.

'Sounds good.' Bel realised she was hungry. Lunch had been difficult and she hadn't eaten much. It seemed so long ago

'And a nice glass of red?'

'Yes, please!' Wine was just what she needed to chase away her morbid thoughts. She accepted the glass with a smile. She'd forget the future. Leave that to take care of itself. She was here. Matt was here. And they had another night together.

*

After dinner it felt quite natural to Bel to be in Matt's bed again. He was a gentle lover. While there was none of the youthful wild passion she'd experienced with Callum, neither was there the indignity of Pete's indifference to her wishes. Matt carefully undressed her, taking care not to disturb her foot. Though it was less painful than it had been earlier, it still ached with any sudden movement. When they were both naked, Matt lay beside Bel and gently stroked and kissed her all over till her entire body was throbbing with desire.

Then, when she thought she would burst with wanting him, Matt slowly lowered himself onto her and gradually began to move inside her, unleashing a torrent of craving for more as she strained against him. This time she couldn't contain herself, and sounds she didn't recognise escaped her lips as the world crashed around her.

'Wow!' A long sigh escaped Matt's lips. 'Glad there are no near neighbours. I might have been accused of murder.'

'Sorry. I don't know… I've never…' Bel felt a tingling on the back of her head. Where had those loud moans come from? She hadn't been able to stifle them. Her pleasure had been so intense, the keening noise had escaped her without any conscious effort on her part. And it was something that had never happened before. For her, sex had always been a silent affair, one in which each participant struggled for his or her own fulfilment. But this! Matt had made her body sing in a way none of her other lovers had. She had no words to describe how she'd felt, how she still felt.

'Shh.' Matt wrapped Bel in his arms, his chin resting on the top of her head.

She could feel his lips moving slowly in her hair. She shivered. Her hands found his shoulders and she began to stroke them. 'That was incredible,' she whispered. 'I've never...'

'Not bad for an old fellow?'

'You're not old.'

'Not young either. And there's many wouldn't agree with you. I think my kids think I should be past all this – at least Elspeth does.'

The mention of Matt's daughter broke the spell, and Bel disengaged herself from his embrace and lay on her back. 'She doesn't like me much.'

'You're not her mother. That's the problem. She's never come to terms with Ailsa's death.' Matt moved closer to Bel and took her hand, linking his fingers with hers. 'I sometimes think she feels guilty it was Ailsa in the car and not her. She pleaded a headache that morning, and wee Fiona wanted to go into town so much that Ailsa offered to drive her. She's been overprotective of Fi – and me – ever since.'

Bel tried to digest this new information. It was a new insight into what she'd imagined to be Elspeth's controlling and jealous manner. 'She began to mellow when she heard about Aunt Isobel's plans.'

'And when you said you'd be going back to Australia.'

'Mmm.'

'But let's not talk about her now. She'd have a wheen of fits if she could see us here like this.' He turned on his side and deftly slid Bel onto hers so that he could cuddle up behind her, wrapping both arms around her waist. 'Comfy?'

'Mmm.' Bel was almost asleep.

Twenty-four

Isobel - 1962

We'd seen Maisie, the spey-wife over the years. She'd seemed old to me before the war, so goodness knows how old she was now, but she hadn't changed much. She'd never foreseen anything of note for me again, and I'd never told my sisters how accurate her prediction about Bob Smith had been. I wouldn't dare, for fear they'd make fun of me, or wonder why I hadn't shared it with them at the time.

Soon after we opened the shop, Maisie had come in to buy some wool. Then she'd taken to dropping in from time to time for a cup of tea with us and she always liked to read the tealeaves afterwards. 'Och you'd think it was true,' was her favourite saying, and, regardless of what the others might think, I knew it was, or could be.

So, one Thursday around lunchtime, we weren't surprised when Maisie's now grey head appeared in the doorway. 'Is there a cup of tea going?'

'Always for you,' Nan replied. She'd joined us in the shop when she returned to Glasgow, and the three of us loved working together. 'The kettle's on the boil. You must have smelt it.' We left the shop in Kate's charge, and Nan and I joined the old woman over a cuppa in the back shop. When we'd finished, we automatically turned our cups upside down to release any remaining tea and allow the tealeaves to set.

Nan handed over her cup first. We listened to the expected tales of holidays, Isobel's success in school which would make her mother proud, and laughed at the mention of a new beau for Nan. There were always men asking her on dates and "giving her the eye" but Col had been the only man for her.

'Well, I'll get through to relieve Kate,' Nan said, when Maisie had finished with her and put down the cup she'd been peering into. 'Thanks again, Maisie.' She rose and left.

'Och, you'd think it was true,' Maisie said, true to fashion. 'Now, yours, Isobel.' She picked up my cup and a ripple of something I couldn't identify swept through me.

I knew the others looked on Maisie's reading of the tealeaves as harmless fun. I wasn't so sure. I always remembered how accurate she'd been all those years ago, or had it just been a lucky chance? I had the most ominous feeling she had more to tell me.

I don't know why I felt so apprehensive this particular day. I tried to still my trembling and clasped my hands tightly in my lap as the woman opposite me gazed into my teacup, empty except for the clustering of tealeaves around the edge and sides.

There was silence except for the dull sound of voices seeping in from the shop, then Maisie began to speak. 'You're going to hear a voice from the past,' she said. 'And you'll think that, this time, it'll all work out. But he's going to leave you again.' She raised her eyes and I could see they were filled with pity. I wanted to ask whose voice, who'd leave again, although fearful to hear her answer. But, just as I opened my mouth to speak, Kate breezed through.

'Am I in time?' she asked. 'We just had a bit of a rush, and I couldn't get away.'

My mouth closed of its own accord, and I watched as Kate poured herself some tea.

'Don't stop for me,' she said, clearly seeing Maisie still holding my empty cup.

'No. We're finished.' I stood up and left, my mind in a whirl. Could she have been talking about Bob Smith? Was he the voice from the past? Eileen had kept me informed about his life. I never told her how hurt I felt each time she mentioned him, but listened eagerly, greedily absorbing every scrap of information as if it could bring him closer.

She and Alan had kept up with him and his new wife, so I'd heard when their son was born, when Bob gained promotion, when they'd gone on joint holidays. All the time I was thinking it should have been me, not some faceless woman. Then, three years ago had come the news that stunned me. Mhairi died. It was sudden – a brain aneurism. The poor man! To be widowed with a small child. No, his son must have been eleven or twelve, not so little.

But what a tragedy. My heart had gone out to Bob. Even though he'd hurt me dreadfully, I'd never forgotten him. I wondered how he'd be feeling. Lonely? Overcome with grief? I wanted to be there for him, to comfort him. Any bitterness I'd felt towards him had dissipated long ago, I tried to still the small voice telling me that Bob was free again. I knew it was impossible that he'd ever seek me out again, but in a small corner of my heart, I began to hope.

Although I knew it was foolish, each time I saw Eileen, or she invited me over, I expected her to casually mention that Bob would be there too. But she never did, and he never was. And as the weeks became months and the months became years, I gave up hoping. Now this!

It was daft. Bob had gone out of my life forever. We were different people now. He was a widower with a teenage son and I was… I was still the good sister, the foolish virgin who'd refused to share a room with the man I loved to distraction. But I didn't think that then. And I didn't consider myself to be foolish. I still felt I'd been right. I'd kept my virtue when others had given in to a moment of passion. Surely I didn't deserve to be punished for the rest of my life?

No. I put Maisie's words in the vault where they belonged and decided to get on with my life.

*

I was so successful that, when the phone rang one wet Friday night several months later, it took me a few moments to recognise the voice on the other end. The familiar flutter in my stomach alerted me to its owner. It was Bob!

'It's been a while,' I said, trying to remain calm when my heart was pounding, and my head felt as if it was going to burst. I sat down and took a deep breath as he talked. I barely heard his words so intent was I on feeling composed.

'So, will you?' I heard and realised I'd completely missed his question.

'Will I?' I repeated stupidly.

'Will you agree to meet me? I know it's been years. You've moved on. I've gone through a lot recently and I started to think about you... to remember... We had some good times. Maybe we can talk again.' There was a long pause while I tried to think of what to say. 'Are you still there?'

'Yes.'

'Yes, you're still there, or yes to meeting me?'

'To both.' I wasn't sure whether it was excitement or anxiety, but my stomach was churning in a way it hadn't for years. Not since that fateful weekend in Largs had I felt so mixed up. We made arrangements to meet in a tearoom at Charing Cross the following week when he said his son would be visiting his grandparents. His son! I'd almost forgotten about that. But he must be about fourteen now. Surely he was old enough to look after himself?

I put down the phone and remained sitting as if glued to the chair. I was in a trance. My thoughts were spinning out of control. Did he just mean he wanted to talk or was *talk* code for more? Did he want to recapture our relationship? Surely that's what he must mean. Men didn't mess around at our age, did they? Was he looking for a wife? A mother for his son? Had he discussed me with Eileen and Alan? Should I ring her? My hand was on the phone when a horrifying thought occurred to me. What if this wasn't his idea at all? What if Eileen or Alan or both had put him up to this?

No. I'd say nothing to anyone, I'd wait until we met. Then I'd know. But that was almost a week away. How was I going to survive till then?

*

Somehow I made it through the next few days. Nan, the more perceptive of my sisters, did ask me a few times if I was all right, when I became lost in a daze, when I almost gave the wrong change or showed a customer the wrong garment. But I managed, and the day of my meeting with Bob finally arrived.

On a Sunday afternoon, Charing Cross was pretty empty. In fact, I was surprised to find anywhere open, but Bob was clearly familiar with the small café-cum-tearoom. It was close to the Mitchell Library and seemed to cater mostly for students.

I moistened my lips as I hesitated outside. I'd worn my favourite suit. It was a blue herring-bone tweed which set off my hair – still black, but now longer and coiled in what I thought was a sophisticated bun at the back of my neck – and I'd chosen a paler blue blouse to match it. As I stood there, willing myself to enter, I wondered if we'd recognise each other. It was over twenty years since we met and I was no longer the tightly-wound twenty-year-old, he'd known. No, I reminded myself, I was now an equally tightly-wound forty-four-year-old spinster.

I almost turned away. What if he decided he didn't want to know me? What if it had all been a mistake, some sort of bad joke? What if…?

'Isobel?'

I spun round and there he was. He'd shaved off his Clark Gable moustache, done something different with his hair and gained a bit of weight, but he was the same Bob Smith I remembered. I wanted to throw myself into his arms and tell him I was sorry, that I still loved him and I was thrilled to see him again. Fortunately, some element of good sense held me back.

'Bob,' I said and held out my hand.

He took it in both of his, smiled his old smile, and I was lost.

'It's been a long time,' he said. 'Good to see you again. Thanks for agreeing to meet me. Shall we…?'

Once inside we found a corner table away from the groups of students taking a break from the library and placed our orders. I opted for my favourite Russian tea while Bob chose a coffee, an indication his tastes, at least, had changed. What else had changed? Twenty-four years was a long time. I looked around and wondered why I was here. I felt out-of-place in this predominately student atmosphere. It had never been my scene. But Bob obviously felt quite at home.

We made tentative conversation, each seemingly testing the other. We avoided all talk of our time together, Bob focussing on telling me proudly about his son who was called Rory or the Gaelic version Rhuairi. 'His mother was from the Islands,' he said, but left it there. I felt a pang at the thought of the woman who'd taken my place.

Bob expressed interest in our shop, and I enjoyed explaining how, after the war, Kate and I had set up Plain and Fancy to cater for the post-war demand for fashionable clothes and how Nan had joined us when Col died.

'I'm sorry to hear about Colin,' Bob said. 'He was a good man. We lost a lot of good men in the war.' He sighed. 'To think he survived that, only to… And you say your sister has a child?'

'A daughter. Isobel.'

'Like you.'

'Yes. But not really like me. Young Isobel's more fearless, more adventurous. She'll go far.'

'Like my boy. They must be about an age.'

We talked on about the children. It was as if Isobel was indeed my own daughter, and we were two parents comparing notes. But, of course, we weren't.

'And you're still living in the same place?'

'I am.' But he knew that. He'd called me there. Was he just making polite conversation? *Well, I could play that game too.* 'The house is full these days,' I said, enumerating the various women who now made their home there.

We talked on till the afternoon light was beginning to fade. The café was beginning to empty and the waitresses were looking anxious, clearly wanting to close-up and return to their families.

'I think we should go,' I said, though reluctant to bring the meeting to an end.

'Before we do…' Bob seemed to make a decision. 'I've enjoyed meeting with you. I'd like to see you again. You know my circumstances. I can't promise you anything, but…' He smiled and his eyes twinkled in the way I remembered. I barely heard the disclaimer. My heart started to beat so loudly in my ears I was sure he must hear it.

'I'd like that,' I said.

Twenty-five

Bel – 2015

Bel blinked, the sunlight streaming through the window almost blinding her. Turning to see Matt's face beside her on the pillow, she smiled at the memory of the previous evening. She gently flexed her ankle. It barely ached at all. She might not be able to drive but, if Matt drove her, she could get back to Glasgow. Last night, when she'd called her aunt before dinner, the old woman had sounded frail. Bel was anxious to be back with her.

Her eyes fell again on the man lying beside her and, for a moment, she imagined how it would be to waken beside him every morning. Then, sighing, she dismissed the thought as fanciful. How could that ever happen? She'd already decided this was to be a pleasant interlude, ignoring the small voice that reminded her that was before they'd slept together, before she'd…

Gently, so as not to disturb the sleeping figure, Bel eased herself out of the bed and, leaning on the bedside table for support, tested her injured foot. She winced a little as it took her weight, but as she straightened up, she found she could walk slowly and with only a slight limp.

By the time she'd showered and dressed, Matt was awake.

'You're up. The ankle must be feeling better.'

'Much better. I think I should go back to Aunt Isobel's today, that's if you can drive me. She didn't sound too good last night, and I can't stay here malingering any longer.' Her eyes fell on his sleep-mussed hair and she had a strong urge to run her fingers through it.

'Sure can. I'll be dressed in a tick and fix breakfast. I'm guessing you want to get off soon?'

'Please. It's been good of you to...' Bel blushed, not quite sure what she was thanking him for. His hospitality? His love-making? She decided she'd said enough. 'I'll go through and feed Hamish,' she said, to hide her embarrassment.

By the time Matt appeared in the kitchen, Bel had regained her equilibrium and was fondly watching the little dog enjoy his breakfast. He was so like her own Toby. Her hand went to her throat and she had a sudden longing to be back in Sydney, in her own home. Back with her own little dog, and with the knowledge that she was in control of her life. This... this wasn't real life. Real life was her ordered routine, her boutique, her walks by the harbour on summer evenings, occasional visits to the opera, the theatre. She felt a lump come to her throat.

While Matt was fetching some paperwork from his office, Bel wandered over to the large bookshelf that covered one wall of the open living room. She examined the titles, finding some familiar ones, then noticed one book was sticking out of a shelf. She slid it out and absentmindedly flicked it open, smiling to see a younger Matt had written his name on the flyleaf. A jolt of shocked surprise shot through her as her eyes scanned the name and address written by the young boy:

Matthew Rhuairi Reid Smith.
Anniesland,
Glasgow,
Scotland,
The World.

Matt Reid and Rhuairi Smith were the same person. He was Bob Smith's son!

*

On the drive back to Glasgow Matt was cheerful, seemingly unaware of Bel's unsettled state of mind. She wondered if her aunt knew that

Matthew Reid and Rhuairi Smith were one and the same – that her solicitor was the son of the man she'd loved and lost. Surely not? Should she tell the older woman or leave her to die in peace and ignorance? Maybe Isobel would like to know. Maybe she *should* know. And what about Matt? How would he feel to discover that his father and Isobel had been… not lovers, never that, but close? That his father had been the love of Isobel's life?

Bel didn't speak for much of the trip, allowing Matt to ramble on and only murmuring enough comments to encourage him to continue. There was something niggling at the back of her mind, and it wasn't till they hit the outskirts of the city that it dawned on her. That comment of her aunt's about "finding young Matthew" and Mary's subsequent revelation that Isobel had become excited when she discovered it was a family practice of an uncle and his nephew.

The penny dropped. Isobel had been looking for Rhuairi. She must know who Matt is. She'd set out to discover the whereabouts of the son of the man who'd left her twice, dumped her to marry someone else. What did that say about her aunt? Was she re-living her love for this Bob Smith through a friendship with his son? No wonder she treated him like the son she'd never had. He was! Bel couldn't wait to confront her aunt.

*

'I'm back!' Bel burst through the door and entered the living room expecting to see Isobel sitting in her usual chair reading the paper or completing the crossword. But the room was empty. Everything was neatly in place, but there was no sign of the elderly woman.

'One of the other rooms?' Matt had come in behind her and headed back into the hall, Bel following more slowly. They were about to go down the hall to the kitchen when Betty's wiry figure appeared on the stairs.

'Isobel isn't feeling so well today. She's having a wee nap.'

'Why…?' Bel began.

'She didnae want to worry you all the way out there, so she gave me a call and I changed my days. It wis nae bother. She's done a lot for me over the years. I've just been making sure your room's ready for you.'

'I've only been gone two days.' Immediately she'd spoken, Bel regretted the sharpness of her tone. 'I'm sorry, Betty. I didn't mean to snap at you. It's just… I didn't expect this. We could have left earlier if I'd known.'

'No. She didnae want that. "Let the young ones enjoy their time together." Those were her very words.' Betty nodded as if to confirm what she was saying.

Bel looked at Matt and blushed. What did her aunt know? What *could* she know? Bel hadn't known herself that she and Matt would end up in bed together.

'She's canny, that one. And she's always been fond of you and had your interests at heart. She talked a lot about your coming here, and she was that pleased to see you two together.' Betty said, as if reading Bel's mind, and nodded again. 'Now, I suspect you could both be doing with a cup of tea?'

'Yes please. That would be good,' Matt replied, clearly noting Bel was lost for words.

When Betty disappeared into the kitchen, Bel peeked into Isobel's room, but her aunt was fast asleep, her body looking strangely small and lost in the king-sized bed, her long plait of white hair falling over one shoulder. She closed the door gently and stood still in the hallway, till Betty appeared carrying a tray with the promised tea.

'You okay?' Matt asked, taking a seat beside Bel by the window and picking up his cup. His eyes mirrored Bel's own concern.

'I think so.' Bel sighed. 'I didn't expect to come back to…' She gestured around the room. She couldn't tell Matt what she'd discovered – suspected. Maybe later, when she'd been able to discuss it with Isobel. But she'd have to wait till her aunt had recovered. Then she had the terrible thought. What if Isobel didn't recover? What if this "turn" of hers was the start of her final journey?

She felt dizzy. She wasn't ready for this. She needed…

Bel knew what she must do. As soon as Matt left – if Isobel was still asleep – she must read the rest of the Isobel Saga. She needed to find out what happened when Isobel was reunited with Bob. She knew her aunt had never married, yet her reading so far indicated Isobel's strong belief that she'd become Bob's wife. What had happened to prevent it? Why was Aunt Isobel still alone?

As soon as Matt left, promising to call soon and extracting a promise from Bel to keep him informed about Isobel, Bel retreated to her bedroom and began to read.

Twenty-six

Isobel – 1962

I may not have sat home waiting for Bob's call, but he was never far from my mind. So, it was a relief when I finally picked up the telephone and heard his voice. He suggested we meet for lunch. I agreed, while thinking how different this was from his courting twenty years ago. This *was* courting, wasn't it? We were older and had experienced more of life since then. At least he had, having been through a war, married and become a father. Whereas I…

When I considered, I realised my life hadn't changed much. I'd changed the hair salon for the factory, then our dress shop, dated a few guys, but underneath – inside – I was still the rigidly moral girl Bob had known back then. Is that what he expected? Or did he think I'd altered in that very essential respect? Surely not. Part of me couldn't wait to see him again, while another part hoped he didn't expect more than I was prepared to give. I didn't intend to lose him again, but I knew I couldn't become anything more than I'd been before until there was a ring on my finger.

This sort of thinking was getting me nowhere, and when Eileen rang me the night before my date with Bob, I was relieved to have someone to confide in.

'I hear Bob Smith rang you,' she began without any preliminaries.

'You hear a lot,' I said. So, she didn't know everything. 'I suppose Alan told you.'

'Actually, it was Bob. He came to dinner the other night with Rhuairi – that's his son. He and our Gavin go to school together and are great pals. Are you going to be seeing him?'

I avoided answering the question straight off. 'What's he like these days?' I asked.

'What do you mean?'

'You know,' I said, though she clearly didn't understand what I meant. 'Is he still the same as he was back when he and I were…'

Eileen didn't answer immediately, then she said, 'Well he's older, of course. And Mhairi's death knocked him around a bit. I don't think he's found it easy being the only parent to Rhuairi.'

'Has he…?' I wavered, wondering how I could find out what I really wanted to know. 'Have there been other women since… since his wife died?'

I heard Eileen chuckle. 'How would I know? But he's a man, he's still good-looking, and there are always women on the lookout for a meal ticket.'

How crass. But Eileen had always been like that. Called a spade a bloody shovel as my father would say.

'But he's never brought anyone here… to meet Alan and me, if that's what you mean.'

'Mmm.' Did that mean no one serious, or that he was associating with women he didn't want to introduce to his friends? Where did that leave me?

'So, have you arranged to see him?' Eileen wasn't going to be side-tracked.

'We're having lunch together. Do you think…?'

'I think that's a good thing. You two always made a good couple. I never knew what went wrong, why you let him go.' Eileen's voice rose to indicate a question, but I wouldn't be drawn now, any more than I had been at the time. It was my secret, mine and Bob's; and clearly, he hadn't said anything to Alan either.

'Well,' she said at last. 'Maybe we'll see the two of you for dinner one of these days.'

How I hoped that was the case. I was too nervous to ask if she thought he was serious, if he was looking for a wife, a mother for Rhuairi. The very idea made me shiver with excitement. But we *were* in our forties, not kids anymore, so surely marriage was on the cards? Although scared to get my hopes up, by the time the call ended I'd almost persuaded myself I'd be the next Mrs Smith.

When I hung up the phone, Nan was coming through the hall and looked at me speculatively. 'Was that Eileen? What did she want?'

'Why would she be wanting anything? Can't my friend ring me for a chat?'

'You look a bit strange. It was more than just a chat. You looked a bit odd after that other call you had too – a few days ago. Reminded me of a long time back when you were seeing that guy. When Col and I got engaged.'

Damn my sister for being so observant. I felt a blush rise up my neck and onto my face and raised my hands to my cheeks as if to suppress it.

'It is,' she said gleefully. 'It's him again, isn't it? I heard his wife had died. He's free again. Oh, Izzy, I'm so happy for you.'

I stared at her in amazement. This wasn't the reaction I'd expected from my sister.

'It's early days,' I said, unwilling to share my hopes. *What if I was wrong?* 'But he's invited me to lunch.'

'All very proper,' she said with a smile. 'It'll do you good. There hasn't been anyone since John, has there?'

'Not really,' I said, meaning not at all. After John was killed I didn't see the point of forming a relationship. I knew no one would be able to match up to the memory of Bob Smith. Although I'd gone on a few dates, I'd decided years ago that it was my fate to be the family spinster. I'd been sure Nan would marry again. She was the sort men liked, and Kate… She was more of an unknown quantity, having always been more caught up in her career than menfolk – apart from the Polish guy during the war. Maybe he'd been for her what Bob Smith was for me. He'd been killed too.

*

I dressed carefully in a new tweed suit and pale lemon blouse with a scalloped collar. I patted my hair as I took one last look in the mirror. Some might call the style old-maidish, but I loved the sense of sophistication it gave me.

We'd arranged to meet in the city. I hadn't wanted him to pick me up at home. Something inside me wanted to keep him a secret, though Nan had already found out, and I supposed it wouldn't be long before Kate did too. My niece was too young to bother, but she might be excited if there was to be a wedding. The very thought made me shiver in anticipation, but I was determined to take one step at a time. For now, it was enough that he wanted to see me again.

As soon as I entered the restaurant, I saw Bob sitting at a corner table studying the menu. For a moment, I was able to examine him unobserved. His hair, once thick and jet black was now beginning to thin at the temples and had more than a few flecks of grey. His shoulders, too, had developed a slight slump. Without his moustache, he was no longer the magnificent specimen of manhood I'd swooned over, no longer the Clark Gable lookalike. But he was still my very own heart throb. I took a deep breath to still the flutter of excitement in my gut and made my way towards him.

Bob looked up and stood as I approached. 'Izzy. Good to see you.' He took both my hands in his.

Not the kiss I'd hoped for, but my heart began to pound feverishly at the touch of his hands and my legs felt so weak that, but for his firm grasp, I might have fallen. 'Good to see you too,' I said, my words coming out in a gasp as his grip tightened.

He smiled. 'Shall we sit?'

I slid into a chair, my stomach doing somersaults and my mind in a whirl. Bob handed me a menu, but the words blurred.

'Water?'

'Yes please.'

Once I'd taken a gulp of the cool liquid, I was able to meet his amused eyes. Was he laughing at me? No. His expression was kind.

'So,' he said.

'So.'

Bob took the menu from my hands. 'Shall I order?'

'Please.'

I felt a fool, but it was nice to have him take charge.

'How was your week?'

'It was good.' I relaxed at this very ordinary question and started to tell him about some amusing episodes with customers. The ice was broken and we began to chat like old friends. But was that all we were? He talked about the school – he still taught in the same one – and I chatted about Plain and Fancy. And all the time we were talking, I was wondering about his intentions.

When we stood up to leave, I could barely conceal my disappointment. I surreptitiously crossed my fingers. He had to want to see me again. I couldn't bear to leave without knowing we'd meet another time. We stood outside the restaurant, and I gazed up at him, oblivious of people hurrying past.

'You're looking nice, Izzy.'

I smiled, my mouth dry. Was this it? Was he going to leave me with another promise to call? Was I going to be forced to wait for the phone to ring like a love-sick teenager?

'It's been good to see you. We should do it again.'

I gazed into his eyes and willed him to say more, to…

'How about next Saturday? I have to be in Byres Road. Maybe we could meet there?'

I let out a loud breath and felt a sense of lightness. 'I can do that. Would you like to meet me at the shop?'

'Oh, I don't think I'd fit into a ladies' dress shop.' Bob laughed awkwardly. 'How about we meet outside the Curlers? We can have a bite to eat there.'

It wasn't quite the romantic venue I'd have liked – to be eating while jostling with students from the nearby university, but it was better than nothing. We shook hands, he gave me a peck on the cheek and we parted. I gazed after him as he strode off down the street, before turning to catch my bus home.

'How did it go?' Nan wanted to know as soon as I walked in. 'We won't be interrupted. Isobel's over at Mary's,' she said referring to my niece's friend who lived a few houses down the road. 'She'll be there all afternoon. I'll put the kettle on and you can tell me all about him.' At twelve, Isobel was an inquisitive girl who loved to listen in to our grown-up conversations and there would be no peace if she was here.

'There's not much to tell.' Nan and I were sitting facing each other at the kitchen table. I wrapped both hands around my cup and gazed into the warm tea, the swirling leaves reminding me of Maisie's prediction. While she'd been right about Bob coming back into my life again, I'd decided to ignore the second part of her forecast. She didn't know everything, and this time, I was determined to prove her wrong.

'What did you talk about?' Nan wasn't going to give up easily. She was like a dog with a bone once she got started. I'd thought my sister would find another fellow when she came back to Glasgow, but, although she attracted a lot of interest, she steadfastly refused to encourage any of them, saying that she could never feel for another man the way she'd felt for Col. I could understand that, given my feelings for Bob.

She was waiting for an answer.

'We talked a bit about his teaching, how things had changed since the war, and he wanted to know about Plain and Fancy.'

'And his son? What's his name?'

'Rhuairi. His mother was from the north. He's a little older than Isobel, I think.' I suddenly realised Bob hadn't said much about his son, and made a mental note to ask about him next time. If things went the way I expected – hoped – then I'd no doubt meet the boy one of these days. I felt a slight quiver of apprehension at the thought of becoming stepmother to this boy, a teenager, the son of the woman who'd taken my place in Bob's life.

'Mummy! Auntie Izzy?' Isobel's familiar voice echoed through the hallway, the front door banged and my niece's feet pattered on the linoleum floor. Next moment, her bright face appeared in the doorway, her eyes sparkling with excitement. 'Mary has a puppy,' she announced breathlessly. 'Can we get one, too?' She pulled up a chair and joined us, reaching across the table to help herself to a chocolate digestive.

'Oh, darling. I don't think so. Your aunts and I are out at the shop all day when you're at school. And the aunties are often out too. A dog would get lonely on its own all day. Mary's mum is home so her puppy has someone to keep it company.'

'Ohhh.' Isobel's eyes filled, her smile became a pout, and I could see she was about to burst into tears. I wanted to take her into my arms and comfort her, tell her I'd buy her the puppy if she wanted it so much, bring the smile back to her face. But, as usual, I managed to restrain myself, remind myself that, no matter how much I loved Isobel, I was her aunt, not her mother.

Then I thought again about Bob's boy, about Rhuairi Smith, this time with a tremor of anticipation. And there would perhaps be another child. How would it be to have a child of my own, Bob's son or daughter, a brother or sister for Rhuairi? I began to picture us all sitting here together, three children playing in the corner while we adults looked fondly on. I completely ignored the fact that any child of mine would be years younger than the other two and unlikely to prove company for them.

'Izzy!' Nan's voice interrupted my thoughts.

'Sorry, I was miles away.'

'I was asking if you'll be seeing him again.'

Once more a warm glow engulfed me. 'Next Saturday, for lunch again.'

'Lunch?'

'What's wrong with lunch?'

'Nothing.' But I knew my sister. I could tell something was bothering her.

'Go on. Say what you're thinking.' I felt my face redden at the hint of concern in her tone.

'I just thought he might have suggested a film or even the theatre, with dinner. Didn't you both love films back then?'

We did. Nan knew we did. I could remember every film we'd seen together. I had them written down in an old diary. I smoothed my skirt with one hand, trying not to allow her unease to affect me. 'We're both older now and... he has Rhuairi. I suppose that's why...' It hadn't occurred to me to wonder why Bob chose to meet me in the middle of the day rather than selecting a more romantic evening date. I tossed my head. 'We'll get to that. We've only just got together again.'

I spoke so confidently I believed my own words.

*

It was after a few more lunch dates that I casually mentioned a film I wanted to see. Of course, I could have gone alone or with Nan. Kate was always happy to stay home with Isobel. Films had never appealed to her, and she didn't appear to have any social life to speak of. In recent years, she'd joined the church choir and apart from the Sunday service and the Wednesday evening choir practice, she seemed content to stay home reading one of the books Nan and I joked were "worthy".

'Everyone's talking about this Bond film,' I said as we were preparing to part after yet another lunch date. I drew on my gloves and refused to meet his eyes, trying to pretend I hadn't a care in the world, while my fingers were tingling with nervousness. '*Dr No.* Have you seen it? It has that new Scots film star in it.'

'Sean Connery. Yes, I've heard it's a good one.' He hesitated, and I held my breath. 'Would you like to see it?'

Now it was my turn to be perverse. I felt confident enough to ask, 'What about your son? Can you…?'

'He can look after himself.' Bob seemed to consider for a few moments, then his face lightened as if he'd made a decision. 'What about Friday night? Are you free?'

I understood this wasn't a time to play hard-to-get. 'Yes,' I breathed, 'I'd love to.' I was so confused I didn't know what I was saying.

That film was the first of many, and I began to feel even more confident in our relationship although while I wanted to shout it to the world, I also wanted to keep it private – to keep Bob to myself. A part of me was afraid that, the more people who knew about us, the less of Bob I had. I knew it was foolish, but I couldn't completely shake the fear something would happen to spoil our idyll.

My happiness was almost complete when I received a call from Eileen. We'd barely spoken since Bob and I started seeing each other again, and I was wary of sharing too much with her. Alan was still close to Bob, and I worried what he might be saying about me – about us.

So, when I heard her voice, I felt my stomach contract and a lump came to my throat. But I managed to disguise my concern and put on my cheeriest voice. 'Eileen! How lovely to hear from you.' I smiled as I spoke, having read somewhere that it helped give a good impression.

'I haven't heard from you for a while. Is everything okay?'

'Sure. I've been busy with the shop and…'

'I hear you and Bob Smith are still on.'

'I suppose he's told Alan.'

While I'd assumed it would happen, I still felt a tiny niggle that

Bob felt free to talk about me behind my back, while I'd been more circumspect.

'Actually, no. Alan says Bob never mentions you.'

Now, I felt let down. I knew it was irrational, but that's how unreasonable I was.

'No, it was Helen Brown who told me she'd seen the two of you together in Sauchiehall Street the other week.'

'Right.'

'I mentioned it to Alan, and we thought it would be nice to have the pair of you to dinner.'

'Oh!' I was lost for words. If Bob accepted the invitation to dinner at Eileen's it would be a clear sign he was serious. He was, wasn't he? 'Will I...?' I finally said when I found my voice again.

'No, better let Alan broach it with him. See how he takes it. I take it you've no objection?'

'No.' What did she mean "see how he takes it"? Did Eileen think Bob wouldn't want to take me to dinner with them? The four of us had gone out together often enough in the old days. But I guessed it was different now. They were married and we weren't.

Bob hadn't even mentioned he was seeing me again to Alan, his best friend. Was he ashamed of me, or just keeping his cards close to his chest as I had been? I didn't know what to think. 'So, I'll wait for Bob to mention it?'

'I think that would be best, don't you? I mean, he's been pretty cagey about his personal life in recent years. We've only ever seen him and Rhuairi together. Maybe...'

I could hear the doubt in her voice and remembered her telling me he hadn't taken anyone to meet them since Mhairi died. But surely, I was different? I wasn't some casual acquaintance, a woman he'd taken out a few times, someone who meant nothing to him. I was... What was I? I hoped I was the next Mrs Smith, but I didn't dare let anyone guess.

Nan probably did. She knew me better than anyone and wanted the best for me, but I hadn't let on to anyone else. I wasn't even sure Kate knew who I was spending time with. I'd never allowed Bob to pick me up at home, preferring to keep our relationship private – secret some might say. Deep down, I think I may have been worrying about his feelings, scared to talk about us as a couple in case I jinxed everything we had together.

'I'll speak to Alan, then. I'll be in touch.'

I hung up the phone and sat staring at it. I wondered how Bob would react.

When he'd tell me.

If he'd tell me.

Thoughts were whirling around in my head. I felt dizzy.

*

We were drinking tea in a café in Central Station before going to a film, when Bob made the remark I'd been waiting for. 'I had a beer with Alan Davison last night. Remember Alan and Eileen back then?'

'Of course. I still see Eileen occasionally, but she's been pretty busy since she married and now they have a young boy.'

'Aye. Their Gavin is good pals with Rhuairi.'

I waited.

'Alan and Eileen. They'd like us to go to dinner at their place.' He glanced at me out of the corner of his eye. 'What d'you think?'

'That's good of them. Do you want us to go?'

Bob coughed before replying. 'It's you I wonder about. You've been at great pains to keep quiet about us meeting. I wasn't sure… I hadn't said anything to Alan, not since I got back in touch. Seems some friend of Eileen's saw us together. Women and their gossip!' He shook his head, and I couldn't tell if he was pleased or annoyed.

'Well, we did a lot together in the old days. We were a good foursome back then.'

'Do you want to go?'

'If you do.' I tried to sound nonchalant, while my heart was racing. This invitation was important to me. It would be the first time we'd gone anywhere as a recognised couple. I would be the first woman Bob had taken to Alan and Eileen's for dinner since Mhairi. I closed my mind to thoughts of his wife. I wanted to pretend he'd always been my Bob.

It was only right Alan and Eileen should invite us as a couple. They'd introduced us. We'd both stood up at their wedding. Now they'd be the first to recognise our relationship. I exhaled with relief. 'Did they suggest a date?'

'Next Friday.'

'Sounds good.'

'You're sure?' It occurred to me that perhaps Bob wasn't sure himself, that he'd only asked me to please Alan. Maybe he'd expected me to refuse. But I immediately dismissed that idea. Why on earth would he want me to refuse an invitation to dinner from the couple who'd been our best friends?

"I'm sure.' I smiled, took his hand across the table and checked my watch. 'Now we should make a move if we don't want to miss the beginning of the film.'

Bob visibly relaxed. I thought I detected a hint of something I couldn't identify, then it was gone. I was too relieved he'd been thinking of my feelings to pay too much attention to what was probably only in my imagination.

*

On Friday evening, I took more care than usual getting ready. It was a cold night – winter was drawing in – so I decided to wear a new red woollen dress I'd picked out of our latest display. It was knee-length and clung to me in all the right places. I smiled as I contemplated Eileen's reaction. She'd let herself go since Gavin was born and now bore little resemblance to the slim and fiery friend who'd been so much more daring than me in every way. I covered the dress with my camel swagger coat, pulled my favourite black boucle wool hat over my hair, slipped on my matching gloves and I was ready to go.

'You're off to Eileen's tonight?' Nan came out of the kitchen as I was walking downstairs. 'See and enjoy yourself. Don't make too much of it.'

I stared at my sister. What did she mean?

'You're looking very glam for Eileen's. Watch you don't go over on your ankle in those heels.'

I glanced down at the black patent leather shoes, the heels were higher than I was used to, and pursed my lips. Tonight was going to be special. I wanted to look my best.

'Och, go on with you.' Nan almost pushed me out the door but, before I left I saw a face peer over the banister and heard my niece's voice. 'You look nice, Auntie Izzy. Are you going somewhere special?'

I nodded and closed the door behind me.

Bob was waiting for me in his car. He didn't understand why I wouldn't permit him to come to the door for me. I didn't either. Maybe after tonight I would. But I got a peculiar thrill out of the secrecy of our meetings, though I know I couldn't keep it up. If our relationship was to progress in the way I wanted, I'd have to become more open. I shivered at the thought.

*

I thought I'd feel pleased to be dining at Eileen and Alan's with Bob, enjoy being part of our old foursome again. But the evening didn't go as I'd expected. I couldn't put my finger on it, but right from the start, something felt wrong.

Alan was his usual jovial self, greeting Bob with a wink and a slap on the back, and me with a kiss on the cheek. 'Good to see you two back together.' He rubbed his hands, then poured a Scotch for Bob and a sherry for me. Bob accepted his drink awkwardly and coughed. I drank mine down quickly to hide my uneasiness. Meanwhile Eileen fussed around, and Gavin, after saying hello to us both, sidled off to bed.

We sat on the overstuffed lounge chairs making awkward conversation till Eileen jumped up. 'Dinner should be ready, now,' she said and headed for the door.

I followed her into the kitchen. 'Can I help?' I asked, watching her remove a casserole dish from the oven.

'It's all done. Beef Wellington. Bob's favourite.'

I stood there feeling useless and realising I knew nothing about Bob's taste in food – favourite or otherwise. Our relationship had been conducted in a bubble, a bubble which didn't allow for the sharing of any really private information. Not for the first time, I wondered if he felt the same way I did.

By the time we started to eat, I'd already downed three glasses of sherry and could feel my head beginning to spin. I tried to keep up my end of the conversation, but kept losing the thread of what was being said. I felt confused. This wasn't the evening I'd been looking forward to.

We had finished our dessert – a delicious concoction of berries, meringue, and whipped cream, and I was beginning to feel more like myself when Alan raised his wine glass in Bob and my direction.

'To you both.'

I waited expectantly for Bob's response. There was none. I peeked at him out of the corner of my eye to see him draw a finger along inside his collar. He pushed his chair back. 'We should be going. It was good of you to invite us both. Thanks for the lovely meal, Eileen. You outdid yourself yet again. Izzy?'

He stretched out his hand to help me rise, and I was forced to join him in thanking Eileen and Alan for their hospitality. The cold evening air hit me as we walked to the car, completely sobering me up. *What was that about? Why the sudden decision to leave? Was it Alan's toast? Something I'd said?*

Bob was silent on the drive back, but by the time we stopped outside the Kelvin Drive house, he seemed to have forgotten whatever it was that had disturbed him. He turned towards me for our usual kiss and cuddle, and I snuggled into him, enjoying the warmth of his skin against my cold cheeks.

'Next Friday?' he asked, as we drew apart.

'Mmm.'

'Same time. Pick you up here?'

I nodded and slipped out of the car, standing by the kerb to watch him drive off and feeling confused. Something was bothering him. I puzzled for a moment, then shrugged. It couldn't be too much. He still wanted to see me next week as usual.

But as I pushed open the front door I had a knot in my belly.

Twenty-seven

Isobel – 1963

Christmas came and went and my relationship with Bob hadn't seemed to have progressed. We still met most Friday evenings, but sometimes I felt we were just marking time, waiting for something to happen.

We were finishing a quiet dinner in what I had come to regard as *our* restaurant when Bob surprised me.

'I have something for you.' He ferreted around in his pocket, and my eyes widened as he drew what looked like a ring box out of his pocket. 'A little bird told me it was your birthday.'

'Oh!' My heart began to beat madly and my fingers became slippery as I clumsily unwrapped the package to reveal a beautiful garnet ring. It wasn't the diamond I'd been hoping for and the stone was small, but it took my breath away. I was about to remove it from the box when Bob forestalled me.

'Let me see if it fits,' he said as he carefully freed it from the wrappings and placed it on the third finger of… *my right hand.*

I tried to hide my disappointment and held my hand up to admire the ring, letting it catch the light while I held back my tears.

Bob didn't notice. He was too caught up in what he imagined was my delight at his gift.

Belatedly, I kissed his cheek. 'Thanks,' I said, my voice almost breaking with what he probably imagined was pleasure. I was pleased he'd remembered my birthday after all those years, of course I was. But this wasn't the gift I wanted.

'I thought you'd like it,' he said, taking my hand in his and rubbing his thumb over the ring. 'It's the one you admired, isn't it?'

I was puzzled. Then I remembered one evening when we'd been standing outside a jewellery store. I'd been admiring the engagement rings. When Bob had asked me what I was looking at, I'd pointed blindly at something in the back of the window, to distract him from the real source of my interest. It was a beautiful ring with a unique setting, the small dark red stone held by what appeared to be two golden hands.

'Yes.' I swallowed hard to disguise the sudden nausea that threatened. 'It's lovely, Bob. Thank you.' I looked down at the ring, its many-faceted surface glinting in the light. I turned my hand this way and that, as if I could change it into the diamond I'd been hoping for. A ring was a ring, and it was a step in the right direction, or so I managed to persuade myself.

But I wasn't getting any younger and if I – we – were to have a child, we didn't have too many years left. It had never occurred to me that Bob might not want another child. He had Rhuairi, but surely, he'd like his son to have a sibling – a little brother or sister to share his life with? My imagination was working overtime, so I was glad when Bob proposed a toast.

'To another wonderful year.' He raised his glass, his eyes twinkling, and I fell under his spell again and raised my glass to join his.

'To us,' I said daringly, holding my breath as I remembered his reaction to Alan's similar toast. He didn't contradict me, but his eyes took on that faraway look I'd been seeing recently.

I wasn't sure what it meant, but sometimes I had the feeling that even though we were in the same room, sitting together, he was with me in body, but not in spirit. His mind was elsewhere. I shook my head slightly to dismiss those suspicions, for that's all they were. They were the thoughts that came in the dark of night when sleep eluded me, when Maisie's words came back to haunt me, to tell me he'd leave me again.

I took a deep breath and asked the question I'd planned before Bob had surprised me with the ring.

'My sisters and I wondered if you – and Rhuairi of course – would join us for Sunday lunch?' I held my breath as I waited for his reply.

We'd been seeing each other for almost a year and I had yet to meet his son. Nan had suggested this invitation as a way of expediting the meeting – an informal get-together. 'My niece must be around his age…' I found myself babbling and bit my tongue to allow Bob to reply.

'I'm not sure,' he said, slowly. 'We usually go to his grandparents on Sundays – Mhairi's folks. They like to see the boy. His uncle and aunt are there too. They've no children of their own.' He looked down, avoiding my eyes.

I twisted the ring on my finger, willing him to agree. Surely they could miss one Sunday with the boy's family? I didn't think of them as Bob's family. They belonged to that part of his life I wanted to forget. I knew Bob's own family were dead. He'd told me. His brothers had both been killed in the war and his parents had died not long after. We were both orphans. I liked that. It gave us something in common. We could be all things to each other if only…

He hesitated, picked up his glass then put it down again. 'Maybe… just this once. Which Sunday did you have in mind?'

My stomach took a wild leap. *He was going to agree!* 'How about Sunday week?' I suggested, pretending to be calm, while a rush of adrenaline overtook me.

'I'll have to ask Rhuairi.'

And with that I had to be content.

*

'Well?' Nan called to me as soon as I walked in.

I ignored her while I hung up my coat, then joined her by the radio which was playing softly. 'Isobel in bed?' I asked, helping myself from the bowl of sweets on the low table, making sure my new ring was in her line of sight.

'What's that? Did Bob…'

'Birthday present.' I flourished the ring in front of her. 'But, it's not an engagement ring.' I could hear the disappointment in my voice and turned away to avoid the look of pity in her eyes.

I blinked away the tears and tried to inject a note of excitement into my voice before speaking again. 'He's agreed to lunch. Next Sunday, with Rhuairi.' I turned back to face my sister. 'It's a good sign, isn't it?' My voice wobbled. I wasn't sure. I wasn't sure of anything anymore.

*

By the time Sunday arrived, I was a bag of nerves. I'd seen Bob once since he gave me the ring, but it had been a rushed cup of tea in the city and, although he'd seemed to act normally, the extra something I'd been looking for wasn't there. I knew I was probably making a mountain out of a molehill, but the memory of his odd behaviour at Eileen's kept forcing itself into my mind.

I'd shared my misgivings with Nan who'd told me not to be silly, that Bob had, no doubt, more to think about than me and it would all come out in the wash – a favourite expression of Mother's which did nothing to calm my fears.

One person who was excited about the lunch was young Isobel. She couldn't wait to meet the unknown Rhuairi and was full of questions about him – none of which I could answer. She was just at the age when a visit from a new boy, especially one with an exotic name, was the highlight of her week. Her eagerness amused me, and I wished I could feel some of her youthful exuberance. I wasn't sure why, but I was dreading this lunch which I'd been at such pains to arrange.

'Sit down and take a deep breath,' Nan said, pushing me into a chair. 'He's only a man. You're acting as if the Prime Minister himself is coming to lunch.'

'I'm sorry.' I took a deep breath, but couldn't sit still. This lunch was a big deal. It was the first time I'd introduced Bob to my family. For me, it was tantamount to announcing our relationship to the world.

Did Bob see it that way too? Was that why he'd hesitated? But he *had* agreed to come, I reminded myself. Maybe Nan was right and I was making too much of what was, after all, only a family Sunday lunch. Part of the family, at least. The aunts who'd been living with us since the war and had outlived our parents, were making their weekly pilgrimage to the cemetery followed by lunch with a group of friends.

'They're here!' Isobel's voice called from the hallway where she'd been waiting impatiently.

'On you go,' Nan pulled me up. 'They're your guests. You need to let them in.'

I opened the door to see Bob standing awkwardly. My gaze went past him, expecting to see Rhuairi. My eyes widened. There was no-one there. Bob coughed and shuffled his feet. 'Rhuairi... he wanted to show his grandparents his... I left him off there on the way.'

'Oh!' I tried to hide my disappointment. This was to be the grand meeting of both families. Instead, it was only to be Bob. What did it mean? Did he want to keep his son away from me? What would Nan think? And Isobel? She'd been looking forward to meeting the fourteen-year-old.

Bob came forward to give me a peck on the cheek, while I forced a smile. Not an auspicious start.

'Come on in.' I ushered him into the living room and introduced Nan and Kate.

Nan offered Bob a glass of sherry while I tried to find something to say and looked wildly around for Isobel.

Kate sat on the sofa, her face giving nothing away. This wasn't how I'd planned it. If I'd thought about it at all, I'd pictured a smiling Bob graciously greeting my sisters, his arm around me possessively while Rhuairi and Isobel ran off hand-in-hand.

Instead, the four of us sat awkwardly on the edge of our seats like strangers.

'Hello,' Isobel shyly peered round the door. 'Where's...?'

'He couldn't come.' I could hear the tension in my voice.

'Oh!' She disappeared again.

Lunch was difficult. Instead of the easy-going conversation I'd envisaged, we lurched awkwardly from talk of the weather to the anti-nuclear marchers, the defection of Philby, and the possible future of the EEC.

Isobel's contribution was to ask Bob if his son was a fan of Cliff Richard, at which he looked blank. Popular music was evidently not something he was familiar with, whereas Nan, Kate and I had become used to the sounds of the English singer blaring out from the record player my niece had received for her birthday.

When we'd finished eating, Nan and Kate cleared the plates leaving Bob and me sitting at the dining room table looking at each other. I felt frozen. What had happened to the easy chat we'd been used to? Thinking back, it had all started to go wrong at Eileen's when Alan had been so jovial. *How could I regain our former warm companionship?*

As if sensing my uneasiness, Nan breezed in, a coat over her arm. 'Isobel and I are going out to the pictures and Kate's off to visit a friend. You two might like to take your tea into the living room and relax. It can't have been easy, Bob, being subjected to Izzy's family like this. I've left a tray in there for you both.' She disappeared and we could hear her urging Isobel into her outdoor garments, the murmur of Kate's voice, then the door closed and there was silence.

'Shall we?' I rose, feeling more relaxed than I had since I met Bob at the door. We were on our own again. It would be all right. It seemed that it was only when other people were present that I got into a blue funk and Bob became a stranger.

We moved into the front room, and I poured the tea. Bob sat beside me on the sofa, looking decidedly awkward and making me wonder yet again what the problem was. He picked up his cup, then put it down again and turned to face me. But he didn't speak.

He hesitated for so long I began to tremble, convinced what he wanted to say would change my entire future. This was it, the moment I'd been waiting for. I felt anticipation build up inside me until I thought I would burst with excitement. I had to fight to keep still.

When he finally spoke, I barely heard the words. 'Isobel, I need to tell you before you hear it from anyone else. I'm getting married again.'

I heard the words *married* and *again*, but the rest flew past my ears. I shuddered at the thought that my day had come. After all the waiting, I'd finally have Bob's ring on my finger. So what if it was twenty years too late and came with the added complication of a son from his previous marriage? But where was the hug and kiss? Bob was still talking.

I forced myself to listen as a chill of fear crept though me, my skin tingling with shock.

'I shouldn't have come today.' He dragged a hand through his hair. 'I know you'll feel I've led you on and let you down again. I'm sorry if you expected more from our relationship. But I've met someone else. Annie…'

He finally reached out his hands to me, but I pushed him away. 'Go!

Get out! Leave me alone!' I yelled, standing up and turning my back on him. I didn't want him to see the tears streaming down my cheeks.

I heard the door open and close and slowly turned around to face the empty room. I was humiliated. How could he? How could I have let myself get into this situation again? I berated myself as being all sorts of a fool. What did he want in a woman? Why had he started to see me again? Continued to see me, led me to believe… I obviously wasn't his sort of woman, never had been. I'd made sure we were never completely alone – not like last time. So there had been no opportunity for him to try to take things further, and he'd never tried to… Was that why he'd looked elsewhere? Had he found someone who'd give in to him?

I hadn't changed and neither, it seemed, had he. For the first time, I regretted my rigid moral stance. Because of my strict principles I was doomed to remain single for the rest of my life.

I sat there until the room grew dark, until I heard the door open and close again, the click of the light switch in the hall and feet running up the stairs. The door to the living room opened and the light was switched on. I blinked at the sudden brightness.

'What on earth are you doing sitting here in the dark? And you haven't even drawn the curtains.' My sister walked over to pull the green velvet drapes closed, then turned to face me.

I must have looked a mess. I could feel my hair escaping from the bun I'd coiled up so elegantly earlier in the day and I knew my eyes must be red from the tears I'd shed. My sodden handkerchief was crumpled in my hand. I half-rose then collapsed back down into the sofa. I raised my hand to cover my face, ashamed to be discovered in this state.

'Has Bob left? What's happened?'

Nan sat down beside me, still wearing her coat. She unbuttoned it, then grasped my hands. 'What is it, Izzy? Whatever's the matter.'

'What's wrong with me?' I wailed, the tears streaming down my cheeks. 'Why doesn't he want to marry me?'

'Maybe he doesn't want to get married again. He has…'

'You don't understand. He *is* getting married again – he's just not marrying *me*! He's marrying someone called Annie.' I pushed aside my sister's hands, leapt up and rushed upstairs flinging myself down on my bed, curling up into a ball and sobbing, my breath coming in gasps. My heart was broken.

Twenty-eight

Isobel – 1985

Bob was dead!

I heard the news from Eileen who believed I'd got over what she called my *ill-fated romance* years earlier.

But when that woman – Bob's widow – appeared at my door, and I heard her words… It made his death real and brought back all the regrets I'd bottled up over the years. What if I'd been different, if I hadn't been so self-righteous? What would my life have been like?

Her harsh words echoed through my head again and again while I twisted his ring on my finger. What could I do now?

There *was* something I needed to do. I was filled with the longing to see Bob's son, to meet him, the one person alive who had known him well, the son I might have had. But how was I to find him? Rhuairi wasn't a common name, but Smith was. There was no use looking in the telephone directory. Glasgow was a big city. And he might not even live in Glasgow. He could be anywhere.

I'd have to use my longstanding source of information, my old friend, Eileen, but I'd need to be subtle. She'd think I was mad trying to track down Bob's son. Perhaps I was, but it was something I knew I had to do, even though I wasn't clear what I'd do with the information when I had it. The boy would be grown now. He must be in his thirties, no doubt with a family of his own. That made me all the more eager to find him. I didn't intend to stalk him. I just wanted to see him, maybe even meet him, then I'd be satisfied.

I picked up the phone and dialled Eileen's number.

*

'This is nice.'

Eileen and I were eating lunch in a new Italian restaurant on Byres Road. It had been easy to persuade her we should meet there when I told her I wanted to see what the new owners had done to our old shop. The restaurant, just across the street from our old shop, was her choice. I've never been partial to Italian food, but I was so keen to get information from Eileen, I'd have agreed to anything. And she didn't appear surprised when I made no objection to her suggested venue.

We chatted about the shop which had been turned into a bookshop, Eileen's daughter and granddaughter, young Isobel's latest news from Australia, and Nan's worsening health, then I threw in my question.

'Do you keep up with Bob Smith's family? His son, Rhuairi wasn't it?'

She gave me an astonished stare. 'Bob Smith? You're not still fixated on him, are you? The man's dead. I did tell you, didn't I?'

'Yes. You told me.' I crossed my fingers under the table. 'His son. Did he follow him into teaching?' I forked up another mouthful of the spaghetti carbonara I now regretted ordering, it being far too rich for my taste, and pretended indifference.

'Teach?' she said. 'No, teaching wasn't good enough for Rhuairi Smith. He was a bright lad, studied law. I think I heard he'd joined his uncle's firm. His mother's brother.'

I was about to ask another question when she changed the subject, and I never found the opportunity to get back to it without seeming obvious. She drew out the latest photos of her family which she expected me to enjoy as much as she did, and we spent the rest of lunch in meaningless chatter. Afterwards we parted, vowing as usual to meet more regularly in future, but neither of us meaning it. We'd grown apart over the years and had little in common these days.

As I walked home, all I could think of was Rhuairi Smith. A

solicitor – that should make him easier to find. As long as he was still in Glasgow.

As soon as I got in, I took out the phone book.

'What are you looking for?' Nan appeared in the doorway, looking pale.

'Should you be up? What did the doctor say?' I asked, knowing my sister had been confined to bed for the past few weeks with a bad bout of bronchitis – the same illness that had seen off our mother.

'I'll be fine. I can't stay in bed all the time. If my time's come, it's come, and lying there doing nothing won't change matters. I just wish our Isobel was here.' She looked wistful, thinking of her daughter who hadn't returned home since she left fifteen years earlier. 'But she has her own life now,' she sighed. 'And I'm able to imagine her there. I don't want her to see me like this.'

I put the phone book away and helped my sister back to bed, relegating my desire to find Bob's son to the back burner while I took care of my sister. Nan had been unable to work for the past few months and, since Kate had been gone for several years now, we'd taken on a couple of staff. They could be trusted to keep the shop going as long as necessary, until I was able to get back to it. The speed with which Nan was failing led me to believe it wouldn't be for much longer.

'If you want Isobel to be here, I could ring…,' I offered.

'No. It'll be time enough when…'

I knew what she meant. Isobel would have come like a shot if she knew how sick her mum was and she'd definitely be here for the funeral. A plan began to take shape in my mind. If I could just find this Rhuairi Smith in time, maybe he and Isobel could meet, maybe even… Then reality took hold. He'd be married, of course. And, if he was anything like his father… But how I hoped he was. The thought of meeting Bob's son, of having the opportunity to get to know him, filled all my waking hours.

*

Nan didn't last long after that. What had originally been diagnosed as bronchitis turned out to be cancer. She'd always suspected she wouldn't make old bones and, after Col died, she'd lived for her daughter. When Isobel left for Australia, it was as if the spirit went out of her and she was putting in time. The trip to Sydney had bucked her up for a bit. But I think, seeing how happy Isobel was there, she finally gave up hope of her return and began to accept me as her only remaining family here in Scotland.

Unlike me, young Isobel had had no qualms about giving up her virginity when she met that art student. Callum, I think his name was. It was the time of what some called *free love*. I didn't approve one little bit. Nothing's free in my view. And I had a strong suspicion my niece had a narrow escape, and that's what sent her off to Australia. Of course, she got married there, but it didn't last. However, I was pleased she'd known the love of a man, even if it didn't turn out well. That was men for you. They tended to end up disappointing us.

Nan and I thought Isobel might have come home when her marriage broke up, but she had her business and seemed to enjoy the lifestyle, if her letters could be believed. When Nan came home from her trip she was full of praise for the life Isobel had made for herself.

She came home for her mother's funeral and, if she was angry we hadn't told her of her mother's illness, she hid it well. She'd changed. She now called herself Bel. The rebellious adolescent and anxious twenty-something had become an independent organised woman with a mind of her own. She'd always had that – one of our contentious issues – but now she appeared to be at peace with herself and life. She reminded me of myself, of the person I'd liked to have been.

After Nan's funeral, Isobel was off again. She left the next day. I'd hoped we'd have time to talk about old times, maybe for me to show her around the city, but she said she'd her business to get back to and there was nothing to keep her here. I had difficulty holding in the tears as I farewelled her at the airport wondering if I'd ever set eyes on my niece again.

With Nan and Kate now gone, Plain and Fancy had lost its appeal for me. We'd set it up as a family business, now I was the only one left. And I wasn't getting any younger. I decided to sell the shop, though had no idea what I'd do with myself rattling around in the house all alone.

Twenty-nine

Bel – 2015

Bel read on, turning page after page as the story of her aunt's life came alive for her. It was a fascinating and sad story.

Her eyes filled with tears reading how her mother had missed her, but had kept her in the dark about the seriousness of her illness. The first intimation was the call to tell Bel of her mother's death. She'd left at once and been there in time for the funeral. She'd always regretted not being able to say goodbye, but her aunt had told her it was so sudden there had been no time to let her know. Now it was apparent she'd lied.

Bel dropped the page she'd been reading and walked over to the window, seeing the scene outside as if for the first time.

She shivered. Scotland was not her favourite place. This house was not her favourite place. Had her mother known that when she decided to keep her sickness a secret? Bel would never know.

But Isobel had had no such qualms. She'd reached out to Bel, and Bel had responded. She'd come back and… she'd met Matt. Had that been Isobel's intention all along? Was her illness and the legacy only a ploy to bring the two of them together? Surely not. Bel's overactive imagination was running away with her. There was no way her aunt could have anticipated the immediate attraction between them, the chemistry, the…

Bel abruptly moved back from the window and looked at the now scattered pages lying on the floor where she'd dropped them. She didn't want to read any more. She wanted to talk with her aunt. To get some answers.

'I'm away now.' Betty's voice carried up the stairs, and Bel heard the door close behind her. She walked down slowly, her hand sliding on the wooden stair rail, her feet sinking into the carpet, and paused at the door of her aunt's bedroom. She turned the handle gently and pushed the door open.

'You're back!'

Isobel was sitting up in bed, her hands gripping the edge of the bedspread and looking directly at Bel. 'Come away in. Don't stand there looking glaikit. I'm not dead yet. How did you and young Matthew get on? What was all the nonsense about a twisted ankle? Did the pair of you need an excuse?' She gave a chuckle which turned into a cough.

Bel pulled up a stool and sat down beside the bed. To her relief, her aunt seemed to have made a rapid recovery, though her voice had lost some of its usual determination.

'You old fraud. From what Betty said, I thought you were at death's door. I did twist my ankle, tripped over a clump of heather or something. Matt was good enough to put me up until it would take my weight again.'

'Mmm.'

Bel wondered how to approach what she wanted to know and decided a direct question was the only way to go. 'While I was there,' she began. Isobel leaned forward and grasped Bel's hand, making it difficult for Bel to think straight. 'I found a book.'

'A book?'

'It was one Matt had as a child…' Bel forced herself to meet her aunt's eyes. 'He'd written his name in it.' She took a deep breath before reciting, 'Matthew Rhuairi Reid Smith.'

The hint of a twinkle appeared in Isobel's eyes and she nodded with a satisfied smile.

'You knew, didn't you?' But Bel didn't need a reply. She could see the answer in her aunt's expression. 'Why didn't you tell me?'

'What difference would it have made? Matthew is who he is whether he calls himself Rhuairi Smith, Matthew Reid or anything else.'

'But why…?' Bel wasn't sure what she was asking. Why Isobel had sought him out? Why Matt had changed his name?

Isobel chose to answer her second unspoken question. 'You'll have to ask him. Something to do with his uncle is my guess. Keeping the firm in the family name or some such.'

'But Matt, not Rhuairi? Does he know? About you and his dad?'

Isobel shook her head. 'No, I could never tell him. Maybe it's time, now that… He reminds me so much of Bob. It's almost been like having him back again.' A faint smile appeared on Isobel's face and her eyes glazed over, then she seemed to recollect herself. 'Of course, he's not the man his father was. He takes after his mother's side of the family, I guess. There's a sense of loyalty, integrity that… But you don't want to hear all those old tales. You've been reading my bits and pieces?'

Bel nodded. 'I know he married someone else – a second time. How could you bear it? I'd have…'

'We bear what we have to.' Isobel's voice was becoming weaker. She gripped Bel's hand. 'And I had you. You were an unexpected blessing. My sister's wee girl. I was sorry when your dad died, but it meant you grew up here, in this house with all of us, with me.'

Bel's eyes began to mist at her aunt's words. When had the familiar Auntie Izzy of her childhood morphed into the more formal Aunt Isobel? Bel couldn't remember. Probably somewhere in her teens when she was at pains to establish her independence and rebelled against all the adults in her life. She now realised how much her attitude must have hurt those around her, how selfish and uncaring she'd been to those who loved her.

'How much have you read?' Isobel's question took Bel by surprise.

'Mum's death. I hadn't realised… Why didn't she let me know how sick she was? I could have…'

'She didn't want that. There was nothing you could have done. She had a wonderful visit with you, loved seeing your home. She could picture you there. She often spoke about it. She was proud of what you'd achieved. And she went very quickly once the cancer took hold. There would barely have been time.'

'I could have come,' Bel repeated, almost to herself.

'So, you and Matthew?'

Bel was surprised when her aunt changed the subject again. 'Me and Matt,' she stammered.

'How did it go out there when you *twisted your ankle?*'

Bel wrinkled her forehead. Her aunt couldn't be asking what Bel thought she was. 'His daughter dropped in with Fiona.'

'And I guess she wasn't the best pleased to see you. I remember when we met her. And I've heard that one is a might possessive of her dad. But the wee one?' Isobel's eyes were eager.

'You're right about Elspeth. I didn't make a friend there. But Fiona is a different matter. She's delightful. They were both interested in your plans for the house. And Fiona is interested in talking with you about it, giving you her opinions. She's a bright wee thing.'

'Aye. Too late for that. I'm thinking I don't have long.'

'Nooo.' Bel couldn't stop the wail of denial. 'You're looking so well.' But even as she spoke, Bel could see the lines on her aunt's face had become more pronounced, her complexion paler, her skin almost transparent, and she seemed to be finding it more difficult to breathe.

'I'm a bit tired now, our Bel. Maybe you can come back later?'

'Can I get you anything?' Bel had to hold back the tears.

'Not at the moment. Maybe later.'

There was a bell on the bedside table. Bel moved it closer to her aunt. 'Be sure to ring this if you need me.' She walked out slowly, closing the door after one last glance towards the bed where Isobel's eyes had already closed.

It was lunchtime, but Bel didn't feel hungry. She considered calling Matt, but knew she had to sort out how to tell him about Isobel and his dad. She wasn't ready for that conversation just yet. She roamed through the house ending up in the kitchen, the kitchen that had always been the heart of the place. For Bel, it was filled with ghosts and memories, some pleasant, some not. She sighed and leaned on the back of a chair, her ankle suddenly aching with the unaccustomed movements. If Aunt Isobel was to be believed, it would soon all be over. The house would be made ready for its new occupants, she'd be back home in Australia, and all of this would be just a memory.

Bel pulled out the chair and sat down. Her feelings were confused. Last night with Matt had rekindled emotions she'd thought gone forever. And this trip had reunited her with a side of her aunt she'd forgotten. What had set out to be the fulfilling of an unwelcome obligation had turned into something more, much more. She stroked the scarred wood of the table with a finger.

Lost in memories of the past, Bel jumped when her mobile rang. Taking it out of her pocket, she saw Matt's name.

'How's Isobel?' he asked without waiting for her to speak.

Although she'd decided it was too soon for her to talk with Matt, Bel was surprised how relieved she felt to hear his voice. 'She wakened and rallied for a bit, but she's sleeping again.'

'And how are you? What are you up to?'

'Nothing much. Sitting. Waiting.'

'I'm coming over.'

'There's no need.'

'I'm in the Anniesland office. I can be there in ten minutes. I'll see you then.' Matt ended the call before she could say any more.

Bel clutched the phone as if it could transfer to her the confidence Matt's voice had conveyed. Although she was hesitant about seeing him, about what she needed to say to him, to ask him, it was comforting to have him take charge. She'd been in charge of her own life for so long, she'd forgotten how to accept help.

Isobel was still asleep when Bel saw Matt's car drive up. She'd been watching from the window and hurried to open the door. 'She's still asleep,' she whispered, leading Matt through to the kitchen. 'Tea? I'm afraid there's no coffee.'

'I'm used to that. Tea'll be fine.'

Bel was stirring her tea, when Matt stilled her hand. 'What's up? You've been a bit quiet since we left Invergulas. Is it something I've done? Are you having second thoughts about…?'

Bel raised her eyes to meet his and shook her head. 'No, it's something else. About Aunt Isobel.' She was torn between wanting to share what she had read with him, and being wary of revealing her aunt's story without her permission.

Matt took her hand in both of his. 'You must be worried about her. Did she say much before she fell asleep again?'

'No. I mean…, yes. It's about that…' She took a deep breath. 'When I was waiting for you, before we left. You were in the office and I was wandering around. I went over to the bookcase and picked up a book – a Biggles book.'

'That old thing? I should have thrown it out or given it to Robbie years ago. But what's that got to do with Isobel?'

Bel let out a great sigh. 'Nothing and everything. You'd written your name in it...'

'I used to do that all the time. Didn't everyone?'

'Matthew Rhuairi Reid Smith.'

'That's me. So?' Matt furrowed his brow.

'But your name is Matthew Reid.'

'Yes. It's not so unusual. When I joined Uncle Don's firm he wanted me to take his name – keep it in the family. Reid's my middle name so it wasn't so hard. A bit more memorable than Smith, don't you think?'

Bel managed a smile. 'But Rhuairi?'

'A family name. Mother's family. Her grandfather, actually. Mum and Dad called me that – a weird Scottish custom of giving a guy one name and calling him by another. Rhuairi! Imagine? When I was growing up I could barely spell it. As soon as I started uni I became Matt. Dad still called me Rhuairi of course, but I've been Matt to my friends for as long as I like to remember. Why is it important to you?'

'Rhuairi Smith.'

Matt looked puzzled.

'Aunt Isobel knew you as Rhuairi Smith, son of Bob Smith.'

Matt's eyes widened. 'I don't think so. When Isobel came to the firm I was Matthew Reid, partner in Reid Solicitors. Where did all this come from?'

'Come with me.' Still holding Matt's hand, Bel led him upstairs to her room where the pages of Isobel's Saga were still strewn across the floor. She bent and picked them up, carefully shuffling them into order.

'This is what's it's about,' she said, clutching the bundle to her chest. 'It's Aunt Isobel's... memoir, I suppose you could call it. It's not exactly a diary. It starts in 1938 and skips years, only describing incidents she deemed important. Your dad's in there.'

'Isobel knew my dad?' Matt's expression told Bel it was news to him too.

'You should ask her.'

Bel was still unsure how much to share when the tinkle of a bell sounded from downstairs. 'It's Aunt Isobel. She's awake.' She dropped the papers onto the bed and, with Matt following, headed downstairs. Taking a deep breath, Bel opened the door to Isobel's bedroom.

'What took you so long?' the frail voice asked, then Bel saw her aunt's eyes move beyond her to where Matt was standing. The old lady's face lit up, smoothing out some of the wrinkles and making Bel remember her aunt as a younger woman. 'Matthew! You're here too?'

'I popped in to see how you were.' Matt moved toward the bed, past Bel who was too surprised by the apparent change in her aunt to go through the doorway.

'It's good to see you two together. I'd hoped…' Isobel's voice faded and she brought a handkerchief up to her mouth to stifle a hacking cough. When she took it away from her face, Bel thought she could see spots of blood on the white poplin.

'Should we call Dr Ramage?' Bel asked Matt, but was interrupted by her aunt.

'No need to bother William. He's done all he can. All he can do now is sign my death certificate.' She tried to laugh, but ended up coughing again.

Bel rushed forward and helped Isobel prop herself up against the pillows. 'There. That should help your breathing. What can we do?'

'Just sit down the pair of you. You're making me nervous hovering over me like that. I need to talk to you – both of you – before it's too late.'

It was like a royal command. Matt pulled up a couple of stools, and the pair sat down, one on either side of the bed. Isobel reached her hands out to clasp those of the young couple. 'Seeing you two together, it's like the closing of a circle; a story that started many years ago before either of you were born.' She turned towards Matt and her eyes grew tender. 'You're so like him,' she murmured.

'Are you sure…?' Bel asked, feeling uncomfortable and unsure how much of her story Isobel wanted to reveal.

'Haud your wheesht. It's my story and I'll tell it when I want. I dinnae ken how much you've told this lad.' She turned to face Matt again. 'Your dad – Bob Smith – he was a fine young man when we met, but it was never to be, and yet… If I hadn't been such a good girl, been more like my sisters, and my friend, Eileen, maybe…' She shook her head. 'That's why I had to find you, Rhuairi Smith. You didn't make it easy, but I did it. Then I had to inveigle young Bel to come here. Had to be near dying to do it.' She chuckled and squeezed her niece's hand, making Bel wonder exactly what her aunt meant. Her mind seemed to be wandering. She wasn't making sense. 'I gave you my story,' she said to Bel. 'Did you read to the end?'

Bel shook her head. 'Not yet,' she whispered. She saw the old woman's eyes close and tried to extricate herself, but the hand holding her tightened its grasp. For a dying woman, her grip was still strong.

'Has Matt read it?'

'No. I wasn't sure… Isn't it your private…?'

'When I'm gone nothing will be private. That's something I've learned. Best you read it now, before…' She took a breath. 'You *are* my solicitor, after all, and Bob's son.' Her voice lingered over his name, caressing it. 'I'll be seeing him soon enough. It's about time you found out what it was all about and why I chose *you* to look after my affairs. Now, off the two of you go and let me have a rest. And I hope you haven't wasted as much time as I did.' Her last words followed them out of the room.

Bel closed the door and the two stood looking at each other. 'I guess we'd better do as we're told,' Bel said.

'Maybe you can fill me in on the story so far. I'm bamboozled. What has Isobel's life – her story – got to do with me? How did she know Dad? Did she know Mum too? And Annie… You met her. They married when I was in my teens and…'

'I know. It's all there.'

'How about I make some tea, and you bring it all downstairs? We'll be right there if Isobel needs us. I have to make sense of all this.' He dragged a hand through his hair. 'It's as if she planned for us to meet, to…'

'She didn't plan all of it,' Bel smiled. 'I think we had something to do with it. That and a clump of heather.'

'Oh, I think we'd have got around to it sooner or later. I had my eye on you.' He drew her towards him and planted a kiss on her lips. 'Mmm. Isobel knew a thing or two when she introduced us.'

'But how could she know? We could have hated each other on sight.'

'I guess that was a risk she was willing to take. Or maybe it didn't occur to her. Do you really think she's intending us to channel her and Dad? Sounds weird when you put it like that.'

'Get on with you.' Bel gave Matt a slight push and headed upstairs.

*

'So that's it.' Bel laid both hands flat on the table as she finished bringing Matt up to speed on Isobel's story. Their tea had become cold as the tale progressed. 'As far as I've got anyway. Maybe we should read the rest together?'

'It doesn't seem real. I wonder if Dad knew.' Matt pulled on his ear. 'To think that she carried a torch for him all those years… that they never even…'

'A bit hard to believe, but times were different then I suppose.'

'Not that different.'

'More tea?'

Matt's hand went to his cup before nodding. 'I guess so. We may need some sustenance for the final chapter, though I don't know what more there can be.'

Thirty

Isobel – 1985

Weeks went by, and I had no luck in finding Rhuairi's whereabouts. It had become my obsession. I felt my life would be so much better if only I could see him, meet him. Maybe I could relive that time when… I think I went a bit mad.

It was Mary Anderson who unwittingly helped me. Isobel's old school friend still lived along the road and, over the years, had kept in touch. Her parents were older than Nan and I and didn't enjoy good health. The poor girl had cared for them, one after the other, and my sister and I had taken pity on her, welcoming the visits which gave her some respite from the house of sickness.

'I'm seeing the solicitor today,' Mary said, as she sat drinking tea with me one Tuesday morning. It was a couple of months after Nan died. I had the shop on the market and was too depressed to go in every day. It wasn't right that I was the only one left, that even my wee sister had died before me.

'Mmm.' Another solicitor. Glasgow seemed to be full of them, and none of them were Rhuairi Smith.

'Maybe…' Mary hesitated as if she was worried she might be overstepping the mark. 'Have *you* found a good one?'

'What?' *How could she know I was scouring the city to find the one who could remind me of my lost love?*

'I was just thinking. Now you're on your own here…' She gazed around the room, and I could see her taking in the dust which had begun to accumulate, the papers which lay in a heap on the floor. 'Excuse me if I'm speaking out of turn, but have you thought of putting your affairs in order?'

My first reaction was to tell her to mind her own business, but she made sense. I did need to speak to a solicitor. When the shop sold, I'd have a nice nest egg, then there was the legacy from my parents, and this big house. It would all go to Nan's Isobel one day, but I needed to ensure my wishes were carried out when that day came. I'd been so focussed on finding Rhuairi that I'd completely forgotten my own affairs.

'Maybe you should give me the name of the man you're seeing?'

'His name's Reid, Don Reid. In Anniesland. He's in partnership with... his nephew I think it is.'

I couldn't believe it! I'd been searching all over Glasgow and wee Mary from along the road had the answer. It had to be him. I ignored the fact that there must be lots of law practices which were uncle and nephew partnerships. My gut told me this was it.

'You'd better give me their details,' I said, trying to hide my excitement.

*

I rang the office next morning only to be asked, 'Is it the older or younger Mr Reid you want to see?' My heart plummeted. They were both called Reid! Of course, it would have been too easy if Mary's man proved to be the one I was looking for. 'Either,' I replied, realising I might never be able to locate Bob's son, though I didn't intend to stop searching. When the day came for my meeting with the solicitor, I dressed carefully in a new tweed suit with a favourite pale blue blouse and, after some thought, added my mother's pearls. I rubbed my thumb over the garnet ring that never left my finger – a habit I'd developed over the years whether to give me confidence or bring me luck, I wasn't sure.

As I rode up to the fourth floor in the lift, I realised I was shaking and my heart was fluttering at the prospect of perhaps meeting Bob's son at long last. I'd dismissed the fact the nephew was called Reid and had almost forgotten the real reason for this visit.

It was to set my affairs in order, as Mary had put it. I suppose that meant write my will, decide what would happen to the house and any money that was left when I finally shuffled off this mortal coil. I rather liked that phrase as it rolled around in my head. But this was a serious business. Apart from young Isobel in Australia, I was the last in the family and, since she had no children and wasn't likely to have any now, the family would die out with the two of us.

I took a seat in the outer office, furnished in what appeared to be the latest minimalist style, and waited. I shifted uncomfortably on the firm fabric seat, watching a receptionist with a wild head of hair juggling with phone calls and a typewriter.

All of a sudden, the outer door swung open and a young man with black hair hurried in. He called out a greeting to the receptionist before walking past me and disappearing through a wood-panelled door. My heart leapt. He was the image of the Bob Smith I'd met all those years ago albeit clean-shaven and with a different hairstyle. This had to be his son. It had to be Rhuairi Smith.

A few minutes later, an older man with thin grey hair and wearing a pair of gold-rimmed spectacles emerged and held out his hand. 'Miss MacDonald? I'm Don Reid. Sorry to keep you waiting. Come along in.'

I followed him into a large office where the morning sun shone through a ceiling to floor plate-glass window. He showed me to a seat before settling himself on the other side of a heavy wooden desk. He picked up a pen and rolled it in his fingers. 'How can I help you?'

I desperately wanted to ask about the young man I'd seen, but instead set out my requirements and, before long, he had made a few suggestions I hadn't considered and the meeting was at a close.

He handed me his card. The only names were Don Reid and Matthew Reid. Nowhere was there any mention of a solicitor called Smith. I fingered it in surprise. 'Are there just the two of you in the practice?'

'Just young Matthew – my nephew, my sister's boy – and myself. Ah, here he is now.'

The young man I'd seen earlier popped his head around the door.

'Matthew, this is Miss MacDonald. She's been recommended to us by another client – Mary Anderson. You've been dealing with her parents' estate, I believe.'

I couldn't take my eyes off the nephew. He was Bob's double. I was so wrapped up in my memories, I barely heard the conversation. It was only when Don Reid asked, 'Will that be all, Miss MacDonald?', that I looked up to see both men smiling at me.

'Sorry?'

'I was asking if you were satisfied with our decisions today. We should make another appointment when I have the paperwork ready for your signature. And I was suggesting that young Mathew here take you over. I'm trying to reduce my client load as I plan to retire soon. We thought maybe you'd prefer dealing with a younger man who'd be able to handle your affairs until...' He coughed.

'Yes. That would be quite satisfactory,' I said. Matthew Reid looked so like the image I'd kept in my heart all those years, I was delighted to have him looking after my affairs. I could pretend he was Rhuairi Smith and enjoy our meetings which I was determined would be on a regular basis.

It wasn't till years later that my initial suspicions were confirmed when Matthew revealed to me how his uncle had asked him to change his name in order to retain the family name of Reid for the practice. By then I'd convinced myself that, even if Matthew wasn't Bob's son, he must be related to him in some way. The likeness was too strong to be a coincidence. And by then, Matthew Rhuairi Reid Smith had become a surrogate son to me.

Thirty-one

Bel – 2105

'That's all?' Matt flipped through the pages in what seemed to be an effort to uncover a section they'd missed. 'What did Annie say to her? Why did she visit? How did she even know Isobel existed?'

'Frustrating! I guess Aunt Isobel wanted to keep something to herself. That was in…'

'1985. That's when Dad died – in the March. Annie visited Isobel that same year. And it was in November Isobel approached our firm looking for a solicitor.' He rubbed his chin. 'I remember she said she'd be happy to have a young man to represent her, one who could "see her out" as she put it. Uncle Don and I, we didn't think anything of it at the time. The old guy was getting on, thinking of retirement, so I seemed to be the obvious choice. But now… I wonder.'

'That's not exactly how she describes it. And the only one who can tell us the truth is lying through there.' Bel sipped her tea. She stared down into the teacup. Despite the tea, her mouth felt dry. 'I don't think she has much longer…'

'No.'

'She knows.' Bel lifted her head and her eyes met Matt's, seeing an answering sadness in their brown depths. She sighed. 'I wish there was something we could do…'

Matt covered Bel's hand with his. 'She's ready to go. She's had a good life.'

'But has she? That's always what people say when someone of her age dies, but life wasn't always easy for Aunt Isobel. She was a lonely old woman and I... I had no idea how much I meant to her.'

They sat without speaking, the warmth from Matt's hand comforting Bel. He began to stroke the back of her hand with his thumb.

'She wanted us to get together. I can't believe the old dear manipulated our meeting after all those years, that she managed to set us up,' Bel said.

'I guess she wanted us to experience what she missed out on.'

'What she threw away, you mean? But she was right – about us.'

Matt's hand tightened on Bel's and his other one reached up to her chin to turn her face towards his. 'She surely was. But... what happens now? When Isobel has gone, do you still plan to return to Sydney?'

Bel shifted uncomfortably. This was the problem, the issue she'd been wrestling with since she awoke that morning. Even before she found that book and made the discovery of Matt's true identity. 'I... I can't stay here.' She rose abruptly and walked over to the window, staring out blindly.

She took a deep breath and turned back to the room, both hands holding the sink behind her for support. 'What we have is special, Matt, but... my life isn't here. I made that decision a long time ago and I'm too old to change it now.'

'Maybe not. I bet you thought you were too old for what happened last night, too. But it did, and we can't go back. You say what we have is special, so why not give us a chance? At least stay for a bit, until everything is settled here. It's what Isobel would want you to do.'

Bel could see the logic in Matt's suggestion. It would give them both time to... to what? To discover whether last night had been a flash in the pan or if they had the basis for a lasting relationship? But she didn't need time for that. Even before last night, she'd been aware that in Matt, she'd met someone unlike anyone she'd known before, someone she could spend the rest of her life with, if only...

'We'll see,' she said.

*

Isobel had wakened briefly, managed to take a little of the chicken soup Bel heated up, then drifted off again. Matt had wanted to stay overnight, but Bel couldn't face sleeping with him in this house. There were too many memories, and there was something about the place that made her reluctant to trust her newfound emotions to its care.

She shivered as she extricated herself from his embrace.

'You know I can be here in a trice if you need me,' he said, pulling her back into his arms and moving his lips against her hair.

Bel almost weakened. It would be so easy to give in, to allow herself to be engulfed in the ecstasy of the previous night again, to fall asleep in Matt's arms, to… She stiffened and pulled away. No. There were too many ghosts here. 'Thanks,' she whispered.

'Call me in the morning?'

'Promise.' She watched him drive off, stood for a moment gazing at the empty road, the streetlights glinting in the shadows, then closed the door and made her way upstairs.

Once in bed, Bel pulled out the Isobel saga one more time, in the hope she and Matt had missed something, that another page had been tucked away. That there was something to explain what Matt's stepmother had said to make Isobel start searching for him. But she came up empty-handed. Sighing, she dropped the bundle of papers onto the bedside table and closed her eyes.

*

Bel had barely slept all night, worrying that her aunt might call out to her. She'd tossed and turned, only falling into a light doze as the sky began to lighten. The papers were the first thing Bel saw when she awoke. She picked them up and stroked them carefully. Isobel's story – the part of it she was willing to share with Bel at any rate.

Bel dressed quickly and made her way downstairs. She tapped gently at her aunt's door before letting herself in. Isobel was lying propped up against the pillows. She seemed to have aged in the past twenty-four hours and looked every one of her ninety-seven years; her entire body appeared to have shrunk, her eyes were sunken, the lines on her face had become more pronounced and her skin had developed a greyish tinge. The illness had drained her face of its customary liveliness. For the first time, Bel saw Isobel as the old woman she was and knew it was only a matter of time – hours or days – before she'd be gone.

Stifling the tears that threatened to overwhelm her, Bel walked to the bedside and touched her aunt's frail hand, the skin feeling paper-thin under her fingers. 'How did you sleep?'

'So-so.' Isobel's voice came out as a croak.

'Can I get you anything?'

'I could maybe manage a wee bowl of porridge.'

'Right.' Bel patted Isobel's hand and left. Once in the kitchen she stood staring out the window, but everything was a blur. Exhaling loudly, she turned back to the room to prepare the porridge for her aunt and the tea she knew she'd enjoy with it.

*

'Now sit down,' Isobel said, when Bel returned to fetch the empty bowl. 'I need to talk to you.'

Bel sat, cupping the bowl in her lap with her hands.

'You and young Matthew,' Isobel began. 'I saw the way you looked at each other yesterday. I'm not too sick to notice these things. It reminded me of the way Nan and Col looked at each other. The way they…'

Bel shifted in her seat, feeling a blush rise to her cheeks, but unable to prevent it. The reference to her parents caught her unaware. She didn't really remember them together. The mother she remembered best was the one of her teenage years, busy with work and keeping the house in order, and telling Bel what she could and couldn't do. She'd been so young when her dad had died, she barely remembered him.

'What I wanted to say is this,' the frail voice continued. 'Don't let what you two have pass you by. If I'm right, it's a chance for you both. A chance to…' Isobel stopped and coughed loudly, bringing her hand up to her mouth. After a pause, she continued, 'I got a second chance with Matthew's dad and I let it slip through my fingers. I don't know why… Maybe there was something I could have done…' She gazed into space as if seeing the man who'd left her twice; the man who'd chosen to marry other women; the man for whom she still carried a torch.

She grasped Bel's hand, loosening its grip on the bowl. 'Don't make the same mistake. Matthew's a good man.' She coughed again.

'Would you like some water?'

'No. I need to…' She leant back on the pillows and closed her eyes.

Bel was about to slip out quietly when her aunt spoke again. 'When I… I know I don't have long. When I'm gone… Don't be in a rush to go back home. I never knew what it was like to be with a man. I tried so hard to be good, unlike my sisters – and my best friend. They weren't bad women, ye ken, but that's how I labelled them.

'Yes,' she said, as if talking to herself,' I was the good sister, the one who refused to compromise my principles, and as a result I lost the one thing I wanted above all else.' She sighed heavily. 'You've known love, known a man, and I'm thinking you and young Matthew…'

Isobel coughed again, and without asking, Bel handed her a glass of water, supporting her aunt's grasp on it, and wiping her mouth with a tissue afterwards. 'Don't make the same mistake I did.' She paused. 'But I'm thinking…'

Bel saw a twinkle in the older woman's rheumy eyes. She was a witch. How did she know what Bel and Matt had got up to? Were they so obvious?

'I know, my dear. I could tell when you got back yesterday. There was a glow about the pair of you, the same glow your dear mother had when she told me that she and your dad had *done it* up in Crieff. Back then, the obvious solution, the only solution was marriage. But these days…' She shook her head. 'But I think with you and Matthew, it's more than what they call a one-night stand.'

Bel almost choked. The term coming from her staid aunt's lips was incongruous. But the old woman was right. What she and Matt had *was* special. She didn't know what to say.

Isobel grasped Bel's hand. 'You *will* give him a chance, won't you? It would make me so happy if I knew that my niece and Bob's son…' Her voice faltered, then seemed to regain its strength. 'It would be fitting. I could die happy.' Her eyes closed, and the hand holding Bel's loosened.

Bel sat still for a moment, trying to take in what her aunt had just said. Had she heard her correctly? Was Isobel trying to indicate that if Bel and Matt became a couple, they would somehow channel Isobel and Bob, complete the relationship that had failed twice in no small measure due to Isobel's reluctance to consummate it? It was all too weird. She shook her head and, tucking the covers around her aunt's hands, left the room.

*

'How is Isobel this morning?' Matt's voice on the phone was welcome. She'd been sitting in the kitchen thinking about Isobel's bizarre conversation. The sound of his soft Scottish burr provided the comfort she hadn't realised she needed. Maybe she wasn't quite as self-sufficient as she'd thought, though the position she found herself in wasn't one she'd experienced before.

'Much the same. She's very frail and sleeping a lot. I think...'

'I'll be there as soon as I can.'

Thank God! Bel let out a huge breath and pressed her palms to her eyes. She felt a sudden release from the tension of being alone in a house which was about to become... what? She had the strongest feeling that her aunt wouldn't last out the day and was glad she wouldn't be alone when Isobel's final moment came.

She tidied up in the kitchen, then went into her aunt's room. Isobel was asleep, her breathing laboured. She'd barely touched the tea Bel had prepared earlier, falling asleep again after only a few sips. Bel dropped a kiss on the sleeping woman's forehead, then closed the door gently.

Unable to settle to anything, she opened her iPad and scrolled down the large number of emails which had appeared in the last few days when she'd been too occupied with other matters to check them. Opening one at random, she saw it was from Jan, asking when she planned to return. Sydney, Isabella and her home were so far away. It seemed ages since she'd left, when it was only a couple of months ago that she'd set foot in this house. It was strange to think of everything carrying on there without her. She'd be glad to get back.

Then she remembered her aunt's words: *Don't be in rush to go back home. You will give him a chance, won't you? It would make me so happy if*

I knew that my niece and Bob's son… It would be fitting. I could die happy.

Could she? Stay here? Give their relationship a chance? Bel's mind spun. Glasgow was the one place she'd vowed never to return to. Yet here she was. She'd come at the bidding of a dying woman and found… She wouldn't call it love – not yet. But the very fact the word love came to mind was inconceivable. It was a word she'd never thought to use again, not in relation to a man, anyway.

She rose hurriedly in an attempt to dismiss the unwelcome thoughts. But they persisted as she moved through the house, her eye catching sight of specks of dust Betty had missed and swiping at them with her hand.

She was walking through the hall when she heard a car draw up, followed by footfalls on the steps and the doorbell. *Matt!*

'Hi!' Her greeting was muffled by Matt's shoulder as he gave her a warm hug. She sank into the embrace she hadn't realised she was yearning for. His presence alone was making her feel better. How could this man have such an effect on her?

'How're you coping?'

'Not well.' It was a relief to say it out loud. 'Thanks for coming.'

'Have you eaten this morning?'

'I…' Bel thought back. She remembered taking tea in to her aunt, but had she made any for herself? 'I can't remember.'

'You need to eat. Today won't be an easy one. I can rustle up some breakfast if…'

'I can do it.'

'Sit down and relax. You're wound up so tight if you were a watch spring you'd snap.'

Matt's attempt at humour fell flat, but Bel followed him into the kitchen and sat down at the table, automatically sitting in her usual chair. The one opposite – the one Isobel usually sat in – looked abandoned. Bel shifted her eyes to avoid the sight of the empty space, turning instead to face Matt.

'Scrambled eggs on toast?' Matt's head swivelled around from the fridge where he'd been inspecting the contents.

Bel nodded, not sure if she could stomach anything, but willing to agree to please him.

'And tea, hot and sweet.'

Bel began to shake her head and tell him she didn't take sugar, then realised that hot, sweet tea did sound good. There was something surprisingly pleasant about being taken care of. She leant back in her chair and exhaled loudly. 'Thanks for coming,' she said again. 'I wouldn't like to go through this on my own.'

Bel looked at the plate of eggs on toast Matt laid before her. He really was house-trained and quite unlike any man she'd known. But she still didn't feel hungry. She took a sip of the tea, grimacing at the sweetness, nonetheless it did send a warm glow through her.

'Try to eat a little,' Matt said, as Bel made no attempt to pick up her knife and fork. 'I'll just take a peek in at Isobel, shall I?'

'Mmm.' Bel slowly picked up her fork and took a small mouthful of the eggs, washing it down with more of the sweet tea.

'She's still asleep, and her breathing…' Matt hovered just inside the door.

Bel looked up quickly. 'It was laboured earlier. Do you think…?'

'We should send for William? Yes.'

Bel felt a prickling in her scalp. Was this it? She cleared her throat. 'I'll call him.'

Dr William Ramage was in his surgery, but promised to come as soon as he could. Bel returned to the kitchen, looked at the half-eaten plate of scrambled eggs and scraped it into the bin.

'Thanks,' she said to Matt, and pushed a hand through her hair. 'I'm sorry, but…'

'It's okay. Do you want to sit with her?'

'I think so.'

The pair made their way to Isobel's bedroom and sat one on either side of the bed. It was peaceful in the room, the only sound the old woman's heavy breathing, interspersed with the occasional croaking sound as her breath seemed to catch, almost stopping before it resumed its regular rhythm.

Time seemed to stand still, the loud ringing of the doorbell startling the silent couple.

'That'll be William now. I'll go.' Matt rose and squeezed Bel's shoulder on the way out.

When he'd gone, Bel stroked her aunt's forehead and rearranged the long white plait on the candlewick bedspread.

Isobel's eyes opened. 'Bel?'

'I'm here, Aunt Isobel.' Bel took her aunt's hand. 'Dr Ramage is here too. He's just arrived.'

'Och. There was no need to bother the puir man. There's nothing he can do for me. My time's about come.' Her eyes closed again, but her hand tightened slightly in Bel's indicating she was still awake.

'And how are you today, Isobel?'

At the doctor's hearty greeting, Isobel's eyes blinked open again. 'As you can see, I'm still in the land of the living, William,' she said testily, her weak voice coming out in gasps.

'Well, let's have a look at you. Maybe...?' He glanced at Bel and Matt and raised his eyebrows.

'We'll leave you with your patient,' Matt said, ushering Bel out of the room. 'Bel and I'll be in the kitchen.'

Once there, Bel couldn't sit still. She paced up and down the narrow room.

'Will you sit down, woman,' Matt said at last. 'You'll drive me mad with all that marching about.'

'Sorry.' Bel stood still and wrapped her arms around her body, trying to stop herself from shivering.

'Come here, you.' Matt took Bel in his arms, resting his chin on her head. 'Is that better?'

'Mmm. Oh, I hate this. I hate the whole thing – death and funerals.' Bel shuddered, and drew away slightly. 'I remember my mother's as if it was yesterday. This dark house with all the curtains closed, the dampness on the street outside. The dismal Scottish weather that seemed to seep right through me, reminding me that I'd left the brilliant sunshine of a Sydney summer to come to this godforsaken place. I couldn't wait to leave.'

'She has it all planned, you know.'

Bel looked up at him. 'Planned?'

'Her funeral. She's chosen the hymns, the readings, even the flowers she'd like.'

'Oh!'

But Bel wasn't surprised. Aunt Isobel had always seemed organised, on top of things. It was only in reading her story that Bel had come to know the real Isobel – to understand the vulnerable side of the woman who had normal goals and fears, the woman to whom life hadn't been too kind.

'Fiona never got to meet her again.'

'No.' Matt gave a slight smile, so slight it was barely noticeable. 'But she could still visit the house if...'

'I know. If I don't run off back home immediately afterwards.'

'Have you thought any more about that?'

Bel hesitated before replying. She'd thought about little else since Isobel's words, but was still far from making a decision. 'Yes, and no I haven't decided.' She paused, thinking of the wishes of the woman dying in the room at the front of the house, of the comfort of the man who still held her, of the life waiting for her back home. 'It's all too difficult.'

'Now's not the time, I know, not with Isobel... But I want you to know that *Barkis is willing.*'

Despite her grief, Bel couldn't prevent a smile escape at this reference to one of her favourite novels. She knew it was one of Matt's favourites too, having seen a well-worn copy of Dickens' *David Copperfield* on his bookshelf.

'Thanks. I'll remember,' she whispered, her voice almost breaking at this, yet another sign of his thoughtfulness.

'It's as we thought.' The couple broke apart as William Ramage walked into the kitchen and placed his bag on the table. 'A cup of tea wouldn't go amiss.'

'Sure.'

The three sat around the table, their faces drawn in mutual sorrow. Bel swallowed repeatedly as she listened to the doctor explain that all they could do now was keep her aunt comfortable.

'She's had a good innings,' he said, emptying his cup, 'and she's ready to go. It comes to us all.' He sighed. 'She was so pleased when you arrived, Bel. She'd been hoping to see you again before...' He cleared his throat. 'And it's good you'll not be on your own.' His eyes met Matt's in a question.

'I'll stay with Bel,' Matt said.

But once the doctor had left, Bel turned to Matt. 'There's no need,' she began, only to find herself silenced by a firm finger on her lips.

'There's every need,' he said. 'I have a few things in the car. I packed a bag, just in case...'

'Okay.' It was easier to give in, and Bel was grateful she'd have Matt's company. William had said it could happen any time, and it would be good to have someone to lean on, to share the burden – and the grief.

As he was making for the door, Bel placed a hand on his arm. 'Matt, I don't want you to... I do value what we have together. I'd like to think...'

He covered her hand with his and smiled, a weary smile. 'That's all I needed to know We'll work something out, when all this is over.'

'Yes.' She loosened her grip and allowed him to go.

*

Bel and Matt took turns to sit with Isobel throughout the night. Neither could bear the thought of her awakening – and maybe dying – alone. But as the morning sun began to streak through a gap in the curtains, there was no change in Isobel.

'Tea?' Matt pushed open the door and handed Bel a cup, joining her at the bedside. He'd already showered and dressed and smelt of soap and the tangy aftershave Bel had noticed before. 'You should get some sleep. It may be a long day.'

Bel drank her tea, gave one more glance toward the sleeping figure in the bed and agreed. She'd dozed off a little in the early hours, but felt as if she'd been run over by a bus. Surely she could manage a few hours' sleep?

But once she'd showered and lain down in her bed, sleep wouldn't come. Her overactive brain was filled with questions, the main one being what she'd do after it was all over. The sensible part of her told her she'd pack her bags and return home, pick up her life where she'd left off, and consign Matt and their time together as a pleasant memory. But there was another part of her that urged a different path. That was the side she'd managed to suppress for years; the side that had been released when she and Matt were together; the side that told her there was hope of a future in which she wasn't alone, in which she could have someone to love her, someone to rely on, someone to spend the rest of her life with.

But it was when she got to that point and started to imagine a life in which Matt played a part, that she became confused. His life was here with his home and family, while hers was on the other side of the world. How could they make a life together without one of them giving up their home, their lifestyle? It was all too hard.

Coming to the conclusion that there was no way she was going to get any rest, Bel rose, dressed and went downstairs again. She helped herself to another cup of tea and a slice of toast, then slipped into Isobel's bedroom. Her aunt was still asleep. Matt had a book open in his lap, but didn't appear to be reading it. He was gazing into space as if deep in thought.

'No change?' she whispered.

Matt almost jumped. 'No. Did you get some sleep?'

'Not really. Too much to think about.'

'Hmm.'

'I can take over now.'

'Are you sure? I'm happy to stay for a bit.'

'Okay.'

It was peaceful in the room. Isobel's breathing seemed to have settled down to a level where she was barely breathing at all. Only the slight rise and fall of the covers told them she was still alive.

Isobel's eyelids flickered, and Bel took her aunt's hand. The old woman's eyes opened. 'Aunt Isobel?' Bel's voice wavered.

Standing behind her, Matt put his arm around Bel's shoulders and squeezed firmly.

'Aunt Isobel,' Bel repeated. 'We're here. Matt and I.'

But it seemed that the older woman couldn't hear them.

Isobel was already seeing and hearing something or someone beyond their line of vision. Her eyes glazed over and a wide smile formed on her lips, which began to open as if to speak.

*

I feel young Isobel's hand grasping mine. I know she wants me to stay, but my time has come and with it a sense of release. Bob's son is standing behind her, his hand on her shoulder. It's as it should be. As the room begins to fade, I hear again the shrill voice, the words which have followed me through the years. They're fainter now, and the woman who spoke them is only a shadow.

'Are you Isobel MacDonald?'

Without waiting for a reply, she continues, 'I'm Bob Smith's widow. He died with your name on his lips.'

The memory of her voice and figure fades, as another, brighter figure appears moving towards me.

Bob, the young Bob I've loved all of my life, is walking forward with outstretched hands. He smiles and speaks. 'Come with me. We have all the time in the world.' I feel my spirit leave my earthly body.

I'm young again as we join hands and move on together.

*

'She's gone!' Matt's hand tightened on Bel's shoulder as she leant over to place a kiss on her aunt's forehead. She turned and buried her face in Matt's chest, her shoulders heaving in anguish.

'It's too soon. I...' she sobbed, her voice breaking.

'Hush.' Matt patted Bel's back, his hand moving in small circles. Then, with a finger under her chin, he tilted up her tearful face. 'She's at peace now. She was glad to go. It was her time.'

Bel heard his words through a fog, but the comfort of his presence calmed her. She sniffed and gave a teary smile. 'You're right. I'm being silly. Oh, Matt. I'm so glad you're here. I don't know what I'd have done if...'

'Shhh. I'll always be here for you. I don't want to let you go.' He rocked Bel in his arms till her sobbing subsided. 'I love you. I want you with me always,' he murmured into her hair.

'It's what I want too,' Bel said, suddenly realising the truth. In these arms, with this man who provided her with such a sense of comfort and safety, who could take her to heights of pleasure she'd only ever imagined. This was where she needed to be – where she wanted to spend the rest of her life.

As their lips met, a beam of sunlight lit up the face of the dead woman. It was as if she was smiling.

From the Author

Dear Reader,

First, I'd like to thank you for choosing to read The Good Sister. I hope you enjoyed Isobel and Bel's stories and, if you've already read Broken Threads, I hope you enjoyed meeting Bel again.

If you did enjoy it, I'd love it if you could write a review. It doesn't need to be long, just a few words, but it is the best way for me to help new readers discover my books.

If you'd like to stay up to date with my new releases and special offers you can sign up to my reader's group at https://maggiechristensenauthor. lpages.co/free-book-signup/ and you'll also get a FREE book.

I'll never share your email address, and you can unsubscribe at any time. You can also contact me via Facebook Twitter or by email. I love hearing from my readers and will always reply.

Thanks again.

Acknowledgements

As always, this book could not have been written without the help and advice of a number of people.

Firstly, my husband Jim for listening to my plotlines without complaint, for his patience and insights as I discuss my characters and storyline with him and for being there when I need him.

John Hudspith, editor extraordinaire for his ideas, suggestions, encouragement and attention to detail.

Jane Dixon-Smith for her patience and for working her magic on my beautiful cover and interior.

The Inkstained Groupies and The Noosa Writers who saw early drafts of this novel for their support and encouragement, my critique partner, Karen, for her eagle eye and continuing patience and my beta readers, Louise, Anne and Cynthia for their willingness to read the final draft of this novel.

Annie of *Annie's books at Peregian* for her ongoing support and advice.

And all of my readers. Your support and comments make it all worthwhile.

About the Author

After a career in education, Maggie Christensen began writing contemporary women's fiction portraying mature women facing life-changing situations. Her travels inspire her writing, be it her frequent visits to family in Oregon, USA or her home on Queensland's beautiful Sunshine Coast. Maggie writes of mature heroines coming to terms with changes in their lives and the heroes worthy of them.

From her native Glasgow, Scotland, Maggie was lured by the call 'Come and teach in the sun' to Australia, where she worked as a primary school teacher, university lecturer and in educational management. Now living with her husband of thirty years on Queensland's Sunshine Coast, she loves walking on the deserted beach in the early mornings and having coffee by the river on weekends. Her days are spent surrounded by books, either reading or writing them – her idea of heaven!

She continues her love of books as a volunteer with her local library where she selects and delivers books to the housebound.

A member of Queensland Writer's Centre, RWA, ALLIA, and a local critique group, Maggie enjoys meeting her readers at book signings and library talks. In 2014 she self-published *Band of Gold* and *The Sand Dollar, Book One of the Oregon Coast Series*, in 2015 *The Dreamcatcher, Book Two of the Oregon Coast Series* and *Broken Threads*, in 2016 *book Three of the Oregon Coast Series, Madeline House,* and in 2017 *Champagne or Breakfast,* set in Noosa on Australia's Sunshine Coast, in which characters from the Oregon Coast books make a reappearance.

The Good Sister while a stand-alone novel, follows the story of Bel who readers first met in *Broken Threads,* when she returns to her native Scotland to visit her terminally ill aunt.

Maggie can be found on Facebook, Twitter, Goodreads, Instagram or on her website.

www.facebook.com/maggiechristensenauthor
www.twitter.com/MaggieChriste33
www.goodreads.com/author/show/8120020.Maggie_Christensen
www.instagram.com/maggiechriste33/
www.maggiechristensenauthor.com/

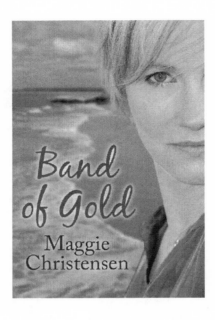

A relationship after a failed marriage. Can Anna love again? Does she dare?

Anna Hollis believes she has a happy marriage. A schoolteacher in Sydney, Anna juggles her busy life with a daughter in the throes of first love and increasingly demanding aging parents.

When Anna's husband of twenty-five years leaves her, on Christmas morning, without warning or explanation, her safe and secure world collapses.

Marcus King returns to Australia from the USA, leaving behind a broken marriage and a young son.

When he takes up the position of Headmaster at Anna's school, they form a fragile friendship through their mutual hurt and loneliness.

Can Anna leave the past behind and make a new life for herself, and does Marcus have a part to play in her future?

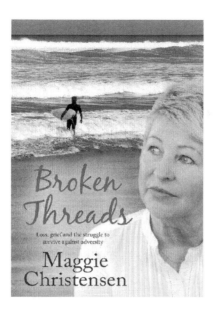

A story of loss, grief and the struggle to survive against adversity.

Jan Turnbull's life takes a sharp turn towards chaos the instant her eldest son, Simon takes a tumble in the surf and loses his life.

Blame competes with grief and Jan's husband turns against her. She finds herself ousted from the family home and separated from their remaining son, Andy.

As Jan tries to cope with her grief and prepares to build a new life, it soon becomes known that Simon has left behind a bombshell, and her younger son seeks ways of compensating for his loss, leading to further issues for her to deal with.

Can Jan hold it all together and save her marriage and her family?

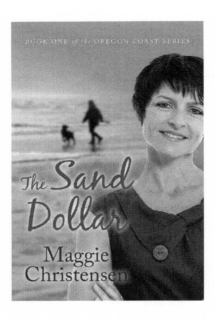

A well–kept secret and a magical sand dollar. Can Jenny unravel the puzzle of her past?

What if you discover everything you believed to be true about yourself has been a lie?

Stunned by news of an impending redundancy, and impelled by the magic of a long-forgotten sand dollar, Jenny retreats to her godmother in Oregon to consider her future.

What she doesn't bargain for is to uncover the secret of her adoption at birth and her Native American heritage. This revelation sees her embark on a journey of self-discovery such as she'd never envisaged.

Moving between Australia's Sunshine Coast and the Oregon Coast, *The Sand Dollar* is a story of new beginnings, of a woman whose life is suddenly turned upside down, and the reclusive man who helps her solve the puzzle of her past.

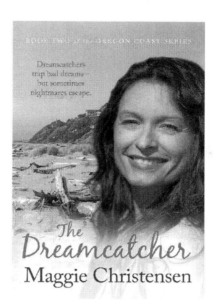

The
Dreamcatcher
Maggie Christensen

Dreamcatchers trap bad dreams – but sometimes nightmares escape.

Ellen Williams, a Native American with a gift for foretelling the future, is at a loss to explain her terrifying nightmares and the portentous feeling of dread that seems to hang over her like a shroud.

When Travis Petersen – an old friend of her brother's – appears in her bookshop *The Reading Nook*, Ellen can't shake the idea there's a strange connection between her nightmares and Travis' arrival.

Suffering from guilt of the car accident which took the lives of his wife and son, Travis is struggling to salvage his life, and believes he has nothing to offer a woman. But Ellen's nightmares come true when developers announce a fancy new build, which means pulling down *The Reading Nook* – and she needs Travis' help.

Can Ellen and Travis uncover the link between them and save her bookshop? And will it lead to happiness?

A tale of dreams, romance, and of doing the right thing, set on the beautiful Oregon coast.

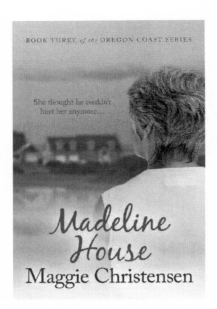

She thought he couldn't hurt her anymore – she was wrong.

When Beth Carson flees her controlling husband, a Sydney surgeon, and travels to Florence, Oregon, she is unsure what her future holds. Although her only knowledge of Florence comes from a few postcards found in her late mother's effects, she immediately feels at home there and begins to put down roots.

But Beth's past returns to haunt her in ways she could never have imagined. Distraught over alarming reports from Australia and bewildered by revelations from the past, Beth turns to new friends to help her.

Tom Harrison, a local lawyer, has spent the past five years coming to terms with his wife's death, and building a solitary existence which he has come to enjoy. Adept at ignoring the overtures of local women and fending off his meddling daughter, he is intrigued by this feisty Australian and, almost against his will, finds himself drawn to her when she seeks his legal advice.

What forces are at work to bring the two together, and can Beth overcome her past and find a way forward?

Set on the beautiful Oregon Coast this is a tale of a woman who seeks to rise above the challenges life has thrown at her and establish a new life for herself.

Rosa Taylor is celebrating her fiftieth birthday with champagne. By the river. On her own.

After finishing her six-year long affair with her boss, Rosa is desperate to avoid him in the workplace and determined to forge a new life for herself.

Harry Kennedy has sailed away from a messy Sydney divorce and is resolute in kick-starting a new life on Queensland's Sunshine Coast.

Thrown together at work, Rosa and Harry discover a secret. One that their employer is desperate to keep hidden. To reveal it they must work together, but first they must learn to trust not only each other but their own rising attraction.

Are these two damaged people willing to risk their hard won independence for the promise of love again?

Made in the USA
Coppell, TX
21 February 2021

50631703R10155